touch left right even if it was wrong . . .

we TAKE THIS man

Candice Dow
and Daaimah S. Poole

GRAND CENTRAL
PUBLISHING

NEW YORK   BOSTON

Copyright © 2009 by Candice Dow and Daaimah S. Poole

Grand Central Publishing
Hachette Book Group
237 Park Avenue
New York, NY 10017

Visit our Web site at www.HachetteBookGroup.com.

Printed in the United States of America

First Edition: January 2009
10 9 8 7 6 5 4 3 2 1

Grand Central Publishing is a division of Hachette Book Group, Inc.
The Grand Central Publishing name and logo is a trademark of Hachette Book Group, Inc.

Library of Congress Cataloging-in-Publication Data
Dow, Candice.
    We take this man / Candice Dow and Daaimah S. Poole. — 1st ed.
        p. cm.
    ISBN-13: 978-0-446-50183-5
    1. African American yuppies—Fiction. 2. Marital conflict—Fiction.
3. Triangles (Interpersonal relations)—Fiction. I. Poole, Daaimah S. II. Title.
    PS3604.O938W43 2009
    813'.6—dc22

                                2008017645

Book design and text composition by L&G McRee

ACKNOWLEDGMENTS

I would like to thank God for blessing me in every way possible and being faithful to His promises. Thanks to my readers for giving me a reason to write! Thanks to my parents, Morris Dow, Beverly Corporal, and Randolph Corporal for loving me unconditionally. Thanks to my sister and good girlfriend, Lisa, for understanding me and growing with me. Thanks to all of my nieces; your existence inspires me. Special thanks to my niece Candice for being such a good girl while Auntie worked on this book. Thanks to my auntie, Oria Sewell, for being the best employee ever. My best friend, Anika, for always being just who I need you to be. Thanks to all my girls in the circle of trust. Special thanks to my good friend Sencera for always coming up with a new good idea and encouraging me to do the same; and to my soul mate for being able to deal with me even when my personality transforms into the character I'm writing and for having my back emotionally, spiritually, and creatively. My agent and friend, Audra Barrett. My editor, Karen

Thomas, and her assistant, Latoya Smith. Thanks to all the book clubs and reviewers that have read and reviewed my work. You are appreciated!

CANDICE DOW

Thank you, Allah, for my talent and blessing me with great family and friends. I have to thank my mother, father, children, extended family, and friends. I love you all without naming names, but you know who you are.

Special thanks to all my readers, who continue to support me. Also, much love to Karen E. Quinones Miller and Liza Dawson, my agents, and to my editor, Karen Thomas.

DAAIMAH S. POOLE

AUTHORS' NOTE

This novel started out as a hypothetical question between the two of us. We were hanging out one weekend, and one of us ran into an old friend who actually had two wives. He claimed that his situation was not about getting over on anyone; it was more about loving two women and wanting to live together as a family. We were thinking, are you serious? Who would really agree to that? But for some reason we were intrigued and couldn't stop talking about it.

Later, we went to a friend's house to watch a football game. As we sat around with a group of men, we began asking them what they thought about having two wives. We received mixed responses. Some of them realized the responsibility associated with mutually satisfying two women and said they would pass. Others looked at it as a solution to infidelity. Needless to say, the topic spawned so much attention and various perspectives from men and women, we knew this discussion was one we wanted to share with our readers. Initially, we considered writing an article. Somehow, as the discussion evolved, it only made sense to write a novel about a man married to two women.

We had opposing views on this topic. One of us thought it could possibly work, while the other said absolutely not! Still, within days, we began mapping out the story. In about a week, we had come up with the concept and title for *We Take This Man*. As we were writing this book, we experienced the same emotional struggles with each other as the characters in the book. So, we hope you enjoy reading it. Although we wrote it primarily for entertainment purposes, we hope it will enlighten you and make you ponder this question: Can two women be happily married to one man?

Thank you,

CANDICE DOW and DAAIMAH S. POOLE

Alicia

My vision blurred as my brain did somersaults. I scratched my wavy roots. How could this be? As I backtracked in my mind, I held my BlackBerry in my hand and scrolled through my calendar just to be sure. Ever since I was twenty years old, I marked the days I'd taken my birth-control pills. And just as I thought, I hadn't missed a day in the entire two months Dwight and I had been seeing each other. This is impossible. My nerves percolated and my purple lace panties draped around my ankles when I stood up from the toilet. The Ocean Water scented–Yankee candle sitting on top of the bathroom sink flickered behind me, back and forth in the same motion that my knees rocked. I shook the hell out of that little indicator stick and still it told me the same thing. Here I was, thirty-two, in love with a married man, and pregnant with his child.

My head pounded as I staggered onto the side of my garden-style tub, pushing my wicker storage boxes to the side. How was I going to explain this to Dwight? Shit!

Why do they make it such a hassle to tie your tubes when you've never had a baby? More than that, why didn't he use a damn condom like most married men?

The two things I swore I didn't want to experience were here in front of me, demanding my attention. Love and life were both inside of me and I didn't know how to proceed. I vowed to myself a long time ago never to fall in love again or to have a baby. It seemed like having a man's child granted a woman the freedom to be as stupid as she wanted to be for him. And I would never be anyone's fool. I watched my mother cry for twenty years over my father, a married man who denied her and me.

As I sat there, grasping my hair, twirling my two-strand twists, tears would not come. I was angry at myself—angry at my heart. Me and love just don't mix. That shit always lands my dumb ass in the wrong place at the wrong time, facing a life with a monkey on my back. Finally, when tears began streaming down my face, I thought about my last experience with love. Nearly ten years ago to the day, I stepped out of the shower to find federal police raiding my off-campus apartment at the University of Maryland. My then boyfriend, Deshaun Francis, was one of the biggest hustlers in the DC area *and* my fellow classmate. He was an upstanding student on a full scholarship, which is why I was able to turn a blind eye to his illegal dealings.

Love has a weird way of making you pay for its existence in your life. I attempted to argue with the police. "Let him go. He didn't do anything," I yelled at the top of my lungs, thinking they would somehow listen. And damn if they didn't tell me to shut the hell up and put some clothes on. Not only were they locking my man up, I was going, too. My life flashed before my eyes. I was in my senior year, steps away from the real world and a well-paying job waiting for me. But instead of that, I was headed to jail in the name of love. No one ever told me that if you pillow-talk with a criminal, bitch, you're a criminal, too. If I planned to stay out of jail, I had to enter a plea. It killed me to go free and leave Deshaun to suffer, but I knew that's what he wanted me to do. For the rest of the semester, I had Erykah Badu's "Otherside of the Game" on repeat and began letting my hair grow natural. I prayed that my holistic, sacrificial, spiritualistic ways would convince the universe's cipher to evolve and mystically drop all the charges against Deshaun. Obviously, I was out of my natural damn mind and the love of my life got twenty years on kingpin charges. Once I snapped out of it, I swore I'd never fall into a situation that I wasn't in control of again.

So please tell me why the hell I'm sitting here, banging the back of my head against beige ceramic tile, staring into the shower glass doors with a distorted, stupid me staring back. If I don't abort this baby, I'll have to carry this illegitimate, unexpected child for the next nine months. *That's some bullshit.*

Suddenly, I had the answer to this dilemma. Just get up and run this baby out of me. I sprang up and rushed into my bedroom. My mind was delirious. Where were my gym clothes? My heart crashed against my chest. Sweat beaded on my forehead. I panted. Then I paused, trying to catch my breath and remember what I was doing. The black wall I'd painted in the name of being fashion-forward stared back at me. It defined my destiny, a damn black hole.

I flung each piece of my workout set from my dresser drawer and tossed it on my sleigh bed, the place where my adulterous acts occurred. Regis and Kelly giggled loudly in my ear. I glared at the television inside my mahogany armoire. What the hell was so funny?

Just as I stepped out of my underwear, my home phone rang. Then my cell phone rang. I knew it was Dwight. I just couldn't talk. I really didn't know what to say. I turned up the black iHome speaker beside the phone on my nightstand to drown out the constant ringing. During the past few months, I'd be playing Alanis Morissette's "Ironic," just because of the one line: *Isn't it ironic that you meet the man of your dreams and then meet his beautiful wife?* How fucking ironic is it that I'm pregnant? Initially, that song blasted out and I rushed back to my iPod to change it. I scrolled forward to "You Oughta Know." The rapid rhythm rushed through me, fueling my confusion. After I put on my workout clothes, I was armed to fend off all of my wrongdoings.

I pulled my iPod from the speaker base and plugged my earphones into it. I jogged out of my bedroom, through the living/dining room, to my front door, and down the stairs of the condominium building. Hoping the shock from pounding on concrete would make this all disappear, I stomped harder with each step. I wanted this to go away. I had to sweat this thing out. The brisk air crashed into my face. Yesterday, it felt like springtime, but Maryland temperature fluctuates like a seesaw and the sun outside my window deceived me. I considered turning around to get a hat, but I kept going.

Moments later the cold temperature felt more like a sauna as buckets of water poured from my body. Nearly ten miles in, a sour taste hijacked my mouth and I began to feel nauseated. My jog turned into a slow trot and suddenly my legs were too weak to move. I stood on the side of Route 198 and Route 1, right in the middle of the roundabout, and my insides splashed out. I prayed that somehow, the baby had been discarded, too. Once I lifted my head, I felt dizzy. As I checked my jacket pocket for a mint, my body swayed. Heavy morning traffic full of suburbanites rushed toward Route 95 heading to all the technology companies on the outskirts of DC. The rapid speed jerked my already-disoriented body. Staggering left and right, I tried to stand. A strong wind whipped past and threw me into the street. It was my punishment for trying to rid my body of its infirmity. I was sick. I was stupid. And I was on the ground, facing oncoming traffic. Raising my hands in the air, I tried to block the car about to run me over. I prayed . . . I prayed hard. Brakes screeched in my ear as I lay defenseless.

CHAPTER 1

Tracey

Four Months Earlier

A gentle morning breeze blew my white translucent curtains open, allowing the Florida sun to beam brightly in. I felt my husband's hands caress my creamy butter skin. I removed his hand from my shoulder and lightly kissed it.

"Good morning, baby girl," he said as he nibbled on my neck.

"Morning, baby," I said, turning over to snuggle my waist into his pelvis and wrap myself in the warmth of his arms. I closed my eyes and attempted to go back to sleep, when I felt Dwight getting out of bed.

"And where do you think you are going?" I asked, trying to prevent him from moving.

"I have to get to the office."

"No, don't go to the office. Just stay in the bed with me," I whined, sitting up and allowing him out of my clutches.

"As good as that sounds, I can't, Trace. I have to get to the office. I have a lot of work to do."

"But it's Sunday, baby."

"My job doesn't care about the day of the week. You know that."

"Damn, every time I want to just spend some time alone, you always have to work. Sometimes I think you are married to your work."

"No, I'm not married to my work. If I could I would stay home with you. But I can't."

"Can't it wait a little while longer? I wanted to have breakfast with you and then just lay in the bed until the girls come home," I said, trying to convince him that our bed was the only place he needed to be.

"Tracey, I really have to get to the office."

Instead of arguing with Dwight, I lay back down, turned over, and wrapped the sheets over my naked body, adjusted my pillow and continued to rest. There was no way I was leaving the comfort of my California king bed. My mother-in-law would be bringing the girls home this afternoon and I was going to relax with or without my husband. I heard Dwight turn the shower on. I thought about joining him. But sleep was calling me.

Fifteen minutes later I opened my eyes long enough to see Dwight walk out of the bathroom. He had a green towel wrapped around his waist and moisture all over his brown, stocky body. Dwight pulled his Ralph Lauren teal polo shirt over his head and zipped up his tan khakis. Then he sprayed on his Chrome cologne and splashed a little aftershave on his jawline.

"I'm outta here," he said as he grabbed his cell phone and keys off the dresser and leaned over to me and kissed my forehead. "I love you. Don't be mad at me."

"I love you, too. I'll try not to," I said groggily.

"Don't sleep your day away."
"I won't."

Hours later I awoke and still wasn't ready to leave the comfort of my bed. I looked around my spacious master bedroom and then reached for my robe. I walked into my bathroom and began running my bathwater.

I stood in front of the mirror wiping a piece of a sleep out of my eye and began cleansing my golden yellow skin. I pulled my chocolate brown hair back into a ponytail and noticed a purplish mark on my neck. Dwight still nibbled on and kissed my neck like we were kids. We had been together since I was thirteen and he was fourteen. Almost twenty years together—that sounded strange coming from a thirty-two-year-old woman. But it is true I had known my baby for almost my whole life. He played basketball with my brother and came over to our house all the time. My grandmother raised us because my parents died when I was younger. Then Nana passed away about twelve years ago. I guess that's why I am so close to my husband's family. My only real family is my older brother, Wade. He has two years on me but acts like the younger sibling. He is so immature and ain't never been nothing but cute his whole life. He passed through school and a little bit of college just because he had hazel eyes and curly hair.

Dwight and I wanted to get married when I turned eighteen, but our family and friends talked us out of it. They convinced us to wait until we finished college. I thought they were hating, but I thank them for it now. I got to pledge Sigma Gamma Rho and experience college life. I went to Bethune-Cookman and Dwight went to Georgia

Tech. He stayed for about a half a semester and transferred to Bethune-Cookman with me. He couldn't stand being away from me or his mama. Since then we have been inseparable. We married and settled here in Jacksonville, with our two daughters, Jordan, who's six, and Destiny, who's four.

Dwight is hands-on with our daughters. He irons their clothes, feeds them breakfast, and drops them off at school, all before I wake up sometimes. Then he heads to the office; he's a systems engineer at Horizon South. My husband is such a good man and I have his mother to thank. Dwight's father walked away when he was younger. And I guess his mother just wanted to raise a good man, and she did. Dwight treats me, his mama, and his sister like queens. Dwight said I'm materialistic and I shop too much, but that doesn't stop him from spoiling me. I do hide shoeboxes and new bags from him after I go shopping. I blame my need for everything on being raised by my grandmother. My grandmother loved me, but kept me unfashionable like grandmothers do. The minute I could get a job I did, so I could buy my own clothes. And now I'm just addicted. I shop so much I have filled up my walk-in closet and halfway took over Dwight's. I walked out of the bedroom and into my large open hallway and took in the beauty of my new home.

We just moved in two months ago and it is still taking some getting used to. Sometimes I get up in the middle of the night and can't believe I really live here in this fabulous 3,000-square-foot house. Ever since I was a little girl I dreamed of a house like this. My house has four bedrooms, four and a half bathrooms, an in-law suite, and a den downstairs. I have a fifty-five-inch plasma TV mounted on the wall in the family room. My contemporary kitchen has upgraded honey-maple cabinets, absolute black granite countertops, and an island in the middle. My oldest daughter Jordan's room is decorated with pink butterflies and white clouds on the walls. Destiny's is fuchsia pink with Dora the Explorer accessories. We'd put a contract on our house almost two years ago. The model home for our development wasn't even finished yet. I knew it was my dream home based on the floor plan. So there wouldn't be any problems, we immediately put our townhouse on the market and the first person who saw it, bought it. We had to put our things in storage and move into a cramped apartment. We had only two bedrooms for the four of us and we had to share a bathroom. We were only supposed to live like that for six months before our house was completed. But the construction schedule went nine months over schedule. Our original developer was shut down because he was using illegal immigrants. We were supposed to be moved in by October but the work didn't finish until July.

But now all that was behind us. What matters now is that my daughters get to grow up in a beautiful home that I wished I grew up in. When we moved into our new home, all the rooms were empty, like a blank canvas, and since then I feel like I have created a masterpiece. I turned every room into a page out of a home decor magazine. I drove myself crazy at first with decorating. I wanted to buy everything to match—the borders, the towels, the sheets. But now each room is exactly the way I wanted it to be. And now that they are perfect, I want them to stay that way. I don't want anything out of place. Not even a pillow. I've asked Dwight if can I hire a housekeeper; he told me no.

But I'm going to keep asking him, even though he said only rich people have housekeepers. My response to him was that smart people have housekeepers. He doesn't get it, but he'll give in eventually. He eventually gives in to my every want and need.

As soon as four o'clock came, Mama Dee was stomping across my lawn. She was wearing a pearl-pink pantsuit and beige sandals. She had my little girls in tow and she didn't look happy. My vacation was officially over. Mama Dee's brown flipped wig bounced up and down with her every step. I still wasn't dressed, so I threw a wrap dress over my voluptuous frame. I opened the door and she playfully yelled, "Here, take your little replica divas back." She then handed me their pink Barbie overnight bags.

"Why you call them divas?" I said, laughing and giving my babies a hug. They both look just like their father, with beautiful brown skin and teddy-bear noses.

"Well, let me see. First they said, 'Mama Dee, why you don't have a flat television? How come you don't have any bottled water?' Then that little one right there told me my polish was chipped on my nails and I needed a manicure." She laughed and then asked, "Where is my son?"

"At work."

"On a Sunday? Does he spend any time at home?"

"That's what I told him, but he said it is some important project going on, so I just deal with it."

"Well, I have to get back home. Tell him, although I love flowers, I would love to get a visit from my son."

"I will, Mama Dee. Be safe."

"I will. I got to hurry up and have things ready before Danny and Reggie get back from their honeymoon."

"I can't believe she married that man," I said, shaking my head.

"Me neither. What you going to do?" she said, sighing. "We all told her not to. She didn't listen, so whatever happens happens," she said as she walked back to her car. I closed the door and caught up on my daughters' weekend.

CHAPTER 2

Alicia

When I pulled up to the regular Thursday night happy hour with my girls, I couldn't wait to relax after a stressful week and talk trash with my friends. It is such a blessing to have friends like mine. We are just real with one another, and we've been that way since we all met at college. We all grew up within twenty miles of each other, from Prince Georges County to Montgomery County to Anne Arundel, but didn't meet until we were freshmen at University of Maryland.

We always tried to pick a new point to hit every week. Usually somewhere around the 495 Beltway, but for some reason someone picked DC this evening. It was always a hassle finding parking, especially near the Verizon Center. I drove my silver convertible Saab from G to H streets, back and forth, until I finally settled on valet parking. The parking attendants at IndeBlue were in the street, waiting to get my money. They probably noticed my car circle the block and figured I'd be back. Before I got out, I checked

my BlackBerry and thankfully I hadn't received any messages from work. Then I said a short prayer that there would
be no crisis requiring my attention this evening. I planned
to have a night away from the computer to relax and ana-
lyze life. I slung my black Coach satchel over my shoulder
and handed the guy a five-dollar tip.

The moment I stepped into the lounge, I felt less tense.
The dimly lit bar with walls the color of the sunset and cos-
mopolitan decor reenergized my spirit. Smooth R&B blasted
through the speakers, and just as I was about to text Andrea
to see if she was here, I saw Tammy's red mohawk peeking
out over the crowd. She and Andrea were propped on the
sleek brushed-nickel stools at the opposite end of the room.
It appeared they'd reserved a seat on each side of them for
Gina and me. I adjusted my black-and-white printed wrap
shirt, straightened my posture, and sashayed past all of the
men in business suits surrounding the bar. Andrea and
Tammy were so engrossed in a conversation that they hadn't
noticed me. I crept up to them. "Hey, y'all!"

"Hey, girl . . ." came out in harmony.

I gave hugs and asked, "Where's Gina?"

Tammy said, "She just texted me and said she's looking
for a parking space."

We giggled because Gina was the cheapest of the crew
and I guess we were all thinking the same thing: *Why
couldn't she just valet?* That's our girl, though. I slowly slid
on the stool, adjusting my low-rise trouser-cut jeans; although I got a tattoo of a bird and the words FLY FREE on
the small of my back, I'm still very conscious of my ass
spilling out of my jeans when I sit down. I looped my
forearm in the gold chain handles of my purse and plopped
it on my lap.

Andrea leaned in on the bar and faced me. "So, what the hell is going on with your job?"

Tammy grabbed my wrist. "Wait until Gina gets in here so you won't have to tell the story twice."

While we were waiting on Gina, a male shadow hovered over me. He motioned for the bartender's attention.

"A French martini for the lady and . . ."

His voice sounded familiar, so I turned to see who it was. The caramel-colored man resembling Jay-Z smiled back at me. We'd kicked it a bit a long time ago, but he seemed a lot slimmer than I remembered. Maybe he took my advice and started hitting the gym. His cheap blue dress shirt was tucked nicely into his black pants. He smiled and his brand-new veneers nearly blinded me. His gap was gone.

"How are you, Ms. Alicia?"

When the bartender set the drink down, he slid it in front of me. I blushed. "How did you remember I drank French martinis?"

He laughed. "Because I remember every time we went out you'd have to explain . . ." Imitating me, he continued: "Chambord, pineapple juice, and vodka."

I laughed a little longer than I needed to, because I couldn't remember his name. He said, "You were quite a number."

Thankfully, Tammy, aka Memorex, leaned in and whispered, "Isn't that Byron . . . remember we use to call him Grizzly?"

I wanted to burst out laughing. Instead, I nodded as it all came together—who exactly Byron was and where I'd met him. He was a flunky I met on a Black Ski Weekend in Colorado.

"So, Byron . . . how have you been?"

"Working hard. Playing harder."

He seemed a little more relaxed and less uptight. "So, how do you manage the best of both worlds? I'm always just working. This is the extent of my playing."

"Well, you look like you're having fun."

We laughed and he continued, "I never let work consume me. When five o'clock strikes, I'm out."

"I wish. I can't remember the last time I worked a forty-hour week."

"You need someone to help take that load off."

As attractive as the offer sounded, I'd rather work my ass off than to have to cook, clean, and wash some man's drawers all in the name of taking the load off. I smirked. "I guess."

Gina strutted in and sang, "Hey, y'all."

As she headed down the line with hugs, Byron backed away. "Okay, Ms. Alicia. Go ahead and hang out with your girls."

When he touched my forearm, I noticed a ring on his left hand. I shook my head. Wow, I couldn't believe someone actually married him. If my memory serves me correctly, he was a Teeny-Weeny-I-Don't-Feel-You-in-Me dude. Someone must have been desperate.

When Gina got to me, she asked, "Who was the cutie that just walked away?"

Tammy and Gina were the comedians of the crew. Tammy laughed louder than necessary. "Gina, that was Grizzly. Remember him?"

Gina's preppy black-frame glasses popped off her nose as she threw her head back in complete shock. "No."

"Yes. That's him," I said.

"Oh my goodness. He looks so different. Remember he had more hair on his hands than I have on my head." Gina laughed.

I looked at Gina's crew cut and couldn't suppress my laughter. "I can't stand y'all."

Tammy rolled her pencil neck. "He's still a damn bear."

Andrea chimed in, "That's not nice, y'all."

Gina said, "Dre, stop feeling sorry for dudes. Nobody told him not to shave his knuckles."

Tammy's drink sprayed out of her mouth when she began to howl with laughter. She slid from the barstool and slapped Gina a high five. "Exactly." She rolled her eyes at Andrea, then spoke to everyone, "That's why our girl had to do what she does best." She and Gina laughed as they spoke simultaneously and looked at me. "Le-Le."

Ironically, everyone outside of the crew thought that Le-Le was a cute nickname for Alicia, but Le-Le actually stood for "Love 'Em and Leave 'Em." It was a name that one of those fools came up with sophomore year of college. I huffed and said, "Let's go upstairs."

Andrea gently smirked at me as if to say they didn't have hearts. Gina, standing a mere five feet, always took charge, so we let her be the first to head up the stairs to get the table. She strutted in front of us in a white baby tee with black writing and tight jeans like she owned the place. Somehow, she made that same outfit fly year after year.

After the hostess sat us down at a large round table, all eyes were on me. Gina, the little smart ass, asked, "So, they're trying to take your job, huh?"

Andrea shot a look at her and rephrased the question, "So, what's going on?"

"Well, they claim they're bringing in someone from the company we're merging with to lead the team."

Tammy said, "But haven't you been leading the team all this time?"

"Exactly," I huffed.

Andrea said, "That's horrible. Do you think your job is safe?"

"I really don't know."

Gina asked, "That's fucking ridiculous. As much as you work, they have nerve even coming to you with that bullshit."

I shrugged. "Unfortunately, that's the way it is. It's a conspiracy, I know. But what can I do?"

Tammy folded her arms. "Get into a field where you'll be respected."

"I make too much money for that."

Andrea said, "Or you could marry a man who makes a lot of money."

"When the hell have you known me to wait for the cavalry to come?"

She shook her head. "Well, Le-Le, if you stayed with a man long enough maybe the cavalry would come."

Andrea kept hope alive that maybe just maybe someone would come and validate her existence. Damn if I planned on hopelessly waiting for some man to sweep me up and marry me, so we could live happily ever after in never-never land. I'm a realist and that type of shit happens only in books.

CHAPTER 3

Tracey

For the most part I worked from home as a real estate agent. I scheduled my appointments by phone and did a lot of communication through e-mail. Choosing to go into real estate was a great decision. I get to spend time with my children and I go into the office only three times a week. I show the majority of homes during the day, when the girls are at school, or after dinner, when Dwight is home. My job allows me to be hands-on with them. I go up to their school and volunteer and bring in treats on Friday. I'm the kind of mom I wish I had.

I worked for Harrison Realty. It is a small, family-owned business. There are four other associates. I do all types of deals, from half-million-dollar homes to first-time home buyers. I'm good at what I do. I love selling and almost always make the most sales of the office.

When I walked into the office, Jeff, our receptionist, was on a call. His headset rested on his short brown hair. He signaled me to check my mailbox. I walked over, retrieved my mail, and got a cup of coffee. I had several messages. One was from my two o'clock appointment; she said she was running a little late. I wasn't surprised—folks are always late. However, I was always on time when it came to showing a property. I didn't need any unexpected shit to happen. It is hard to believe, but sometimes people have dishes in the sink, don't make their beds, and let their dogs run loose. And then they get mad when their houses stay on the market for months. I always hide any imperfections: I cover holes in the walls with paintings, and spray a little insect spray if necessary. My trunk is a little convenience store filled with paper towels, Febreze, Lysol disinfectant, and an assortment of cleansers.

"And what brings you to the office on a Monday?" Jen asked. She was my girl at the office. She had dyed black hair with these ugly white streaks painted throughout. She was only twenty-eight, but she looked a little past thirty-five. If I was running late or couldn't handle something, she was there to do it for me. Jen could talk you to deaf about random events. She was one of those women who was always talking about getting married and having kids, and hadn't even met the guy yet. She was nice, but just a mess, and living with her mother didn't help. Her mother always had her running errands. She would pick up her medicine or take her cat to the vet. I felt sorry for her. We chatted until it was time for me to meet my client.

"I have to meet a client," I responded as I popped a peppermint in my mouth.

"You're actually working. I thought you would be somewhere getting a mani and pedi."

"Be quiet. I scheduled that appointment for later," I said.

I opened the lockbox on the three-bedroom ranch house. Everything was neat and orderly. *Thank God*, I thought. I opened the window and allowed some fresh air to seep in. Then I opened the blinds throughout the entire house. The sun makes everything look better.

My client, Miss Chanel Austin, came ten minutes late. I hoped she would like this house, I thought. I showed her three other properties and I wasn't showing her any more. People like her walk in the office wanting to live anywhere and buy anything, but once they realize they are approved, they start thinking they have options. It was my job to let her know that this was her only option. She walked in the door smiling, wearing a tight T-shirt and jeans. She said she was sorry she was late. Her smiled disappeared quickly as she took off her sunglasses like she was unimpressed.

"So let me show you around," I said, leading her to the kitchen. I showed her around the house. "So what do you think so far?" I asked.

"This is okay. The pictures online made it look better."

It was time to turn on my sales skills. "I think this house and this neighborhood have so much potential."

"So where do you live?" she asked, looking around the empty white kitchen.

"In Crescent Hill."

"Oh that's a nice neighborhood. Do you have anything for sale in that area? 'Cause this is kind of far!" I thought about her 594 credit score and nicely explained that she couldn't afford to buy a doorbell in my neighborhood. Basically, she just should be happy that I could even get her ass in a house. I had to let her know this was the best she was going to get for her budget.

"Yeah that's a nice area, but again, this is up and coming.

If you to decide to sell your house, you will have a better chance out here. Plus, your preapproval was for two-fifty. Houses in my area start in the low four hundreds."

"Really? Yeah, I can't afford that. I don't know why I even asked you about a neighborhood like that," she said, second-guessing herself. I smiled and stood in place and let her look around again. When she walked back into the kitchen, I glanced down at my cell phone. The time read four-thirty. She had to hurry up. She was not going to make me miss my nail appointment. When she came out of the kitchen she rubbed her hand on the gold and white wall.

"If I get this, I'm going to have to change the wallpaper. Thank you for showing me this house," she said.

That's more like it, I thought. *Be grateful.* "You're welcome," I said, walking her toward the door. I thought she was about to tell me she wanted to make an offer. But she said the opposite of what I was expecting.

"I'm going to have to bring my boyfriend. He'll make the final decision." She never mentioned her boyfriend in the two months I had been working with her dumb ass.

"And when do you want to bring him?" I asked, disappointed.

"Um, well, he is out of town. He'll be home next week," she stuttered. Just by the way she was fidgeting her fingers I knew she was lying. She was making me mad, playing games. I had something for her.

"So does your boyfriend have access to a computer?" I asked.

"Yes, why?"

"Well, maybe you can send him pictures of the house."

"You are so right, thank you, but I don't know his e-mail address."

"Maybe you can call him up and get it." Once again I called her bluff. Then she pulled her pink RAZR phone out of her purse. I heard her say, "Babe, what's your e-mail address?" She then asked me for a pen. I gave her a pen and piece of paper. She wrote the address down and then gave it to me. I went back to the office and e-mailed pictures of the house. I couldn't let this dumb young girl who had to ask her boyfriend not her husband if she should buy a house discourage me. She is going to buy this house.

After dealing with Chanel's idiotic ass, I had just enough time to pick up Jordan from dance class and Destiny from day care. Jordan was sitting against the mirrored wall, chatting with her friends. She saw me and picked up her bag and ran toward me.

"How was class?" I asked.

"It was good. We are having a recital." Her dance instructor handed me a yellow reminder slip for the recital. I saw Jordan's friend Leah's mom, Sophia. Sophia irritated me. I called her grandmom mommy. She was only in her forties, but technically she was old enough to be her daughter's grandmother. She wanted to be my friend so bad, and always invited us out, and I always declined. She had her daughter Leah in everything: dance, karate, swimming. She even bought her daughter Rosetta Stone software, so she could learn to speak Spanish and French. She has that poor little girl on overdrive. I'm not surprised her husband works out of town twenty days out of each month. I waved to her before she could come over and start up a conversation. *Not today, girlfriend, not today*, I thought as I hurried out of the building. I instructed Jordan to put her seat belt on and pulled out before Sophia caught up with us.

• • •

We picked up Destiny from day care and headed straight to the nail salon. We were regulars. I didn't let the girls get full pedicures yet, but they do get manicures and their toes polished with designs. Lynn, the owner, came over and welcomed us. She was a petite Asian woman in her mid-thirties.

"Hi, Lynn. I'm getting a pedicure and a refill."

"I'll be right with you. Pick out a color," she said. She spoke in Vietnamese to her worker to run my pedicure water. I dipped my feet in the hot soapy water as Lynn took the old polish off of my nails. I was beginning to relax a little when the loud shriek of Jordan's voice filled the nail salon.

"Mommy, tell Destiny to stop copying," Jordan yelled as she picked her polish.

"Pink is my favorite color, too!" Destiny screamed.

"It wasn't your favorite color yesterday. You said it was red."

"Pick another color, Destiny," I said, trying to end their squabbling.

"Why, Mommy? I like pink, too!" she said as she began to cry. I had to get out of my seat and calm her down. I picked up a lilac polish and showed it to her.

"This is pretty, Des. You should get this color." She turned the polish upside down and then said okay and licked her tongue at Jordan.

The girls bickered for the next thirty minutes. They were sitting under the dryers letting their nails dry and their legs swing back. *Next time I'm coming by myself*, I thought. My phone rang and I put down the *Vogue* that I was reading and answered it. "Tracey Wilson."

"Hi, Miss Wilson, this is Chanel. My boyfriend got the

pictures and he said that he loved it and told me to make an offer. So could you please not show the house to anyone and I can come by your office with a check and sign the contract?" I was excited about the sale but I didn't let her know it.

"That's fine. Just give me a call tomorrow." I probably should have felt bad for doubting her, but I didn't. I just continued getting pampered and thought about everything I could buy when she signed on the dotted line.

After me and the girls left the nail salon, we drove home. I was trying to beat Dwight home, but we both turned into the driveway at the same time. I didn't feel like hearing his mouth about me spending unnecessary money on the girls. He always accused me of creating mini divas. Destiny ran out of the car and up to him and said, "Daddy, look at my nails." Dwight looked over at me and shook his head.

"They look so pretty, right, Daddy?" Destiny asked as he picked her up.

"Daddy, my recital is coming up. You coming?" Jordan asked, hanging on to his free arm.

"You know I'm going to be there, princess."

"I'm your princess, too, Daddy, right?" Destiny said, turning his attention back to her.

"Yes, Des," he said as he turned from the girls to me. "What's for dinner?"

"I was going to ask you that. You know we just got our nails done," I joked.

"Yes, I know nails are priority over food. Just order a pizza. I'm going to get in the shower. I'm tired and have a big day tomorrow," Dwight said as he shooed us in the house.

CHAPTER 4

Tracey

Mama Dee and Mr. Randy, her boyfriend, were sitting in the row in the small auditorium with me. I was looking all around for Dwight. Every other minute, I looked at the stage and back to the aisle to see if Dwight was coming. Work was taking over his life. I told that man that he was going to have to separate family time and work. Work ends at five p.m. no matter what. If he doesn't make Jordan's recital I am going to be so upset. I finally saw him two rows over, looking for us. I stood up and waved my arms to get his attention.

"Did I miss Jordan?" he asked as he wiped perspiration off his forehead.

"No, you didn't miss her yet."

"Good," he said, relieved.

"Why are you late?" I huffed at him.

"Long story, I'll talk to you about it later," he said as Destiny got up off her seat and gave her daddy a kiss. He kissed her on her cheek and told her to go and have a seat.

• • •

After Jordan's dance recital, we had dinner at the Macaroni Grill. We sat in a big booth. Jordan was still talking about what happened at her recital.

"You were the best dancer up there, Jordan," Mama Dee said.

"Did you see when Leah messed up? I knew she was going to mess up. She always messes up. She was crying backstage."

"Well, next time she'll get it together. You did a great job. You were perfect, princess," Dwight said as he gave Jordan a sideways hug.

"Mommy, am I going to go to dance class, too?" Destiny asked.

"Yes."

"When? Tomorrow?"

"No."

"Mommy, why?"

"Des, you have to be five years old to start. Next year, okay?" She finally agreed and we enjoyed the rest of our dinner.

After dinner we all came into the house. I wanted to go straight to bed, but I had to get everything ready for the next day. I went into the laundry room and put a load of clothes in the washer. Dwight bathed and washed the girls for bed. I poured the last of the Gain in the washing machine. I hate doing laundry—it is such a chore. I wished I had someone to do this for me. I so can't see me doing my own laundry for the rest of my life. You have to wash, dry, and then fold them. Oh, how I hate it.

Destiny peeped down the steps in her Dora the Explorer pink nightgown and said, "Good night, Mommy."

"Night, Des. Go to sleep. No playing tonight. Okay?"

"Yes, Mommy," she said as she hugged me. Jordan came down and hugged me too. Then they ran back into their bedrooms. I placed the towels and washed clothes into a basket and brought them upstairs to fold. I dumped the towels on the bed and began folding them into squares. Dwight walked in the bedroom, closed the door, and said, "Sit down. There is something I need to talk to you about."

"What's wrong with you?" I asked as Dwight reluctantly came and had a seat next to me. I looked him directly in his eyes to try to get a gauge of what he was about to say.

"Remember the project we have been working on that's taken up all my time?" he asked.

"Yes. What's going on? Don't tell me they fired you," I asked as I placed my hand over my mouth and closed my eyes then took a deep breath and stood up.

"No, they didn't fire me."

I said "Praise God" in my mind. "So what's going on?" I asked.

"Well, Horizon South bought another company in Maryland, and they are making some changes within the company. They offered me a better position to move with them to Maryland."

"Maryland! I know you told them they were crazy. Right?"

"I told them as soon as they made the offer that I couldn't accept it. I had to talk it over with my wife. Then they insisted I think about it overnight."

"And you said you would? Oh my God. I need to sit. Dwight, we just bought this house," I said as I sighed. *Why was he doing this to me?* I asked myself. I got up off the bed and looked him straight in his face.

"Tell them that I say no. Absolutely not. How can they ask a married father to move to another city? So if you already told them no, why are we having this conversation?"

Dwight scratched the side of his face and chin and said, "I am going to tell them no again tomorrow."

"I can't tell. It seems like you were considering it. I can't believe you."

"Tracey, I was considering it. If I took the job we would be more secure. We can put all the money back in our retirement that we used for the down payment. Plus I would be getting more experience. Then I could come home and start my own consulting firm. I think the time is right, Tracey. I think it is better to move the girls while they are young. I want us to be financially secure and this will help us."

"We don't need more money, Dwight. I'm one hundred percent against it. I'm tired of this stupid company. They pay well. But there are other companies that pay just as well. My answer is no," I said as I shook my head once again. I walked into the bathroom and took a shower. Dwight tried to follow me but I shut the door in his face and locked it.

Dwight and I have not been communicating since he tried to spring that mess about moving on me. He's barely been getting a good morning out of me. I've been stomping around the house and rolling my eyes at him. And if it wasn't for the girls, he would not be eating. I was in the middle of cooking when I told Jordan to call her father and tell him to hurry up home. I had to show a home. She handed me the phone. Before I could say anything he said, "I'm on my way now, Tracey."

"How long? I can't be late."

"I know. I'll be there—I'm around the corner." Jordan hung up the phone for me. I ran upstairs and changed back into my navy suit and slid my mules on.

Ten minutes later Dwight was still not home. I hated that he lied and said he was right around the corner and he wasn't. I dialed his cell phone again.

"You almost here? I have to go, Dwight, come on!" I yelled into the phone. I only had fifteen minutes to get to the property. I went back downstairs and waited by the door. Still no Dwight.

"Jordan, when Daddy gets in here make sure he goes over your homework with you." As soon as Dwight pulled up, I wanted to pull off. I saw car headlights turn into the driveway. I raced out the door as Dwight walked in and placed the car keys in my hand, saying, "Surprise." I looked over and saw an all-white BMW X5.

"What is this?"

"Your new car, baby," he said as he planted a kiss on my cheek.

"New car. Really? Oh, Dwight. Oh my God, thank you," I said as I jumped in the car and looked all around at the gadgets.

He came in on the passenger side and said, "Let me show you this. You'll never get lost going anywhere. It has a navigational system."

"Baby, thank you so much for the car. It is so beautiful. But I still have to get out of here. Make sure the girls eat and go over Jordan's homework with her." I shut the car door and pulled off.

• • •

By the time I returned to the house the girls were already asleep. Their clothes were hanging up already pressed for the next day. And the kitchen was cleaned. Dwight was sitting on the sofa reading *Black Enterprise.*

"Babe. I'm shocked. What made you buy me a new car?"

"I just thought you deserved it. We can afford it now that I make forty thousand dollars more a year."

"What are you talking about?" I said as I unhooked my earrings and sat next to him.

"I accepted the job in Maryland."

"So there's strings attached to the car? Unfucking believable, Dwight," I said, shaking my head.

"No, I wanted you to have the car regardless. I have to go to Maryland."

"We talked about this and we decided no." *Was I the only person who remembered our conversation?* I thought.

"You decided no, Tracey. I had to take the job."

I stood up, my voice slightly elevated, and said, "You had to take the job. Did they have a gun up to your head?"

"Tracey, sit down and listen. It was forty thousand more to go or stay with thirty thousand less. They backed me into a corner. I didn't have any other choice."

"Couldn't you just go to another company?"

"You know they are the biggest company in the south."

I couldn't do anything but cry. As much as I was opposed to him leaving, there was no way we could afford to keep our lifestyle with him taking a thirty-thousand-dollar pay cut. "I can't believe you would really make this decision without me. I don't know what to say. I'm so hurt."

"I wasn't trying to hurt you. I want to do what's best for the family. I really want you to move with me. We can do this, Trace. They will pay for housing. Just try it out."

"And leave our house, are you crazy? We just waited damn near two years to move in here. I spent all these months decorating and you expect me to move." I was furious. I couldn't understand why he would make such a big move without me. "Dwight, you are not going to force or bribe me to move."

"I'm not. This is not just for me; it is for the betterment of our family. I understand you're upset," he said calmly.

"You don't understand how I feel. This is not right and you know it. I'm not going to uproot me and the girls. I'm just not going to do it," I said, still in disbelief.

"I don't expect you to, sweetheart. I just want us all to have a comfortable life. And I know I made the final decision without you and it was wrong, but I made the best choice for our family," he said as he massaged my shoulders, comforting me.

I walked away, threw up my hands, and said, "I'm not moving, Dwight. I didn't wait for this house to abandon it." It infuriated me that he finalized a move that will affect our entire family without consulting me first. I didn't know what else to say. For everything I attempted to say he had a quick response. Like he had prepared for this conversation. That made me even angrier. Tears just started falling and shooting down my face. I fell onto the bed and Dwight took me in his arms and held me. His consoling tone, warm arms, and telling me I was right lessened my anger. At least temporarily.

CHAPTER 5

Alicia

I walked into the office with an attitude the morning the new guy was expected to start. Why couldn't they just promote me and have that other person take my position? Too much like right. It was okay for me to be the Software Team Lead, but I'm not good enough to be the Software Development Manager. It's all a damn play on words. I write software development documents, I code software, I plan the development schedule, I decide which requirements will be included in each installment, I hire developers, and I'm the customer liaison. So, can someone tell me again why the hell I need another manager over me?

If I go in there to find a snot-nosed rookie overseeing me, everyone is going to have a hard time. I promise to God that I will not train him. I won't hand over anything, except my damn resignation letter. Dwight Wilson. When my project managers sat me down to tell me about the new organizational structure, I didn't question his demographics. I couldn't stomach blatant prejudices. Instead, I hid my fury and smiled tightly. If I wasn't so comfortable with my job and my cushy extended cubicle, I probably would have quit that day. Instead, I decided it was worth a chance. Go in with an open mind. My team and I were too close to let this injustice ruin our bond.

By the time I strolled in fashionably late, through the maze of cubicles in our second-floor office space, my stomach was bubbling. I wore a navy polo shirt layered over a white T-shirt, with my beige and navy slip-on Pumas, just in case a fight broke out. I crept up on the team, all gathered at Desiree's desk, and pushed my way into the circle.

"Okay, have you guys seen him yet?"

"He's in the office with Chavis and them."

I frowned. "I don't like change."

Desiree tapped on her keyboard. "Who are you telling? I hope they don't come in here wanting to change everything. I don't want to learn any new technology."

Jim added, "I know. I don't want some knucklehead coming in here messing up the program."

A voice vibrated through our little gossip group. "I'm Dwight. Not some knucklehead."

It took everyone a moment to recover from the shock. The sight of this tall, husky black man left us speechless. He extended his hand and no one reciprocated. We all smiled nervously. Why didn't it ever occur to me that the new guy could be a brother? I was actually ecstatic to see him except for the cheesy charcoal suit. I chuckled to myself before finally extending my hand. "Hello, Mr. Wilson. Welcome to Optimus."

He nodded in gratitude and began exchanging small talk, querying our interest and positions. We tried our best to size him up, but he appeared unfazed as answers flowed so eloquently from his tongue. He successfully peeled away our initial layer of opposition. We were all still quite attentive as he said, "So, can we all get together after lunch for a get-to-know session? Around one-fifteen."

I said, "Are you asking or are you telling us that you'd like to meet us at one-fifteen?"

He blushed. "They told me you guys were a rough crowd, but I didn't believe them." He directed his answer to me. "We *are* going to meet at one-fifteen in Conference Room D."

Ray said, "Can you put that on the group calendar?"

"No, my account isn't set up yet and I expect that anyone on the team who may not be standing here will get the invite by word of mouth."

His smooth cockiness left us stunned. Desiree and I looked like *damn*. It's nothing like a man with cocoa skin giving orders. Even as his nemesis, I was forced to blush. In less than five minutes and in fewer than five words, he let us know that he was a no-bullshit kind of manager.

"Damn, there goes the morning runs to Starbucks I let y'all get away with."

When the cubicle cleared, Desiree and I gave each other funny looks. I pouted, "He seems a little arrogant."

She laughed. "Forget him. That's why he got a big nose."

"And big lips."

We laughed. It tickled us that at least we had one negative thing to say about him. In the middle of our amusement, I thought about the source. How the hell can Desiree's auburn-wig-wearing, 1985-glasses-wearing, all-my-clothes-are-from-1992 ass talk about anybody? I shook my head and thought, *I'm going to hell.*

Before I got to my desk, I decided to peep in and do a

more personal introduction. I tapped on his door. "Hi, Dwight. I'm . . ."

"Alicia Dixon."

"That's me. You're good. You remembered everyone's name that fast?"

"No. I remember you, though. During my extensive meetings with the program managers, they mentioned you a lot. So when you said your name, it immediately registered. Have a seat."

I plopped down in the chair and noticed a bunch of unhealthy snacks piled in a box on the floor. Twinkies. M&M'S. Twizzlers. Maybe that would explain the protruding belly. His height definitely reduced the impact of his width, but nonetheless, he could definitely jog around the track a few times. "So, was it hard for you to make the decision to come here?"

"Ah, not really. Horizon South is one of the biggest technology firms in Jacksonville. So it was a choice between getting a large increase in pay or a severe decrease."

We both laughed at the no-brainer decision. "I do understand. How much notice did they give you to make the decision?"

"Two weeks."

"Are you kidding me? You had to make a decision to uproot your life"—noticing his wedding ring, I added—"and your family, in two weeks?"

"Well, my wife and kids haven't come yet. It was too much for my wife to accept so suddenly."

"I bet. That's ludicrous."

He clarified, "That's Corporate America."

"Yeah. That's true."

I stood to leave. He said, "How do you think the initial meeting with the team went?"

"You handled them well. You have to put your foot down or we'll walk all over you."

He laughed. "That's hard to do."

"I bet."

He smiled. "So, you're second-in-command, huh?"

"I'm the Development Lead, but I do so much development that sometimes I feel like I'm just leading myself."

"We'll have to do something about that."

My twists swung around and I frowned. "Like what?"

"If you're the Lead, you have no business doing the work."

"Sometimes if you want it done right, you have to do it yourself. You know what I mean."

I stopped midway through my chuckle when I noticed he wasn't amused. He said, "No, actually, I don't. Maybe we have to reevaluate some things around here."

My eyes shifted. Was that his way of saying that we had to reevaluate my job? Suddenly, we'd hopped off the good foot that we started off on. I was lost for words and it took me a minute to shake off the astonishment.

"Oh well . . . I guess I'll see you at our meeting this afternoon."

I turned to leave and he called my name. "I wasn't trying to offend you when I said we have to reevaluate things. I was talking about the way the software is designed. That's my job, you know?"

"Who said I was offended?"

"The sassy, sista-girl way that you were about to storm out of here."

"Whatever, I'll see you at the one-fifteen meeting."

We both laughed for a minute. He said, "I'm going to enjoy this. I've never worked with a sista in charge."

"Well there's a first time for everything."

"You're right, Ms. Dixon. You're absolutely right."

When I walked out of his office, I immediately began to scrutinize everything he said in the conversation. Maybe he was a male chauvinist. Maybe he thought I wasn't skilled enough for my position. Maybe he was going to be a jerk. Maybe I wasn't going to like him.

In our team meeting, Dwight looked to me to explain a lot of the current organizational procedures as he tried to make us aware of his management style. He had a way of making complexity seem simple. Though I was still taken aback by his forward approach earlier, he seemed to have a good system.

He'd often look at me. "What do you think about that, Ms. Dixon?"

When I would nod, he'd joke, "Gotta make the ladies happy."

The guys in the group seemed to get a kick out of that. He had a way with words that left the entire room clinging to the next one. How could he mesmerize all of us? After my tenth time asking myself that question, it hit me. The first step to leadership is to look like you know even when you don't. Dwight stepped up in here like he'd been working with the team for years and, damn it, he wanted respect. It was really that simple.

Suddenly, I began to question my job and how we would integrate responsibility. If he knows everything, and there are ten developers on the team; the leader is not leading, so what do you need her for? Paying five developers and one good lead would mean they could get rid of me.

In my mind, I was already strategizing my approach to the battle of the sexes. He would not win and I would prevail. As I daydreamed about our power struggle, he called my name.

I looked up and noticed everyone gathering their things. "Let's go to my office and go through this Software Development Document."

My eyes questioned how this post-meeting originated. He continued, "We'll go through it page by page, see whether we may need to add more detail or where we could cut corners."

I smiled tightly. "That should be fine."

"And I need you to help set up my development environment."

When we left the conference room, I said, "You're trying to be here all night, huh?"

"What time do you usually get off?"

"I'm a nine to seven girl."

"So I have you for the next four hours."

Did I say that I wanted to spend the rest of my workday with him? Hell, I have things to do. Why couldn't he be like most people and chill on his first day? He was trying to be an overachiever and disrupting my mode of operation.

"Well let me drop this stuff off at my desk and I'll be over."

I stopped at Desiree's cube before I went into his office and rolled my eyes. Desiree imitated him, "Is that okay with you, Ms. Dixon?"

"Exactly. I think he was trying to be smart."

"Alicia, please. I think he's being respectful."

I shared with her the discussion about reevaluating things around here. She laughed. "Alicia, you're just paranoid. I think you should stop trying to interpret what he's trying to say and listen to what he's actually saying."

The *whatever* look on my face let her know that I didn't agree. She said, "Don't be afraid to learn new things."

"Who me?" I had to laugh because I have that argument with Desiree nearly every day. She is the exact same person I met five years ago. She doesn't like to travel. She doesn't like to eat different food. Look at who needs to try new things.

She clarified, because I'm certain she knew what was going through my mind. "Alicia, yes, you are adventurous in your personal life. But sometimes you can be so closed-minded when it comes to work. Honestly. Maybe if you listen to his game plan, it may help you out." She paused and studied my resistance. "How many hours did you work last week?"

As I headed out of her office, I said, "Too many to discuss. I'll catch you tomorrow if I don't see you before you leave."

"Okay, Ms. Dixon."

A slight smile lingered as I walked into Dwight's office. "Hey, you ready?"

He looked away from his computer screen. "Ms. Dixon. I thought you changed your mind."

"I had to go to the restroom. Is that okay?"

He looked up at me as if he questioned if that is where I'd really gone. "Oh, I'm sorry. I'm all up in your business."

We both laughed and he reclined in his chair. The springs creaked as he rested his hands on top of his bald head. Ah, I figured it was my turn to speak. When I noticed the pictures on his desk, I said, "Oh my, is this your family?"

He gazed momentarily at the pictures. "Yeah, my three girls."

"That's cute. What are their names?"

He pointed to his wife. "That's my Tracey." Then he pointed to the girls. "The oldest is Jordan. She's six and my baby girl is Destiny. She's four."

"They are adorable. You're the only guy in the house, huh? I know that's something. Are you going to try for a boy?"

"Nah, she's done. If it were up to me, I would, but wifey says she's done."

A quick streak of envy rippled through me. It must be nice to be called *wifey*. That holds so much more weight than just simply saying my wife. *Wifey* means the chick who is the center of the world. *Wife* just means a chick I married. If I ever bumped my head and decided to do it, it would only be on the condition that he thought I was *wifey*.

"How long have you guys been married?"

"Almost ten years." He smiled and gazed at the picture. "We were high school sweethearts."

"Really."

"Yeah, really."

He scrutinized my shocked expression. How could anyone be with the same person since they were a teenager and still look so happy?

"I can't imagine. You guys never dated anyone else?"

"Nope. Never dated anyone else. Let's get started."

Still a little amazed about his love story, I paused before speaking, "Do you have the document up on your computer?"

He nodded and began printing a copy of the document. I asked, "When is your family coming?"

He sighed. "She says she's not coming."

"You're kidding."

"Nah, we literally moved into her dream home about two months ago and she just ain't feeling moving yet."

"But isn't this position permanent?"

He chuckled. "Exactly. Try explaining that to my little lady. I think when the novelty of the house wears off, she'll follow her man." As if this was a guarantee, he shifted back to work. "Should I print out two copies and we go through each page together?"

"Yeah that makes sense." I was now interested to know what his wife was thinking. "So, neither of you guys want to bend?"

He squinted. "When I first heard about the merger, coming here wasn't even an option. Then I had to decide whether I should take a pay cut or a pay increase. With my salary here, I can afford to maintain a home here and there and still come out better than I would have there. I'm going to buy a house just as nice here and that should change her mind."

"You know the company reimburses up to twenty thousand for settlement and anything over that, but up to twenty percent of the purchase price can be borrowed interest-free. If you leave, they apply interest, though."

"Yeah, I know. That's my plan. You know all the rules. Did you relocate from anywhere?"

"Unfortunately not, I'm from around here. I know the rules 'cause I was pissed that I couldn't use them."

"Well as long as I find a house comparable, she'll come here, I'm sure."

I nodded slowly. "If you think so."

When he refocused the conversation on work, I decided not to pry any longer, but I thought it was crazy that there was no reunion plan. He wasn't the most attractive guy and he was a tad bit overweight, but still, to let your husband run free in the wilderness for the sake of a house was beyond me.

After sitting in his office until eight o'clock discussing new strategies, I gained an entirely new perspective of him. Dwight was smart and organized. He knew just how to delegate and I knew the software like the back of my hand. His presence would definitely free up some of my time.

CHAPTER 6

Tracey

Dwight moved and I'd been dealing with it. He was trying to do his best, calling and keeping up with us. So far it was okay. I got a new car out of the deal, and he planned a trip for us all to go to Disney World. The other good thing about Dwight not being home was that I got to shop as often as I liked and I didn't have to hide any bags. As the girls and I headed home from Kohl's, my cell phone rang. PAIN IN THE ASS came across the screen. It was my brother, Wade, calling.

"Sister, I love you and I think you are the best."

"What do you want, Wade?"

"I don't want nothing. I want to come and check on you."

"Check on me."

"Yeah, my nieces there?"

"We were out but we almost at the house."

"All right, I'm going to meet you there."

When I pulled up to my house Wade was sitting in front

of my door with his seat all the way back. I blew the horn and pressed my garage opener. He stepped out of his car wearing black khakis and a striped green-and-blue shirt. His hair was in a curly fro. He looked more like a college student than thirtysomething. He gave me a hug and lifted Destiny up in the air.

"What's up, little nieces?"

"Uncle Wade!" Jordan shouted. "Can you take us to the toy store?"

"Not today."

"You always say not today," Destiny said.

I opened my trunk and walked to the back of my car to show him what I needed him to bring in the house. When I glanced over at his car, I saw a woman staring over at me. I turned to him and said, "Who is that?"

"A friend."

"You just going to let that girl just sit in the car?"

"She cool. She know how to wait."

"You so wrong, Wade," I said as I glanced back over at the car. Who was I to fight for the girl's right, if she was dumb enough to let some man leave her in the car? We went into the house.

"So what you want, Wade?" I asked. I knew he wanted something.

"Baby girl, I need a favor. I need to borrow some money."

"Wade, I am not a bank. You're not going to keep borrowing money from me."

"Please, I need to pay my car note. I only need six hundred," he said, stepping in front of me and pleading with his hands together.

"Six hundred dollars," I said as I raised my eyebrow.

"Yeah, I gave them a partial payment last month and I

have to pay the rest and this month's payment. I'm starting a job Monday. I promise I'm going to pay you back," he begged as he knelt in front of me.

"Get up, silly. I'm going to give it to you. But you're going to give me all my money back altogether, not in pieces, Wade."

"I promise you can have my first paycheck." I reluctantly took out my ATM card and gave him my PIN. He went to the ATM to take the money out. The damn bank that financed his car needs to be put out of business. He saw a commercial that said all he needed was one pay stub and a driver's license and he could get the car. The next week he got fired. Now every month he's running around to pay the damn car note. I wish he would stop quitting jobs and become a stable grown-ass man.

After Wade left, I ordered a pizza and prepared to watch another episode of *That's So Raven*. Both Jordan and Destiny knew every line by heart.

"Mommy, can we call Daddy?" Jordan asked.

I dialed his phone and got his voice mail. I said, "Daddy's working. Let's eat and then we will call him again later."

While they ate dinner and watched television, I was going to try to get some work done and put a load of clothes in the washer. As soon as I sat at my desk and turned on my computer, Jordan walked in and pouted. "I miss Daddy."

"Me, too! Can we call him again, Mommy?" Destiny said, running into the room and climbing onto my lap.

"Bring the phone here and I'll call him." I dialed Dwight again. This time Dwight answered and Jordan screamed.

"Where are you? Daddy, I miss you."

"Let me speak to him," Destiny said, as she snatched the phone out of Jordan's hands.

"Daddy, when you come home?" Jordan pushed Destiny for taking the phone from her and made her fall. Destiny got back up and punched Jordan in her arm.

"Stop it, girls. Give me the phone and go get ready for bed."

"What are y'all doing?" Dwight asked.

"They're watching television and I was trying to get work done. How are you? How is the job?"

"Everything is going pretty good. I just wish y'all were here. I'm not used to coming home to an empty house."

I could tell in his voice that he was lonely. I pretended I didn't hear what he said and changed the subject. "Dwight did you get all the pictures I sent you?"

"Yeah, I got all one hundred sixty-two of them," he said, laughing.

"You know I'm dangerous with a digital camera. Well, I'm going to put the girls to bed, and I'll call you tomorrow."

"You don't want to talk to me."

"I have a lot of work to do. The girls really wanted to talk to you. I love you. I'll call you tomorrow." Before Dwight could say anything else I ended the call. Let him get homesick and bring his ass home.

After I put the girls to sleep I walked through the house picking up toys and missing my husband. I wanted to call Dwight back. But I couldn't give in to him. I had to be strong and he will come running home. I know he will. I sat on the sofa and sighed. I looked over at our family photo and smiled. It was of all of us dressed in black against a white background. We had the traditional stance—me and Dwight standing in the back and the girls sitting down in the front smiling.

"Mommy, tell Destiny to stop crying," Jordan yelled from the top of the steps. I ran up the steps and heard muffled crying.

"Destiny, why are you crying? What's wrong with you?"

She lifted her head from her pillow and cried while hyperventilating. "I miss Dad-dy, Mom-my. I wa-nt Dad-dy to-to come home."

I took a deep breath and sat on the bed. Speaking to her, but trying to convince myself, I said, "Stop crying. He'll be home soon."

She continued to cry. "But I still miss him."

"I miss him, too, but he has to work," I said, patting her back.

"Why he got to work far away? Why, Mom?" She continued to cry.

"His job moved and he had to go with them." My words didn't comfort her. She began crying louder.

"Des, stop crying. Daddy will be home this weekend. And I'll let you call him tomorrow. Okay?"

"Mommy, can I sleep in the bed with you?"

"Me, too!" Jordan asked.

I put my work off until the morning and laid in bed with my daughters. The moment they touched the sheets, they both feel asleep. I laid there and stared at the ceiling. I dreaded how long this might last, because we all wanted Daddy home.

CHAPTER 7

Alicia

Just when I thought my schedule would get better with Dwight around, our team inherited a brand-new system with a bunch of old issues. Dwight and I were spending countless hours at work trying to develop a game plan to tackle it.

Three weeks had passed and I couldn't make it to my Thursday girls' night out, but I was damned if I wouldn't be there tonight. Especially since they agreed to meet somewhere close to my job just so I could work late and still get there in time to unwind. I sat at my desk with pages and pages of database design documents, trying to decipher some kind of reasoning. It was a mess and our job was to figure it out. How do some people get jobs? And more important, how the hell do they get away with shit like this? Their negligence was messing up my personal life. Dwight and I were working parallel, in hopes that two brilliant minds could unravel this foolish design.

The only problem with that is he never knew when to

say quit, and he expected me to work as long as he did. Obviously he had nothing better to do, but I did. When I noticed it was close to eight, I looked at my cell phone and realized my friends had called to ask what I wanted to drink. They were there and I was here. Although I wasn't close to a solution, I started wrapping things up and documenting my conclusions. I was all packed up before I sent Dwight an e-mail message of my status. My plan was to press SEND, wave good-bye, and dash out the door.

Well, I sent the message, waved good-bye, and Dwight darted out of his office. *Shit.* I turned around and before he could speak, I said, "I sent you an update. I have to go. My girls are at P.F. Chang's waiting for me. They've been . . ."

"I'm sorry. I just didn't understand something in your e-mail."

We both laughed because there is no way he read it that quickly. He admitted, "I'm just trying to get you to stay here with me, man."

"I've been working like a field slave. And I . . ."

"You've been doing a spectacular job."

"I'm glad you noticed."

He reached his hand out to give me dap. "I definitely noticed. I think you might be one of the smartest engineers I've ever had the opportunity to work with."

"Don't patronize me."

"Not at all. I'm really impressed."

"Me, too."

Maybe we were both uncomfortable with the compliments because we stood in silence for a minute. Finally, he spoke, "I must admit when they told me that you were a chick, I wasn't real happy about that."

My mouth hung open. He said, "I mean, I know that's

slightly asinine of me, but honestly, most female engineers aren't as smart as you. Most of them are just in it for the check and they know just enough not to get fired. You, on the other hand . . ."

I nodded before he could finish and said, "I, on the other hand, am stupid enough to actually think like a man."

We laughed and he asked, "So, are you really going to leave me here tonight?"

"I am." I said affirmatively.

"You know we have that briefing on Monday morning?"

"Yep, but it's Thursday night and I have a meeting with my girls tonight." He looked bewildered as I wrapped up the conversation. "So, are you leaving early tomorrow? I'll pick up where you leave off so we'll be ready for Monday morning."

"Actually, I canceled my flight. I'll probably stay here this weekend. There's too much riding on the briefing and I don't want to drop the ball."

"I told you that I got it."

"Nah, I'm going to stick around and make sure we get it right."

"Wow . . ."

"What?"

Just when I thought we'd made a breakthrough, we returned to the starting block. He didn't trust me to handle it. I repeated, "Wow . . ."

"Alicia, look. This has absolutely nothing to do with you and all to do with me being a perfectionist."

"Well, go ahead and work yourself to death. I'm going out for a drink."

"Do you think your girls would mind if I tag along?"

"Noooo . . ." I teased. "You have work to do."

"Stop playing. Do you think they'll mind?"

I pulled out my cell phone and called Gina. "Hey . . . my coworker wants to hang out with us."

"With *us*? Where the hell are *you*?"

My eyes shifted, alerting Dwight to the drama on the other end. "I'm coming. I got held up at work."

"We've already had two drinks. Hurry your ass up so you can catch up."

"Is it okay for my coworker to tag along?"

Gina chewed in my ear. "As long as it ain't that dry-ass Desiree."

"No, not Desiree."

"Then who?"

"You haven't met him."

"*Him?*"

"Yeah . . . him."

I could hear Andrea and Tammy in the background questioning her as she questioned me. "Is he cute?"

"We're on our way."

I quickly hung up before Dwight discovered that I was a member of a crew of horny single women. His eyes stretched. "Do we have the green light?"

"Yeah, we're cool. Hurry up and get your things."

Outside in the parking lot, I told him to follow me. Once we hopped on Route 32 heading toward Columbia, I called Gina back to give her the 411 on Dwight. He was off limits and not quite tempting enough to consider lurking with.

When we walked into the restaurant, I heard them giggling before I saw them. Suddenly, I felt like this may have been a bad idea. Dwight seemed cool and definitely down to earth, but a part of me wondered if he was really prepared for my candid friends.

I pointed in their direction. "They're over there."

"Wow, I hope y'all don't get together to male-bash."

We stepped up to the table and I looked at him. "We're here now."

"Ah, man." He looked around. "Just checking for the emergency exits."

"Hey, y'all!"

They all spoke in unison. "Hey, girl."

"This is my new work friend, Dwight."

"Hey, Dwight."

We sat down and Dwight went around the table to get everyone's name. They wasted no time getting his story.

"So, Dwight. What brings you out tonight?" Tammy said.

"This really nice young lady that I work with."

Gina said, "Okay, Dwight. You can cut the act with us. Let me give you the rules."

His neck snapped back. "The rules?"

"Yes, the only rule: We keep it real."

We laughed because we all hated that played-out line. She continued. "I mean, we know that saying is whack, but at the end of the day, that's what we do. No high-level bullshit. You dig?"

Tammy said, "So, again? What are you doing out tonight? Are you pissed off with your wife? Are you checking for our girl or what?"

"None of the above. Your girl and I have been busting our asses this week. I was torn between staying at work or coming out for a drink."

Andrea said, "That was an easy decision."

"Basically," he said.

I felt it was necessary to let them know that Dwight was my manager in hopes they would pipe down their conversation.

Gina exclaimed, "So!"

Dwight seemed to be getting a kick out of them so I eased off. He was rather impressed that we were all good friends and that we'd maintained our friendship since college. Three or four times over the period of an hour, he said, "It's amazing to meet four women that all know enough about each other to finish each other's sentences."

I concluded that he must have been married to one of those chicks who has no girlfriends. Finally, Gina said, "Whatever, we're all we got. Shit, I don't have a choice but to hang out with y'all."

We laughed. Dwight checked his phone and a series of uh-ohs rippled around the table. His smirk questioned our responses.

Gina said, "I guess your wife is telling you to get your ass home."

He shook his head and stuck his phone back in his pocket. I said, "Go ahead and answer. We'll be quiet."

"Nah, I'm cool."

"We don't want your wife to come in here and start spraying," Tammy said from experience.

He laughed. "You don't have to worry about that. She's in Jacksonville."

"What's there? Work?"

He said, "Family."

Andrea said, "Family? Aren't you family?"

Gina said, "When is she coming here?"

He slightly hung his head. "I don't know."

A bombardment of questions followed as they tried to rationalize a situation that I reckoned to simply let go. It was absolutely and unequivocally senseless. A few nods and a few ohs later, Dwight looked at his phone again. I said, "I think you better get that."

Tammy leaned over the table, as if to expose her nonexistent cleavage. "Dwight, does your wife know that the most beautiful black women in the country live in the DC area?"

"You guys are something else."

Gina said, "Nah, for real." She pursed her clear-glossed lips, which always accentuated her high cheekbones. "Does she know that?"

"I'm not sure. I certainly didn't make it my business to let her know."

Although both Gina and Tammy were putting their selves on display, he couldn't keep his eyes away from Andrea. I wasn't sure if it was the simplicity in her little curly ponytail or the slight resemblance to his wife, or that she didn't have a Post-it note on her forehead stating that she was single. I said, "Dwight, I understand. There is no reason to make your wife insecure."

"She really doesn't have a reason to be. She's a beautiful, secure woman."

Just as he said that, his phone rang again. Gina said, "I'm not so sure about that."

He looked at his phone and for the first time I noticed some discomfort in his face. He seemed slightly apologetic as he scooted his chair back and slid a fifty from his wallet.

"Alright, y'all. Wifey is a little impatient tonight. We'll definitely have to do this again."

Tammy said, "Wifey better act like she know and get her ass up here."

He pointed at her, stood up, and said, "Exactly."

Just seconds after he said his good-byes and left the restaurant, I said, "Y'all hookers are so crazy."

Tammy said, "How you gonna just send your husband to a new state alone with all of us up here?"

We burst out laughing. I said, "But y'all didn't have to say anything."

Andrea said, "If you haven't noticed, we have two recovering adulterers right here." She was referring to Tammy and me. "So if she knows like I know, she better get here and get here fast."

I said, "Exactly. I'm an adulterer, not a mistress. There is a difference. I have fun with married men and then send them home to their wives and I never have to deal with them again. I don't want to do that with a man I work with. Plus, he's not even cute enough to take the risk."

"You're not normal anyway. But from the average woman's perspective, he's a black man working a damn good job," Gina said.

Tammy nodded. "He has nice eyes."

"I can't take y'all nowhere," I said, shaking my head.

I felt slightly bad that I'd brought Dwight out and obviously got him in some hot water, but my girls were right. His wife *should* be here.

When I got to work the next morning, I felt as if I'd inadvertently welcomed Dwight into my private world and I wasn't sure how he perceived me anymore. As I eased by his office, he called my name. I continued to walk, while responding, "I'll be back when I get my coffee."

After getting settled and checking e-mail, I returned, holding the cup handle tightly and aimlessly stirring my coffee. I said, "Hey, what's up?"

"Do you really think you'll be okay if I go to Jacksonville this weekend?"

My ego and I tussled for a moment. Had he really come to trust me or was his sudden change of heart due to his wife's lack of trust in him? I hesitated. "It depends . . ."

"On what?"

I sipped my coffee before I said something silly. When I looked up, he raised his eyebrow. "I'm waiting . . ."

"Well, yesterday, you couldn't imagine leaving this all in my hands. Now, today, you wonder if I'll be okay without you," I said.

"What?"

"What happened between seven last night and nine this morning that finally convinced you that I can handle this all by myself?"

"C'mon now."

"No . . . I don't think it will be okay for you to go, because if something goes wrong, you're not blaming me."

"So, you don't think I trust you?"

I laughed. "Do you think you trust me?"

"I trust you and I'm going home. I know you can handle it," he said.

"But I didn't say that I was comfortable."

He shook his head and looked in my eyes. "I know you got it."

"Whatever."

I strolled to my desk, tripping about how powerful a woman is when her man loves her. He had concluded that he wasn't going home and he probably could have gotten away with it had he answered his phone last night.

Around noon, Dwight came over to my desk while I was in the middle of editing the PowerPoint presentation. He peeped over my shoulder and said, "Already thirty pages, huh?"

Sensing a little cynicism, I decided not to respond. He patted his fist into the palm of his hand. "Uh, don't you think you keep the client's interest longer when you shorten it up? You know they . . ."

I spun around in my chair. "You know, Dwight, you're welcome to do this. Either you're putting it in my hands or I can wash my hands of it and you can stay here and get it done."

He laughed hysterically. "I love it."

"Love what?"

"I love your fire. You just . . ."

He paused, and the wrinkles in my forehead disappeared as I suddenly became flattered. "Whatever, Dwight. Don't try to wow me."

"I'm not trying to wow you." He used his fingers as quotes.

"You are. I can't take this—either you trust me or you don't."

He sighed. "I feel you."

That sounded real personal. We both nodded to acknowledge there was something else going on.

"Look, Dwight. Go home to your wife and kids. If I need you, I'll call you. And because you're a control freak, I'll send you the presentation to critique before I do the final printout."

"How many times do I have to say that I trust you?"

"Until I feel it."

There was a moment of discomfort, and Desiree stepped

into the opening of my cubicle. Our eyes darted in her direction. She assumed that she'd startled us as she raised her arms in a defenseless fashion.

"I'm sorry." She looked at me. "I just wanted to know if you still wanted to go to lunch."

Unconsciously, I looked at Dwight. He nodded. "Go ahead. I'm sure you'll have everything done by Monday."

I turned to save the document before I stood. "You have a safe trip home and I'll hit you if I need to clear anything up."

It was around four o'clock when I yearned to speak to Dwight. I'd spent the past three weeks proving my independence. At the same time, I'd inadvertently grown dependent on him. I picked up the phone. Then I put it down. *Don't call this man while he's headed home to see his family.* I knew he had a layover, but I didn't know where, when, or for how long. Why couldn't I shake the feeling that this was somehow inappropriate even though I knew it was all about work?

In the midst of rationalizing the situation, I said, "Hey . . . Dwight."

"What's up?"

I really didn't have a concrete question. Well, actually I did. Where did the desperate need to hear his voice come from?

"Ah . . . are you in Jacksonville yet?"

"Nah, I'm in Charlotte. I had to fly standby 'cause I canceled that flight at the last minute. You a'ight up there?"

"Yeah, I just wanted to know what you consider a short presentation. I have like ninety pages now. And I . . ."

"I'm sure it will be fine. You're doing the presentation and you talk a little faster than me, so it'll be cool."

"You're right."

"Okay."

"Okay."

"What's with the reluctance?"

I laughed off the accusation. "It's not reluctance. It's just that I know how you are."

"You keep asking me to trust you. Do *you* trust you?"

"What?"

He laughed. "I'm just saying, sweetie. I trust you, but I'm sensing that you're not comfortable with this and I just don't know why."

Maybe my lack of trust had very little to do with work and more to do with this sudden vulnerability for my new boss. "Dwight, I don't know. I'm just used to doing what I want to do with no one to critique it and I just really respect your opinion and it's important to me that you are satisfied with my work." His silence made me nervous. I asked, "Are you still there?"

"Yeah, I'm just trippin'. On the real, I'm proud of you."

I frowned at the phone. "Proud of me?"

"Yeah, man." *Man?* "Black women are the worst power-trippers in the game. You just made me change my opinion. Y'all not all the same."

"What do you mean?"

"Man, y'all are a black man's worst enemy. God forbid you're up for the same promotion that he is."

He laughed, but I was wavering between offense and success. I didn't like his assessment of us, but I was proud of his assessment of me. Still, I had to stand up for my girls. "No. History has taught us that we have to fight for ourselves. We never had the chance to sit in our little carriages and be protected from the rain. We've always been on the grind, neck and neck with our men."

"You got a point. But y'all need to learn how to respect men. That ain't cute. Let's make love, not war."

My eyes shifted. Was that a personal invitation? I quickly jumped back into the argument without pondering too much on it. "We're not making war. We're handling our business because we have to."

The wall of misconceptions that initially separated us crumbled as we discussed the dynamics of relationships in our community. Although he was strong and borderline arrogant at work, he had this juvenile innocence when it came to relationships. Most of his knowledge came from books. Compared to me, he was like the pope. He was a committed husband who wanted one thing: to be with his family.

An hour into the conversation, my ear was pinned to the phone and I was holding on to his every word. *Snap out of it.* Suddenly an overwhelming need to end the conversation came over me. "Well, I actually called you to discuss this presentation. I didn't expect to get so deep. So . . ."

"You know you didn't call about the presentation."

His certainty made me stutter. "I . . . I . . ."

"You just wanted to hear my voice."

"Actually, Dwight, I wanted to know if a hundred and ten slides were too many."

He laughed. "I told you earlier that it doesn't matter. I trust you."

I reluctantly ended the call with that confirmation. I gazed at the screen when I hung up and wondered what Dwight's wife thought of him. He seemed so wise and so committed.

CHAPTER 8

Tracey

Dwight has missed two weekends coming home. Once his flight was canceled, the other time he had to work the entire weekend. I've been upset with his neglect of his family, but I am trying to be understanding. Since he has been up there, I've been having an issue managing my time. All the demands of being a single parent are weighing down on me. Like this morning, we awoke at seven-forty-five and Jordan is suppose to be at school by eight-twenty. I had to take them to the drive-thru at Krispy Kreme for breakfast. And Lord knows, I didn't have time to make lunch. My poor baby Jordan had to eat half of her friend Leah's sandwich, so she wouldn't go hungry. I felt terrible. I don't know what's slowing me up in the morning. Doing hair or getting them dressed. I've even tried to pull out their clothes in advance, make lunch the night before—we still walk out the door forty-five minutes late. I must admit this is hard as hell, doing everything by myself. It's not that I don't know how to do everything. It's just that I feel like I shouldn't have to.

• • •

I came into the office just to close the deal with Chanel Austin. She was running late as usual. She called my cell phone and said that she hadn't known she needed a cashier's check to close and she thought she could pay by cash.

"What are you doing in here?" Jeff asked.

"Closing a deal."

"That's great, you be working it. You want a puppy for your girls? Our lease doesn't allow pets."

"What kind of dog is it? I'm not really a dog person."

"Get it for your daughters. She is a Maltese, an expensive dog, but we can't keep her. She is real little and cute. Plus she won't get that big. I could bring her to you."

I told Jeff I didn't know about the dog, but somehow he convinced me to accept the puppy. Once I saw it I couldn't resist; she was so cute and would be a good distraction for the girls with Dad not being home. The dog had fluffy white fur and big brown eyes. I went to the pet store and bought dog food, a pink leash, a cage, and dog toys. When I picked up Jordan from dance class I surprised her with the dog.

"Thank you, Mommy," she screamed. The dog barked a little. Jordan hugged her and gave her a kiss. Destiny was just as excited. The dog jumped up on her and licked her.

"What y'all want to name her?" I asked as we drove home.

"Can we name her Raven?"

"Okay."

"No, I want to name her Princess."

"How about Princess Raven."

"Princess Raven. But now listen—you can't tell Daddy we have a dog. It is a surprise. When he calls let's not say anything to him." We made a little room for Raven in the garage.

The girls were occupied with holding and petting Raven as if she were a real baby. I went into the kitchen and started dinner. I sat down at the kitchen table and then dialed Dwight. He answered then told me to hold on. I put him on speakerphone and the minute the girls heard his voice they ran into the kitchen yelling, "Daddy!" Destiny screamed into the phone, "Daddy, guess what? We got a surprise for you."

"You weren't supposed to tell Daddy," Jordan said.

"Oh yeah. Daddy, never mind," Destiny said as she passed the phone back to me.

"What surprise is Destiny talking about?" Dwight asked.

"I don't know. They said it is a surprise, and I guess they will tell you when you come home."

"Well, I'll be there this weekend. I miss y'all so much."

"I miss you, too. This is becoming a bit much," I sighed.

"I know, I know, Trace. Did you get the pictures of the houses I sent you?"

"Yeah, I got them. But I'm not looking at any houses, because I'm not moving."

"It wouldn't hurt you to look. They have some really nice developments."

"I'm not looking at any houses. Dwight, what part don't you understand? I'll see you tomorrow. What time does your flight get in?"

"I think like six. Tracey, when I get there, we gonna have to have a long talk."

"Well, I'll see you then," I said as I ended the call.

Even with everything I was going through, I couldn't let Dwight forget what kind of woman he had at home. We had only two days together out of the week and I wanted to make the most of them. I dropped the girls off at Mama Dee's and went and got a manicure, pedicure, and my hair done. I thought I had enough time to get everything done, but I didn't. My polish wasn't dry, but I had to risk a smudge because Dwight was already waiting at the airport. He had called three times already, asking how long before I got there. I lied and told him two minutes, but I was still at least twenty minutes away.

When I arrived at the airport, there were taxis and shuttles moving in and out of the lanes. I drove slow and looked for Dwight where he said he was waiting. I spotted him and beeped the horn twice to get his attention. He picked up his luggage and walked over to the car.

"Hey, baby, you look tired," I said as he got in the car and placed his luggage in the backseat.

"I am. Where are my princesses?"

"With Mama Dee. I thought you would want to relax and get some rest. I wanted us to spend some time together and then we can go and pick them up." On the ride home we caught up on our week. My week was all about dance class and bake sales. His was about his programs and his new coworkers. I was in the middle of telling him about Jordan's and Destiny's antics and Dwight kept saying uh-huh to everything I said.

"Did you hear me, Dwight?"

"Yeah yeah, I heard you." He was staring at his Black-Berry.

"What did I say?" I asked him.

"You said, um . . . you said something about Jordan," Dwight said, still staring at his phone and typing into it. Annoyed, I said, "Dwight, why are you texting? What's that about? You are home and this is family time."

"I'm the boss now and . . . I have to make sure everything is moving smoothly."

"Well, I'm sure they wouldn't have the job if they were incompetent," I said, clasping my hands together and becoming more impatient. It was bad enough our time was limited.

"She is competent, but she is a little inexperienced and I have to coach her."

Then Dwight's phone started ringing. He had the audacity to pick it up and start discussing business. I looked at him like *get the hell off the phone*. He stayed on the phone for twenty minutes. He just ignored me and every time I attempted to say something, he waved his hand at me to tell me to shut up. I was heated. I was beginning to get fed up with him being out of town. Now he was trying to carry his week into the weekend, and I wasn't having it. I instantly had an attitude.

After his call was done, we rode home in almost complete silence. He tried to turn the radio station to sports radio. As soon as he did, I popped in a Mary J. Blige CD and turned the volume up as far as it would go. Dwight turned the music down and yelled, "So you just going to ignore me?" When I didn't respond, he said under his breath, "This is what I get for trying to take care of my family." I didn't give him a response. I blocked him out.

"I told you to get off the phone and you told me to be quiet. So now that you are free to talk, I don't have anything to say."

"See, Tracey, this is your damn problem. Every time you don't get your way you go into this baby mode." I looked over at him, rolled my eyes, and kept driving home.

Once we were home we were greeted by Raven's weak barking. Dwight looked at me like *what the hell is that*. I just turned my key in the lock and Raven jumped up on my leg.

"Come here, girl. Don't bark at Daddy, you want him to like you," I said as I stroked her white coat.

"When did you get a dog?" Dwight asked, still trying to be my friend.

"The other day. Jeff at the office couldn't keep her. And you know we need protection. Now that me and the girls are here alone."

"Tracey, you know that little dog is not going to protect y'all."

"Yes, she will," I said as I rubbed Raven and took her into the garage.

"I'm sorry for taking the call. It won't happen again," Dwight said, pulling me into him.

"I forgive you, but please leave work up there."

"You're right," he said as he gave my whole body another squeeze. "I'm so happy to be home." He then wrapped his arms around my waist. His body was so warm. I felt so weak. We just sat in the dark. I felt like an animal. My insides were so wet. I was about to show him why he shouldn't be in Maryland. We had never been apart this long. I began kissing him and our bodies fell into the cushion of the sofa. We caressed and massaged each other's bodies until we were ready. My body snaked vigorously all over his body in a quest to climax.

"Baby, I need you so bad," I moaned as I opened my legs for his entrance. He flexed himself into mine, entering the deep tight region that missed him. He continued loving me until we both were fulfilled. I missed my man and was so glad he was home. The rest of the evening we sat snuggled on the sofa flipping TV stations.

Sunday morning came too soon. I had already washed and folded Dwight's clothes for the week. We were so busy squeezing in our time and family time, we didn't get a chance to argue about him being in Maryland. I was hoping that if I can tolerate another week or two he will come home on his own. As he looked around the room to make sure he wasn't forgetting anything, I playfully asked, "Is this when you tell me how much you love me, but it is time for me to drop you off at the airport?"

"Baby girl, don't do this," he said as he scrunched his face.

"I'm not doing anything. I just want you to quit."

"I can't do that. This week will go by fast, like last week," he said as he pulled me into him and looked me in my eyes. I looked away and my eyes began tearing.

"I know, but I don't know how much I can take."

"Listen, I have to go, but we will discuss this later. Okay?"

"Yes." He was back off to Maryland and I was back to playing superwoman again.

CHAPTER 9

Alicia

My BlackBerry buzzed just as I walked into Bob Evans for breakfast. It was a text from Dwight. The subject was WHAT HAPPENED?

My heart sank as I reached out to hug my mother. "Hey, Ma."

"Hey, baby."

I read the message and wondered why he was up on a Saturday morning thinking about work after reassuring me a million times that he trusted me. He wanted to know why I hadn't forwarded the presentation to him. I responded: I THOUGHT YOU TRUSTED ME.

My phone rang almost immediately after I pressed SEND. My mother rolled her eyes and sighed. "You're always on that thing."

I raised my finger and walked to the front of the waiting area to talk in private. "Hey, Dwight. What's up?"

"Don't send those kinds of elusive messages."

"What?"

He laughed. "That could have easily been read wrong."

"By who?"

"Who do you think?"

"Dwight, you're trippin'."

"Didn't we just talk yesterday about how crazy y'all are?"

He confirmed what I was already thinking. His wife had begun to grow insecure about their arrangement. I asked, "Are you at home?"

"Yeah."

"Well, why are you calling me from your house?"

"To ask you why you didn't send that document."

I was slightly baffled because when I offered he acted as if he didn't need it. "I'll send it when I get home."

"Where are you?"

I huffed. "I'm at breakfast."

"Oh." He paused. "Well, don't forget to send that document when you get home."

"Okay, Dwight. I'll see you Monday morning."

"If I see any room for correction, is it okay to call you later?"

"Yes, Dwight."

I walked over to where my mother had been seated. She looked inquisitively. "Why are you smiling?"

I quickly scrunched my face. "I'm not smiling."

"Who was that?"

"My new manager. He had a question about work."

"Never seen that look on your face when you talk about work."

"Whatever, Ma. How was bingo last night?"

That question always took her mind away from anything else. Bingo had been her other man for as long as I could remember. After my father died, bingo finally had her full heart. When I'd successfully diverted her attention away from me and onto how much money she almost won, I began to regret it.

"So, how's your diet coming along?" I said, trying to switch topics.

She laughed. "I quit."

"Ma."

"I'm not trying to be cute for anyone. I'm at the age now that I can just let it go."

"It's not about being cute. It's about living longer."

Her eyes rolled and a piece of me knew what she thought. She was at the point in life that living didn't matter. She'd rather be in heaven with the love of her life. Maybe they could be in marital bliss in the next lifetime, because since he died twelve years ago, she's been eating herself to death. It was quite alarming watching her go from a size six to a size twenty in a matter of a few years. Her rapid weight gain was the wake-up call that made me start working out. I love food and if I had that same fat gene, I needed to get it under control early, and I figured my mother's weight-management method, *worrying about a man*, wasn't an option.

I added, "Do you realize how much you have to live for?"

"I'm not saying I don't want to live. I'm just saying that I'm too old to worry about what I eat."

The waitress came to take our order. I ordered an omelet with egg whites and she ordered a pound of grease: bacon and sausage, fried potatoes, and pancakes. I turned my face up.

"I don't know who raised you."

"I raised myself, remember?"

She huffed. "Alicia, don't say that."

"It's okay, because I raised you, too."

She always laughed when I said that because we both knew it was partially true.

"Whatever. You don't know anything about being a mother."

"You're right, but that still don't mean I didn't raise you."

She waved her hand at me. "Whatever. So tell me about this new manager that had you blushing."

"Ma, please."

"See, that's a mother's gift. I know how to read my child's emotions."

"Obviously, not because I wasn't blushing. He is married. He's a male chauvinist, and I don't find him the least bit attractive."

She pulled her neck back. "You don't have to lie to me, sweetie. You spend more time defending yourself than you do listening."

"Ma, whatever. Let's talk about something else."

Who the hell would be calling me at midnight on a Sunday? I reached for my phone buzzing on the nightstand. I rubbed my eyes and tried to refocus before I answered. DWIGHT WILSON.

Why was he calling me and what made him think it was okay? I snapped, "Hello."

He sounded like he was running. "Hey, Alicia."

"Yes?"

"I know it's late."

"Yeah. What's going on?"

"I'm just leaving Jacksonville. I actually missed my flight and I'm flying standby. Been here since nine. Not sure if I'll get one tonight."

Suddenly my frustration turned into concern. "What time does the earliest flight leave?"

He chuckled. "At six. Then there's another one at seven."

"I hope you can get on one of those. You might miss the meeting."

"I know, that's why I'm calling."

I turned my television on so that I'd have some light on my way to the bathroom. "What do you want me to do?"

"I just wanted to give you a heads-up. I didn't want you to find out that I'd be late at seven in the morning. At least you'd have a few hours to brush up on anything you didn't feel comfortable with."

"A few hours in the middle of the night, Dwight? Thanks for your consideration."

He laughed. "I'm sorry, but I know it would have been worse if I called you in the morning."

"It would have helped if you called this morning, but it doesn't make much of a difference now. I'm going back to sleep."

"You don't have any questions?"

"No . . . what I don't know I won't know. I'll see you in the morning."

He hesitated. "So . . ."

"So . . . I'll see you when you get in."

"Ah . . ."

"I'm going to bed now, Dwight. Have a safe trip."

"I enjoyed talking to you on the way down."

"I'm glad you did, but I'm going to go now."

"So you're going to let me sit in the airport, lonely without a friend to talk to?"

"Call your wife, Dwight. I have a presentation in the morning."

He sighed. "Man, my wife is upset with me."

"You know, that's too bad, because I am, too, at twelve o'clock at night. I'll see you when you get in."

For some reason, I felt Dwight was playing games. He seemed to be slightly more aggressive after his night out with me and my friends. This entire transaction had me vexed. And more baffling was that I was smiling from ear to ear while taking a piss in the middle of the night.

CHAPTER 10

Tracey

My life has become hectic. I'm trying, but the longer Dwight is gone the harder it is becoming. I had an appointment at seven, and it was six-thirty. I was waiting for Wade to come and get the girls. I looked down at my watch ten minutes later and still no Wade. It was getting late. I should have known better than to trust his irresponsible ass. I called his cell phone one more time and he didn't pick up. Mama Dee was out of town. Danielle was at work and I couldn't leave them home alone. I didn't have any other choice, I had to take them with me everywhere I went. I called Wade one more time and when he didn't pick up I just made the girls get in the car.

"Where we going?" Jordan asked.

"With me to my job. And I need you both to be big girls."

"Mommy, why?" Destiny asked, looking up with puppy eyes.

"Because I have to do my job. And if you let me do my job I'm going to take you to the toy store."

On the way to show the property, I stopped at McDonald's, got them Happy Meals, made them go to the restroom, and turned on a movie. I called to tell the couple I was on my way.

We pulled up in front of the property and my clients were in front of the house waiting. I felt so unprofessional meeting up with a potential buyer with my daughters in the car. It was bad enough I was late and I didn't know how I was going to recover, but I tried my best. I greeted the Sanders and tried to explain my situation.

"Sorry, my nanny took the day off." The husband looked annoyed, but said okay. But he definitely seemed mad. We entered the house and I noticed a musty smell. If I smelled it, I knew they did, too. Then I noticed spots all over the carpet. The carpet cleaner had done a horrible job. I tried to hurry them past all the imperfections and show them the backyard and the pool. They were warming up to me and the house. The husband asked why the owner was selling as he stared at the water marks on the ceiling.

"They are moving to the west coast. I know it needs to be updated a little, but it is a great deal and this school district is one of the best in the state." He agreed and was about to ask me another question when I heard my car horn beeping. I excused myself and walked back to the car.

"What's wrong?"

"Mommy, she said she got to pee."

"You just went, Destiny."

"I got to go again. Real bad," she said as her legs shaked together.

"Just hold it a few minutes." Destiny looked at me and said, "I can't. I can't." And something started running down her leg. I was so mad at her. She peed in my new car.

I was so upset. I was going to kill Wade. Oh, I can't take it. As I went back to the door, the Sanders were walking out.

"Thanks for showing this to us. We'll call you," they said as they walked toward their car. I knew they weren't going to call me. I locked the property and drove home. I'm going to have to get a real nanny. This shit was getting out of control. I called Wade because it was his fault I had them with me. Of course he didn't answer his phone. So I left him a nice nasty message. Even though I was really mad at Wade, I had to be true to myself. And the truth was all of this was Dwight's fault. He should be home and I wouldn't be having all these problems.

Dwight came through the door on Friday like a hero. The girls gave him a king's greeting. I just changed the channel on the television. Dwight dropped his bags, hugged the girls, and tried to hand me some flowers. I looked at him and shook my head.

"What is your problem?" he asked.

"I don't have a problem," I said as I looked past him. He tried to sit next to me and began telling me about his week, explaining all the system problems they had. I kept acting like I was into the television, not even acknowledging that he was speaking.

"Are you listening to me?"

"Not really. Why should I?"

"What is your problem?"

"What's my problem. Let's see. I have the responsibility of ten on me. You promised me you would be home every weekend and that has not been the case. I don't have a problem; you have a problem." I knew I was frustrated and about to cuss him out, so I ordered the girls upstairs. I stood up and said, "I don't know how else to say it, but you got to quit that job. I can't take it anymore. I can't do it all. This little setup is not fair to me. I'm working as hard as I possibly can." He sprung up from the sofa and a look of confusion plagued his face.

"Tracey, I promised you that I would take care of you. It's not your job to work harder. All I need you to do is follow me and I'll take care of you. Do you understand that? You're making this hard on yourself."

"How am I making it hard on myself? Because I want to stay close to my family? What am I supposed to do in Maryland about a job? Who's going to watch the kids when we want to go out?"

He shouted at me in a way he'd never done before. "Damn it, Tracey! I make enough fucking money to hire a nanny if that's what you want."

"I'm not leaving my kids with strangers. I want to stay right here, where your mother, your sister, and my family is. I don't want to go hunting around for nobody to keep my kids."

"I can't quit my job," he said and walked into the den. I stormed behind him, trying to yank his arm. He snatched it away from me. "Dwight!" I yelled. "You act like I'm just supposed to uproot everything and follow you to Maryland. I have everything here. Why would I leave?"

"Everything? What is everything? This fucking house. Is that what you call everything? Hell with the house. I'm your husband."

"Don't talk about this house is all I care about, because you don't care about me or these girls. I have been doing everything by myself while you are living carefree."

"I'm living carefree? I'm working hard every day paying every damn bill in this house. But you just don't appreciate it."

Jordan came to the top of the steps.

"Mommy and Daddy, please stop arguing."

"Stop being grown, Jordan. Go to bed," I yelled.

"Go to bed, Jordan," Dwight scolded her as I walked out the door. I didn't know where I was going; I just got in my car and drove. It was the first time I had to myself in months. I thought the ride would calm me down, but it didn't. I was even more enraged when I returned.

Dwight might as well have stayed in Maryland—he worked the entire weekend and I gave him the silent treatment. Every time he asked me a question, I responded with one-word answers. *You'll get no conversation from me.* We did take the girls to the movies, but I was super evil to him from the time he got off that plane to the moment he got back on. Forget him.

CHAPTER 11

Tracey

I need a damn break! These little divas are killing me. Really, I'm about to hurt somebody. The thought of my husband being seven hundred miles away was transforming me into an Angry Black Woman. This shit wasn't fair. Every other word out of my mouth was a fucking curse word. I was sick and tired. And when I was saying curses I was spelling them out.

"Mommy, when is Daddy coming home?"

"Soon," I said with a smile, but of course I wanted to scream, *Don't ask me that again.* Every day the same thing. Daddy gets drawn pictures, and they write letters professing their love to him. *What about Mommy?* I wanted to ask them; the absent parent gets all the love.

"You said that the last time."

"Is Daddy staying in Mary-land?"

"It's not Mary-land. It is Marilyn-land, Destiny," Jordan said, correcting Destiny like she was pronouncing it right. All their fussing and fighting was too much for one parent. I just wanted to rest. My body needed a mental and physical break. I couldn't wait to just feed these little mamas and put them to bed so I could have some me time. Hell, I really didn't feel like making them anything. I popped frozen macaroni and cheese and chicken nuggets in the microwave.

"I don't like macaroni and cheese," Destiny said, spitting her food out of her mouth and onto the plate.

"Yes you do, Des," I said with my hand on my forehead as I begged God for strength.

"Not no more, Mommy. Can I have a peanut butter and jelly?" she said as she folded her arms and began sulking.

"Destiny, don't make me hurt you, girl. Eat that food," I yelled. Destiny looked at the food then began crying.

"Stop crying and just eat your food!"

"I'm thirsty. Can I have some juice, Mommy?" Jordan asked.

"Get some juice out the refrigerator, Jordan."

She poured the juice and moments later I heard her gasp and say, "Uh-oh."

"Ooh, Mommy, she spilled," Destiny yelled.

"Clean it up, Jordan!"

"Mommy, then I'll get dirt on my hand. Yucky."

"Just clean it off." She looked at me like *are you insane?* It took everything in me not to yank her up. My eyes scorned her. "Jordan don't play with me. Clean that mess up," I yelled. That was it. I left them to fend for themselves.

I went upstairs before I lost my mind. I left the dishes in the sink. I didn't even tell them to take a shower before bed. I just went into my room and closed my door and turned up the volume on the television to block any noise they made.

They started singing the Mommy song. It always started

low and elevated halfway through it. "Mommy, Mommy, Mommy."

Then the knock on the door with another "Mommy, Mommy, she . . ."

I couldn't determine who was saying what and I didn't give a damn, either. I decided to ignore them because if I didn't, I might be on the evening news. *Mother strangles two young daughters.* It seemed like it had worked. They walked away from the door. Just as I began to relax a little, I heard a bunch of banging, jumping on the bed. I opened my door and yelled, "Jordan and Destiny! Go to bed, now!"

It got quiet for a few minutes and then I heard little footsteps approaching my bedroom. There was another knock on the door. "Mommy?"

"What?" I asked.

"I'm sorry."

"I'm sorry, too!"

"Good night, go to bed." I decided I should add, "Love you."

They replied with, "We love you, too."

It wasn't them I was angry with. I was angry with my selfish-ass husband. Why couldn't he be here? Why do I have to do this all alone? I called him. I needed to be reassured of my position in his life. I need him to tell me how much he loved me and how everything was going to be okay. I felt so neglected, like work was his new baby, or maybe it wasn't work—maybe it was something or somebody else. I know something was distracting him. I felt as if something was pulling him away from me, like he was falling in love with his job. He answered and I don't know what came over me, but I surprised myself by asking, "Dwight, are you seeing anyone else?"

He huffed. "Tracey, don't ask me stupid questions."

"There has to be someone else. It is not a stupid question. Why, Dwight, are you extra involved now with your work?"

"Well, if there was, you damn sure aren't worried about it."

"I am worried about it. Why the hell do you think I'm asking? I'm telling you the truth. I'm worried, real worried. Dwight, I feel so lonely in this house without you. I don't like sleeping alone. I miss us. Why can't you just come home?"

"Tracey, you won't even come to see where I live, but you want to ask stupid shit."

"Why are you being so mean when I'm expressing myself? Dwight, you've never talked to me like this. There has to be someone else."

Laughing, he said, "Someone named Work. Tracey, I love you. I love our life and our family, but I can't deal with this right now. I have to go."

"So you hanging up on me, Dwight?"

"No, I'm telling you I can't deal with this right now and I'll talk to you later."

I was so upset that Dwight had just about hung up on me. I looked down at the phone and kept asking myself if I was overreacting and if I was wrong for not following him. I didn't know, but I knew something wasn't right.

A few days later, I felt a little better because Dwight had called and apologized. We both promised to be more understanding until we came up with a solution. I still prayed he would quit his job and come home. But I didn't have the luxury of worrying about Dwight. I was too busy rushing around trying to get out of the house as usual. There was a knock on the front door. I went to the door and the FedEx guy handed me a ProFlowers box. I knew they were from my husband and I started smiling as I signed for them. I opened the box to two dozen red roses. Dwight was really trying and I appreciated that. The note read: I MISS YOU, BABY GIRL. I'LL SEE YOU THIS WEEKEND. We were taking a short family vacation to Disney World and I was anxious to have my family together. I smiled. Maybe he was coming around. Dwight wasn't crazy; he knew family was the most important thing.

I called Dwight to see what time he was meeting us as I packed for our trip to Orlando.

"Dwight, what time will you arrive at the hotel?"

"Tracey, what hotel are you talking about?" he asked, preoccupied.

"Dwight, please tell me that you didn't forget about our vacation."

"We are in the middle of this project. Tracey, oh my God, I really forgot. Damn it."

"You promised these little girls a weekend in Disney World and I'm not going to be the one to tell them their daddy is not coming. So make something happen, Dwight."

"Okay, let me see what I can do. I'm not sure if I can get off. Tracey, I'm going to try."

"Don't try, Dwight—get here! What's more important? Us or that dumb job?"

"You and the girls, but I have to do what I need to do for my job. If you like having a roof over your head, then I have to work."

"Your job! Your work. I am getting tired of hearing about your job. I swear this is making no sense. I wish you would just quit. I need you to be here with me," I said as I began to cry.

"I can't just quit. I made a commitment to this company."

"What about your commitment and responsibility to your family?" I hollered.

"Don't start this shit again. What are you committed to, that house or me? Huh, Tracey? Your fabulous kitchen or your closet full of clothes? Don't talk to me about commitment."

I was silent. I didn't have a response for him. I didn't feel like talking to him right now. We kept having the same argument over and over again, going in circles. I was dead tired of it. Something had to be done.

"Dwight, you better make it. Listen carefully: I'm not going to Disney World alone," I said as I ended the call.

Disney World was only three hours away, and we came right down the Florida Turnpike. We caught a little traffic on the way down, but still made good time. We checked into the hotel and went to our suite. The suite had yellow and white fresh wallpaper. There were two separate bedrooms, a dining area, and a living room.

"Come on, girls, let's get in the pool," I said as we placed our luggage down. They were both so excited. They raced into the bathroom and changed into their swimming suits and floats. I had so much on my mind, but I had to be happy and smile for them. Dwight called to say he was on his way, we were on vacation, and everything was going to work itself out.

• • •

At the pool, Jordan and Destiny swam in the shallow part and splashed water on each other. While they played, I flipped through the latest *Us Weekly*. I loved looking at the fashions and reading the gossip. A warm breeze was blowing and I could almost close my eyes and take a nap. I felt so relaxed just sitting by the pool. A woman with red hair walked up. Her daughter was flipping through the water as she watched.

"Your girls are really good swimmers," she said.

"They both have been swimming forever."

"Are they twins?"

"No, they are two years apart."

"My husband is asleep in the room. I only have the one. I wish I had someone for her to play with We have a big day planned tomorrow. What park are you going to?" she asked.

"Magic Kingdom."

"We are, too! If my husband gets up in time. We might wait until Saturday."

Another mother walked past with a little girl who had her hair up in a bun and was wearing a purple and orange dress.

"Doesn't she look cute," the first woman said as the little girl strutted past the pool.

"Kelsey, don't run," her mother shouted. The little girl realized everyone was looking at her and began to run anyway. We both asked where she got her dress and makeup done at.

"They did it at Bibbidi Bobbidi Boutique at Downtown Disney. It's a little salon where they do your hair and nails and dress you up like your favorite princess."

"Really? I should take my girls to do that. Y'all want to do that, girls?" My girls got out of the pool to look at her.

"Yes, Mommy, I want to be a real princess," Jordan exclaimed. The woman gave us all the information and said we needed to make an appointment. The girls swam for a few more hours and then I took them to get dinner at Burger King and waited for Dwight to arrive.

Dwight crept into our room at two in the morning; I'd left a key for him at the front desk. I was so happy he had made it. The girls would have been disappointed if their father the king didn't make this trip. He knew better than to touch me; he just took his clothes off and went to sleep.

The next morning Jordan and Destiny fought to be first in the shower. They couldn't wait for their day of beauty at the princess hair salon. Dwight was still asleep and I decided to let him rest. By the time he wakes we'll be back, and we can all take on the Magic Kingdom. Just as we were leaving out the door, Dwight sprang up.

"Where are y'all going?" he asked.

"To our princess appointments," I said.

"Princess appointments. Need I ask?" Dwight said, shaking his head.

"Don't look at me like that. They have this salon for little girls where they do their hair, nails, and light makeup."

"We are on vacation. I wanted to spend some time with them."

"It is not going to take all day and they really wanted to do this. Get some rest and we will be back."

• • •

My daughters looked like princesses when they were finished. They had their hair up in buns with a splash of glitter and had tendrils hanging from the sides. Jordan had on a baby blue dress like Cinderella and Destiny had a yellow and blue dress like Sleeping Beauty. Dwight said they looked too grown, but I didn't think so, and he was mad at me for spending almost four hundred dollars on them. I wasn't the only mother who did it, and besides, they loved being real princesses. While we walked around Disney World people complimented them. We took a picture in front of Cinderella's Castle and with Mickey Mouse. The girls rode the teacups and Dumbo over and over until they were sick. I took so many pictures of them I filled my memory card. Destiny and Jordan were having the time of their lives, but I was becoming irritated with the long lines and the hot sun. I also found myself arguing with Dwight over everything from what we should ride on to what they should eat. We had been there plenty of times, but this time I didn't feel like a family. Dwight was just irking me, giving in to the girls' every want. By the time I heard "It's a Small World After All" I was ready to call it a night. I couldn't take another character or song, but Dwight insisted that we stay for the fireworks.

We got back to the hotel and all I wanted to do was get in a hot shower. We all walked past the lit pool. There were parents and children still in and around the pool.

"Mommy, can we swim again?" Jordan asked.

"No, you don't want to mess your hair up."

"Mommy, I was already the princess today. I want to swim. Please," she said, whining.

"I said no, Jordan."

"Let them swim," Dwight said.

I turned around and gave him a look like *shut the fuck up.* "What? You're not going to be here when her hair needs to be done. You will be in Maryland."

"They looked good all day. What's the point? We are on vacation. Let them be kids."

"Stop contradicting me in front of them. I said no."

"Daddy, please!" Jordan said.

"Yes, y'all can go swimming. Let's go get changed."

I gave Dwight a look like *please don't defy me,* but he did it anyway.

When they went back down to the pool I took a shower to try to release some steam. I was mad as hell that Dwight was letting the girls do whatever they wanted. He did it all day and I was so aggravated with him. I say no more candy, he buys them big lollipops. I say, "No, don't get on that ride, you'll get sick." He says, "Destiny, go ahead, get on the teacups again," and she threw up. I was tired of him. He was just trying to make up for all the time he spends away from them, but this was not the way. He could stay by the damn pool, and if they catch a cold in the night air, I'd put them on a plane and let him take care of them. I flopped on the bed. I hated Dwight right now. I'd do anything to get away from him. I couldn't wait for this weekend to be over.

After Dwight bathed the girls, he told them good night and told them to get ready for tomorrow. Then he came into our room and took off his clothes and tried to get in bed with me. He rolled over close to me and I turned my back to him and moved as close to the edge as I possibly could. He turned on the television. He tapped me on my shoulder, trying to hug me. *Yeah I don't think so*, I thought.

"I'm tired. Get off of me," I said.

"Please, I miss you, Tracey."

"I'm trying to sleep."

"You too tired to give your husband that you haven't seen in three weeks love?"

"Dwight, I said I'm sleepy, now leave me alone."

"Tracey, I don't feel appreciated. You don't want me to touch you? Why do I keep trying? I mean, why?" he asked under his breath as he got up off the bed and hit the wall. Now he was taking things too far. Since when did me saying no make him this frustrated? I did want him to touch me, but I was so upset with him. I didn't know how to turn mad off and turn happy back on.

"What's wrong with you? Why are you getting so upset? Get back in bed, I'll give you some," I said.

"No, I don't want any pity sex." I went to try to hug him but he snatched away. He then began redressing, making a bunch of noise.

"Be quiet, you will wake the girls." He paid me no attention and turned the light on.

"I don't care anymore. I don't know what you want from me, Tracey. I'm tired of trying."

"You're tired," I said, sucking my teeth. He didn't say anything, just started mumbling and every other word was a cuss word. He grabbed his keys and walked out of the hotel room. I slipped my dress over my head and put my flip-flops on and ran after him. I sprinted down the hallway. I caught him at the elevator. I was gasping for air and said, "Where are you going? Stop this. This is crazy—let's talk."

"I'm tired of talking. Listen, I had it up to here," he said, pushing the DOWN button on the elevator panel until it illuminated.

"So what are you going to do about it? Run, that's the damn problem. We haven't had an opportunity to sit and talk. Dwight, I'm tired of dealing with you and your mess. You let those girls do whatever they want because you're not around and then I have to deal with it."

"Whatever, it is not about them. It is about us. You want to argue with me about everything, Tracey. I'm trying, you're not."

"Oh my God, I don't know how much more I can take," I yelled.

"Stop threatening me, Tracey. I am not a bad catch. Somebody else might want me and I wouldn't have to beg them for sex. I hope you realize that before it is too late," he said as the elevator door opened.

"And what the hell is that supposed to mean?" I said as I blocked the elevator door with my foot.

"I'm making Maryland my permanent home. You can move or you can stay—the choice is yours. I'm not begging you anymore."

"That's how you want it?"

"No, ask yourself: Is that how you want it?"

"Whatever! I don't need you, Dwight."

I heard one of the other hotel room doors open. I turned to see a couple and said hello as they walked past us. The elevator door opened and a man with a walkie-talkie approached us.

"Excuse me, we've been getting some complaints about noise. Can you try to keep it down?"

"Sir, no problem, we'll keep it down," Dwight said. I

flagged my hand at him and said to get the fuck out of my face.

"Here you go with that evil ghetto-girl shit." Dwight walked back into the room and grabbed his suitcase.

"Where are you going?"

"Why does it matter to you?"

"You're right, it doesn't," I said as I slammed the door on him.

I sat down on the sofa. I was tired of him. I heard sniffling coming from the bathroom. Jordan said, "I'm sorry for making you argue. I'm sorry for getting in the pool."

I hadn't realized that she had heard our entire argument. I got in the bed and said, "No, baby, you didn't make us argue."

"Uh-huh, I heard you say it."

"It wasn't about you, Jordan. Sometimes mommies and daddies have fights, but it doesn't mean they don't love each other. I love daddy very much and he loves me, okay?" I gave her a hug and calmed her down. I wished I believed what I just told my daughter.

When I awoke in Orlando I wished I was dreaming. I tried to call Dwight. I know his back was hurting from sleeping in the car. I dialed his phone but he didn't answer right away.

"Dwight, where are you?"

"I took a flight back to Maryland."

"What? You left us in Orlando?"

"What else was I supposed to do?"

I felt like I wanted to cry, but I held it in. I couldn't deal with him right now. I wiped away my tears. This was our last day here. Tomorrow it was back to work and everyday life for me. I was going to make sure the girls enjoyed themselves. I hung up the phone and walked over to the bed and woke the girls.

"Good morning, princesses. We are going to have break-fast and go to the pool and do whatever you want before we pack up and go home."

"Where's Daddy?" Destiny asked.

"Daddy said he was so sorry, but he had to go back to work. But look what he left for you. He said you can buy whatever you want from Downtown Disney." I pulled out a couple of twenties. They weren't as excited as I thought they would be. They just wanted their dad.

Dwight didn't know where we were. I guess he didn't care to find out. I was so heated on the drive home, I felt like cracking Dwight on his head with a brick.

"Go upstairs and get ready for tomorrow," I said as I dropped my bags at the door and looked through the mail. I walked into the office and turned the computer on. The phone started ringing and I ignored it. But then my cell phone started ringing after that and whoever was trying to get me wasn't giving up. I knew it was Dwight but I didn't care to answer the phone

"You left us at Disney World and now you want to talk to me."

"Yes, I think we need to talk."

"I don't want to talk to you. Fuck you. Fuck Maryland, and I hope you make all the money you want. One day you will realize that family should come first. Who's going to leave their family at Disney World?"

"Who is going to let their husband move by himself?"

"I should divorce your dumb ass." I began crying.

"Every time I don't do something that you want, you always say you're going to divorce me. Well, guess what? I don't care. Most women would die for a husband like me that busts his ass to provide for his family. But not your spoiled ass. You can't leave that house for anything. You can't do what I ask you to do just once, can you?"

"Dwight, are you listening? I want you to listen carefully. This is my last time saying it. I am not ever moving to Maryland. Not today, not tomorrow, not ever. And if you want to save our marriage, you will quit that job and find a new job here or else I will send you divorce papers. And I mean it." He didn't respond so I hung up on him.

CHAPTER 12

Alicia

I hadn't known men like Dwight really existed. After I told him that I wanted nothing to do with a married man, he backed off, way off. Even when he looked at me in what seemed like an inappropriate manner, his eyes quickly shifted. It made me wonder if I still had it. Could it really be that easy not to notice the body I worked so hard to perfect? He obviously realized the ramifications of speaking negatively about his wife to another woman and he stopped. He hadn't mentioned her or their drama in weeks. We went from deep relationship conversations to boy talk: work, sports, drinks. He even stopped hanging out with my friends and me. This was a man trying to save his marriage and be faithful at the same time. His wife was lucky and didn't even know it. Some chicks are just dumb.

Instead of staying at work, keeping his company, talking about Monday Night Football, I decided to skip out and scoop up my mother for our weekly movie date. Just as I was wrapping up my work, Dwight popped his head in my cubicle. Without even turning around, I felt his energy, as the hair on my arms stood. Finally, I acknowledged his presence. "What's up?"

"You tell me."

"Desiree finished the Requirements Document and I've assigned all the modules to a developer. So it looks like we're . . ." I was momentarily distracted by an e-mail that I was reading.

He chuckled. "It looks like I've lost my good friend."

"Dwight, please . . ." I said irritably. Did he even realize that he was the one who had been standoffish?

"Actually, I wanted to know what you were doing this evening. Can we grab a bite to eat?"

"My mother and I are going to the movies, like we do *every* Wednesday."

Nodding suspiciously, he said, "Maybe I'll just have a TV dinner and watch *SportsCenter* alone."

"Or you could go to the mall, grab a slice of pizza, and sightsee until you get sleepy."

"Nah, I'll pass. I thought having dinner with you was a better idea, but since that's not possible, I'll just go home . . ."

"And talk on the phone to your wife."

He hung his head. "Try talking to a woman who's fed up with everything. It ain't fun, I can tell you that."

Inside, I smiled. Things hadn't changed. He was still in a long-distance hell with no water in sight. Just as I celebrated, I looked up into his lonely eyes and pitied him. He was strong, smart, and devoted to a wife who was obviously a complete asshole.

As my mind wandered, he shook his head. "A'ight, Ms. Dixon. You're in another world. Have fun at the movies."

He slouched out of my cubicle and I stared at the emptiness he left behind. Momentarily, I thought about canceling on my mother, but I knew she'd be too disappointed. So I did what good women do: put my mother over men.

My mother was standing in the doorway when I pulled up. She waddled out of the house, carrying a Diet Coke. She smiled from ear to ear as she stuffed herself into my car. "I won big last night."

"Good, so does that mean you're treating?"

She cut her eyes at me. I laughed because I was her return on investment. She stopped treating me a long time ago. The last thing she paid for was that high-priced lawyer who saved me from going to jail with Deshaun. I've been taking care of her since I graduated. Some things you just get used to.

By the time we left the movies, it was close to eleven and I was completely exhausted. I turned my phone on out of habit. Five new voice messages.

"Hey, Alicia. It's Dwight. I need you, baby girl."

My heart dropped. I listened to the rest of the message. "The servers went down and I need you to come in as soon as possible."

By the fifth message, he sounded desperate. I called back. "Yes, Mr. Wilson."

"You ain't gonna believe what happened."

"I already don't believe you," I said, laughing.

"I know you don't. Honestly, though, the servers are down and if you could come back in, I would owe you one."

"You already owe me."

"I know. C'mon, I need you."

"Why didn't you call Desiree?"

"Man, I don't trust her."

"That's your damn problem. I'll be in. I have to drop my mother off first."

When I hung up, I quickly turned up the stereo. My mother snickered and my head snapped in her direction and I couldn't resist shouting, "What?"

"You need a job with regular hours."

"Regular hours can't pay your bills and mine," I said, raising my eyebrow.

"Yeah, I know. But you're never going to have a husband or a family working the way you do."

Although it was something I put out of my mind a long time ago, her words bothered me. Would I be just like her, never worthy of a good man? Just as it crossed my mind, I thought about Dwight. Why were all the good ones with the wrong woman?

"Why should I get married to get divorced?"

She shook her head. "You're so tough, aren't you?"

I zoomed down her street and unlocked the car doors. My brakes screeched as I pulled up in front of her door. "I love you, too, Ma."

"You know I just want the best for you. You're all I got."

Even though she said that all the time, it rattled me. Sure, I had my job and a group of good girlfriends, but did I really want to be fifty-five, hopeless, and alone? I leaned over for a halfhearted hug. "I know. Don't worry, I'm fine."

Her face sagged like she hadn't done all she could do. Like somehow she'd led me wrong. I smiled to lighten the mood. "A'ight, Ma. I gotta go."

When the light from her foyer peeped from the door, I sped off, back on Route 295, heading toward Annapolis Junction, wondering if my life would amount to nothing but a job. I got off at the Route 198 exit so I could stop at Exxon and grab a few cans of low-carb Monster drinks. I needed something to keep me awake.

Before I got back in the car, Dwight called and asked me to pick something up from Wendy's for him. He was definitely pushing it, because I was on my last legs and oh-so-tempted to enter my development, as the stone entrance gates were just yards away from where I stood. Instead I hopped in the car and whizzed over to Wendy's drive-thru.

No matter how many nights I walked into the building from the parking garage, I never felt safe. As usual, I darted from my car into the building and up the stairs. My heart always races even when I swipe my badge on the keypad. I was afraid that the cleaning crew could have carelessly left someone in the closet. As I sprinted to my cubicle, I crashed into Dwight.

I yelled, "Ah!"

He laughed and I felt silly for my paranoia, so I began laughing, too. We giggled uncontrollably for nearly ten minutes. Each time I would stop, he'd start again and vice versa. We leaned back and forth on each other trying to settle the humor until I kissed him. I don't know what came over me, but maybe I needed him as much as he needed me at the moment. He looked at me, questioning, wondering if this was wrong. And my eyes condoned what we both felt. I kissed him again to assure him that it was okay for two needy people to seek comfort from each other. We'd both sacrificed relationships for the sake of work, and who could understand either of us more than us? In the middle of the office, he held me and pushed my hair from my face. My neck tilted back and I looked at him in awe. He held me in his strong arms and his potbelly poked into my flat stomach.

"Are you scared of this?"

He took a deep breath. "Not anymore. Are you?"

"Dwight, it is what it is."

I don't know what got into me, but at that moment I didn't care about his wife or being a mistress or whether my feelings were right or wrong. It felt good and I couldn't apologize for it. Losing his friendship for a mere three weeks left a void in me that I didn't even realize he was filling. So whatever there was to feel—hurt or happiness or temporary satisfaction—I wanted it.

He almost immediately flipped back into work mode, maybe out of nervousness or uncertainty. "Yeah, Alicia. We really have to figure this out."

"What have you done so far?"

"The usual troubleshooting."

I followed him back into the server room and he talked about the problem on the way. After he was done, I asked, "What are we going to do about us?"

"I've never even considered cheating on my wife, I swear."

"I know, Dwight, but I don't believe in fighting what's natural. I don't want to be the other woman. I've never done anything like this before," I lied.

"I know and I don't want to hurt you or tell you that I'm not trying to work on my marriage, because I am."

"I understand and I realize that everything ain't forever, but right now I think I want to experience whatever we're supposed to experience together."

He took a deep breath. "Alicia, I've been trying to fight what I feel and do what's right, because I believe in marriage. My father wasn't there and I never wanted to be that man. But it's hard when you got someone fighting you. I'm getting tired."

Fatigue covered him and I just wanted to kiss him to let him know it would be okay. Maybe it was his honesty or his sincerity or his schoolboy naïveté that made me want to abandon my no-more-married-men philosophy, but I was ready and open. I didn't comment, simply observed him.

"Then there's you. You're smart and funny. You listen. You watch *SportsCenter*. You know how to express yourself without a whole bunch of yelling and screaming. You're a football fanatic. I mean, I'm starting to wonder if Tracey and I ever had anything in common."

Every sensory nerve in my body perked up. He was right where I needed him. Trying not to seem insensitive, I said, "Could it just be cause you guys are so far apart?"

"It could be that, or it could be just that I've had blinders on. You know, I always felt like you get married and you just stick it out. Other women were never an option. But I guess when you're away from home and away from your kids . . ." He sighed deeply, as if that was what pained him most. "You start losing focus and connection, and before you know it, you're here." I raised my eyebrow for him to explain, and he continued, "Thinking about how life would be with someone like you."

"So, one day, you're happily married, and the next you're sitting here with me . . ."

"It's been more than one day since I was happily married. It's gone downhill from the moment I told her I was moving. All she really cares about is how it affects her. I'm a good man and I know it. I've told her several times that she won't be happy till I'm really gone."

"So have you guys discussed breaking up?"

"Well she won't budge. I can't afford to budge; hell, we *are* going to break up. What do you think?" He reached for my hand and scooted his chair close to mine. "I don't know, but I'm glad that we're talking again."

Talking? That didn't really settle well, but he pulled my hand up to his mouth and kissed it. "Maybe some things happen for a reason."

There were no more words needed to describe this feeling. So I made the suggestion to get back to work and Dwight seemed to appreciate it. We began looking at the problem on the computer. He tapped on the keyboard with one hand and casually kissed our clasped hands. As he tried to track down the problem, I admired him and imagined the possibilities.

We primarily discussed work, but as the hours ticked by rapidly, we certainly got more acquainted. My mind had wandered down between his legs, as he rubbed my back, massaged my shoulders, and stared into my eyes. He was Mr. Right Now. Here and now, his touch felt right even if it was wrong.

We probably would have had the systems up before six in the morning if we weren't so touchy-feely. It was clear that neither of us planned on coming into work. I went to my desk to put an out-of-the-office message on my screen and Dwight did the same. We rushed out of the building before the early comers caught us. We felt guilty for doing our job.

As we headed out of the building, he asked, "Where you going?"

"Wherever you're going." He smiled and walked toward me, as if he thought it would be fine for us to ride together. I shook my head. "Dwight, we need to take separate cars."

"Oh yeah, you're right. I'll meet you at Bob Evans."

"Let's go to the one near my house."

As I drove to breakfast, it dawned on me that I hadn't had a bit of sleep and it would only be a matter of minutes before I crashed. What the hell was I surviving on?

Though Dwight pulled into the parking lot immediately after me, he was standing at my car door before I could get out. The morning show radio hosts had posed a question about the increase of men wearing makeup and if you could handle a man that wore foundation. I unlocked the door after he tugged twice on the handle. I said, "I was listening to something."

"I know you're hungry."

"I am but . . ."

I was interrupted by his arm around my shoulder. We went into the restaurant and I was surprised how many people were there at six-thirty on a weekday morning. They were primarily elderly couples. When I commented about them, Dwight said, "That's what it's all for."

"What?"

"The whole stress of marriage and raising kids is so we won't grow old alone."

"That's not what it's all for."

"What do you think is the purpose of stressing yourself out while you're young and vibrant?"

"For love?"

"You don't have to get married to be in love."

"You got a point, but I think marriage is more than just so you don't grow old alone."

He laughed. "Okay."

"Is that why you got married?"

He laughed harder. "I didn't know that was the purpose when I got married. Now that I'm older and I've seen the world, I do believe that whether we accept it or not, that's the purpose of marriage."

"I don't really believe marriage works, but I hope if I ever decided to get married, it would be for more than that."

He gazed over at an older couple. "We all do. In a perfect world, we'd all get married for the right reasons."

"It just seems that so many people do it for the wrong reasons, it makes me say, what the hell?"

"Marriage is good when it's good." He gasped. "But when it's bad, it's bad. You shouldn't rule it out, though."

The waiter came over for our drink orders and he ordered hot chocolate. His raised eyebrows questioned the smile on my face. I ordered coffee and faced him. "That's cute."

"What?"

"A grown-ass man ordering hot chocolate."

"My baby girls got me addicted to hot chocolate."

His eyes lowered like the thought of them made him think about what he was doing here smiling at my face. I looked at the menu so that he wouldn't feel the need to explain his preoccupation.

When our drinks came, he took a sip and the whipped cream got into his mustache. After we ordered our food, I reached over and dabbed it off with my napkin. He closed his eyes and smiled. "That, too."

"What?"

"Having someone who cares just as much about your image as you."

I nodded. "I guess."

"Marriage ain't the worst thing in the world. You should reconsider."

"Why? So that my husband can be sitting at breakfast with the new chick at work?"

His shoulders slouched. "No, because I'd imagine you'd have your man's back."

"What makes you think that?"

"Your personality is strong, but you're supportive. You're an overachiever, but you don't have anything to prove. You're committed to your friends, your mother. It's the same thing."

"I just never saw it in my future. I mean . . ."

"You've been in long-term relationships?"

My eyes wandered as I nodded. Technically, my only legitimate long-term relationship was to Deshaun and that was ten years ago.

Ignoring my discomfort, he continued, "So what's the difference?"

"Ah, well. I just think it's a waste of time. Have you looked at the divorce rate?"

"It's funny. I would have never pegged you as a punk."

"What?"

"Sounds like you're afraid of marriage more than you don't want to get married."

"Whatever."

Our food came and he reached for my hand. I looked down and raised my eyebrow. He smiled. "Let's pray."

He gripped tightly as he thanked God for me and our united brainpower in solving problems. I thought that it was a bit much to be asking God to bless our partnership, but it was cute. Before letting go, I smiled at him and he returned the expression.

After breakfast, I planned to just go home alone, but I wanted to lie beside him. Instead of asking what his plans were, I said, "You know, my house is right over there."

"Yes. I'ma follow you."

Moments later we were in my condominium, standing awkwardly in my bedroom. In hopes to not be overly aggressive, I slipped into a T-shirt and asked if he wanted one.

Probably in an effort to prevent the inevitable, he kept all of his clothes on and told me he didn't mind sleeping on top of the comforter. That wasn't exactly how I envisioned it. I told him it was okay for him to get under the covers with me. We lay close, facing each other, and he wrapped his arm around my waist. I stared into his eyes, wondering what attracted me to him. The once distorted, saggy-jaw face now seemed perfectly pleasing and symmetric. Whatever the case, I seemingly was no longer just mentally stimulated. I was physically stimulated, too. I questioned my own actions. Why was I here, slipping, wallowing in this moment in time?

We lay still, two friends, talking and enjoying each other. I massaged his shoulders, his back, kneading all of his tensed muscles. And watched him become putty from my touch. The crinkles in his forehead diminished and the stress in his face disappeared. Finally, he said, "This is what I need. After fighting wars all day, I need a woman to have compassion for me."

After stroking each other's bodies and egos, we fell asleep. I wanted to make love to him, but I wasn't sure if he was ready to. He was different and I had to strategically plan this out. If I played my cards right, he was probably a man who could be got. Considering he was that rare type of man that I could honestly see myself with, it was worth the effort.

It wasn't until I stepped into the office on Friday morning that my master plan didn't seem so smart anymore. How am I going to manage him going home every weekend? Suddenly, I had an attitude as if he'd made me do something that I didn't want to do. I was angry, but I couldn't understand why. I was losing it. I stormed past his office and casually waved.

His voice lingered behind me. "Ms. Dixon."

As I poured my coffee, I shared conversation with people in the break room and stared up at CNN playing on the hanging flat-screen television. A chill ran up my spine when Dwight rubbed my neck.

"Morning, Ms. Dixon. Did you enjoy your day off yesterday?"

I looked through him. "It was okay."

"Just okay?"

I nodded and left the break room. He didn't immediately follow. I was at my desk for nearly twenty minutes before he stood in my cubicle. "Now, can I get a better greeting?"

"Dwight, it's not appropriate. Not here."

He laughed. "I didn't ask for a kiss or anything."

"What time are you leaving?"

He looked at the clock on the wall. "What time does my boss want me to leave?"

"I don't know. Maybe you should ask him."

"I'm asking her."

"It doesn't matter to me. You can leave now."

"Maybe we should go to lunch before I leave." I shrugged. He said, "Meet you downstairs at twelve."

I nodded and turned to my desk. After checking e-mail and tying up some loose ends, I decided to send an e-mail message to my girls. The subject was: OOPS, I DID IT AGAIN. In so many words, I explained that I appropriately did the inappropriate, but this time I wasn't planning to love 'em and leave 'em. They all wanted to know how the sex was and I had a hard time convincing them that this was different. We didn't have sex . . . I was attracted to him on a deeper level.

After I got yelled at from three separate angles, I realized that no one would understand. Before I knew it, it was lunchtime and time to explain to Dwight that I was wrong and I shouldn't have come on to him. Somehow, it didn't come out that way. I just needed to know more about the state of his marriage before I totally let go. Maybe he was fed up and it would be over in a matter of time. Maybe this was destiny. Maybe his wife was ready to leave him. I said, "Does your wife know how you feel?"

"She knows that I'm tired of running back and forth. I'm burned out. When I get there, we argue like you wouldn't believe. She's mad that I'm not there to help her and I'm mad that she's too stubborn to do what's best for the family."

"So, do you plan to bend?"

"I probably would have, but like I told you, this situation has really exposed a real ugly side of her." His big brown eyes reached out for understanding. "It's bad. I never thought I would regret marrying her. She's just acting like a materialistic brat."

"Do you think she's fallen out of love with you?"

"I just think she's more in love with that house than she ever was with me."

"Wow. That's bad."

"Who are you telling?"

"So whatchu gonna do?"

"I really don't know."

That wasn't exactly what I wanted to hear, but at least he was honest. Clearly, he felt differently about his wife than he did when he arrived. Each time I tried to convince myself to run away and leave this situation alone, something else told me that he was different.

CHAPTER 13

Alicia

The sun had barely peeked through when my phone rang on Sunday morning. Dwight's voice sounded slightly groggy. "Hey, you."

I sat up in my bed with a huge smile. "Good morning. Are you at the airport yet?"

"My flight leaves at four, so I'll be in town around six. You tryna do something this evening?"

I threw out a couple of options and he threw out some, but we ultimately agreed on dinner on the water and watching the sunset. He almost began to share the drama that occurred over the weekend, but I asked him not to. I didn't really need to know the what, how, and where. All I really cared to know was how much longer they planned to pretend this long-distance marriage was working.

It was clear that he and his wife were in a sexual drought as well, based on some casual references he made. It had been a minute for me as well. So we were definitely on the same page.

By the time Dwight called to say he'd arrived in Maryland, I had already showered and put on the skimpy hot pink panty set that I purchased just for the evening. I slipped on a comfortable black dress and pulled my twists back into a ponytail.

Before coming to pick me up, he went home to shower, and by the time he got there, I'd had a glass of Chardonnay and dozed off on the couch. The doorbell startled me. It felt like I'd been asleep much longer than I had. My heart raced as I rushed to the door.

When I opened up, he smiled and I slightly retracted. It was so weird that I'd become attracted to this man. He wore sharp suits, but his casual gear was definitely slacking. His jeans gathered at the bottom. He wore a gray polyester button-down shirt and his shoes were semi-platform. It took me a second to get over the sight, but after he opened his mouth, my superficial preoccupation was erased.

He asked, "Are you okay?"

"I'm fine. I fell asleep and I . . ."

"Can I get a hug?"

He was such a sweetheart. I turned around and gave him a hug. He squeezed me tightly. After I grabbed my purse, I said, "Are you sure you want to hang out? You look tired."

"I want to be with you, whether we hang out or not."

Before I stepped into my shoes, I said, "I wouldn't be mad if we chilled and watched a movie here."

"Wow." I raised my eyebrow. He smiled. "You're one of a kind. You know that, right?"

"Yeah, I know." I laughed. "I'm just joking. Thanks."

We ended up ordering pizza and I poured both of us a glass of wine. He wanted red and I had my regular. We sat

Indian-style in front of my coffee table. When he lifted his glass to toast, he tilted it toward me.

I said, "No, you do it."

"Okay. To peace and happiness and to, as you say, living in the moment."

I nodded my head aggressively and took a sip. Wine dripped from the corner of his mouth and I leaned in. "You got wine on your mouth." He reached to wipe it off and I moved his hand. "Let me taste it."

While still holding my glass, I wrapped my arm around his neck and began kissing him. He moaned. "Hmmm. Does it taste good?"

He yanked off my ponytail holder and ran his fingers through my twists, while pulling my head toward him. His sudden aggression aroused me. I kissed his neck and thrashed my tongue in his ear. I lifted his shirt and poured the remainder of my wine on him and began licking it from his chest and navel. His eyes rolled and I reached down to unbuckle his pants. He pulled my hand from his belt. I looked up and asked, "What's wrong?"

"I think we should wait . . ."

Wait? My body struggled to comprehend this. I knew he wanted me as much as I wanted him. I grabbed his hand and guided it up my dress, so he could feel the ocean gushing from me. I pulled my dress over my hand, so that he could admire my undergarments. He played around down there for a minute, but stopped abruptly. Unlike me, his will was stronger than his nature. I was offended, but at the same time, I was sure he was what I thought he was.

We lay beside each other on the floor, breathing heavily and staring at the ceiling. I was slightly angry that I'd tarnished my good-girl credibility. So I said, "I'm sorry. I'm just really attracted to you and I wasn't . . ."

He reached over and draped his arm over my breast. "I'm the one with the commitment, not you." He leaned over to kiss my shoulder. "I see so much in you and I don't want to ruin what could be. If it becomes physical and I'm still back and forth with Tracey, that could mess up a good thing."

Why did that make me want him more? I was more determined to make him my man than before. I said, "Thank you."

"I can wait. And I'm willing to wait so that in the end we'll respect each other."

I reached for my drink and swallowed the frustration. The doorbell rang and I jumped. I'd completely forgotten about the pizza. He laughed. "Cover yourself up. I'll get the door."

I rushed into the kitchen. By the time he returned with the pizza, his expression looked as if he expected that I would no longer be in my panties. Instead, I sashayed around him just to test his strength. I put soda and glasses with ice on the table.

He said, "Are you going to eat like that?"

When I shrugged, he smiled and sat at the table. After I sat, he began to laugh.

"What?"

"I was getting ready to say grace, but I can't even concentrate right now."

"Why?" He looked me up and down and shook his head. I laughed. "You're funny."

He touched my leg and said, "You're sexy."

After we ate, we relaxed on the floor and talked about

life. What he wanted. What I wanted. And how we planned to get it.

We shared thoughts. We shared vision. His plans were just like my plans. He wanted to own a technology firm and ultimately just do business acquisition. He stared at me. "If I'd only met you ten years ago."

I smiled and he clarified, "This is the area for technology. If I'm going to live my dream, I need to be here."

I nodded. He wrapped his arms around me. "We would be a power couple. Oh, yeah, that's what it's about, too."

"What?"

"Marriage is about sharing a vision. Without a shared vision, it's disposable."

I could do nothing more than nod at everything he said. He made me think of things I'd never even considered. I'd never met anyone who understood me and what I wanted out of life.

CHAPTER 14

Tracey

I was about to meet with a potential seller and on my way there, I dialed Dwight to say hello. After I gave him the ultimatum, he seemed to distance himself emotionally, which made me more distant. But some days, I call out of formality or habit. Neither of us says a whole lot. Our communication is gone, but he still answers every time I call, even if he has to call me right back. However, this time I didn't get him, I got his answering machine. I left him a message telling him that the girls were looking forward to seeing him this weekend. I couldn't bring myself to say that I wanted to see him, too. Men like the chase and I couldn't be too available.

All I saw when I took my shades off and walked up the driveway were patches of missing grass from the yellowish-green lawn. I rang the bell and a young man came to the door.

"Hi, I'm here to meet Mrs. Randolph."

"Come on in. Mama, the door." The young man yelled

and an older woman with thick glasses came to the door with him and said, "Yes?"

"Hi, I'm Tracey Wilson. You called me the other day about selling the house."

"Oh yes, come on in and have a seat."

An older man wearing suspenders and high waters walked into the room. "Glenda, I told you I don't want to sell this damn house. What are y'all doing? Y'all trying to sneak and sell the house? Pops ain't even settled in the ground yet, and y'all already selling the house."

"We had a family meeting and we selling," Mrs. Randolph said.

"That ain't right."

"It is right. Pops ain't leave this house to you. And you ain't finn' to hold us up on the sale."

I didn't know what to say as my eyes went from family member to family member. My weight shifted from one leg to the other, impatiently. I was extremely uncomfortable standing in the middle of a family feud. There was an obituary on the table. The man on the cover had a service uniform on and I could tell the picture was nearly fifty years old. As I glanced at the date, I better understood what was going on. The funeral had been two days ago. I didn't want any part of this.

"Say, how much can we get for this house anyway?" the older man asked.

I pulled out printouts of the other houses that had sold in the neighborhood. "Well, the last house to sell in this neighborhood went for around three hundred thousand. So somewhere in that ballpark. I mean, depending on the condition of the house. That's something I'll be better able to tell you after I look at everything."

I did a once-over and I'm not sure if all these people lived in the house, but it looked worn out. They totally disregarded my last statement, as the eyes of everyone in the room became dollar signs. "That's a hundred thousand apiece."

"Rudy, that money can go towards Toya's college."

"Y'all ain't right. It just don't seem right. We grew up in this house. I rather set this house on fire than see y'all sell it."

My phone buzzed and I assumed it was Dwight returning my call, but it was Danielle telling me not to forget our dinner date. As the family members decided what was right and not right, I excused myself and told them to contact me when they had all reached an agreement.

I walked to my car and sat and put my forehead in my hands. I hated dumb people. I hated the fact that I had to hustle like this. I wished I was just a rich woman with a great husband. But that so wasn't the case. I had an asshole for a husband and I hadn't sold a house since September. I needed him to stay in Maryland to continue to pay all the bills. My head was spinning and I needed a distraction from my drama-filled life.

I couldn't wait to update Mama Dee and Danielle on everything that their son and brother had been putting me through. I know they will side with me—they always do. Unfortunately, tonight was not going to be about me. By the time I had arrived at the Outback Steakhouse, Danny was near tears and Mama Dee was shaking her head. Danielle's tall frame looked malnourished and her brown skin was pale and her usually stylish hair was all over the place. She took one look at me, got up from the table, and took her phone conversation outside.

"Mama Dee, what's going on?" I asked as I had a seat at the table.

"Nothing, I just raised a stupid child. I never seen a girl so smart, so intelligent in all aspects of her life, and so dumb in love."

"What's wrong?"

"Reggie cheated on my child again. They been married for all of four months. I told her to leave the house, but she want to sit and argue with him on the phone. Maybe she needs somebody her own age to talk some sense to her."

"Well what's going on now?"

"He's trying to explain hisself. That bum cheated on her with some girl around the corner from where they live. She up there ready to fight the girl and I told her ain't no man worth fighting over. They both said they didn't do it, but she found e-mails and letters. I told her to pack her stuff and come move with me."

I took in everything Mama Dee said and told her to order me an apple martini. Then I went outside and talked to Danny. I listened to Danielle go on and on about Reggie for fifteen minutes. She needed to realize Reggie was a cheater and she had to deal with it. She was going to have to leave or just deal with the situation and shut up. She said she was leaving him, but I knew she wasn't. She came back to the table a little calmer. I was glad, because I wanted to tell on Dwight and talk about our problems.

"Mama Dee, I told your son to come home or I was going to divorce him."

She turned to me and asked, "Why?"

"Because your son left his family at Disney World."

"He did what?"

"We were having a really bad fight and he left, went

back to Maryland. I can't take him being up there any-more."

"That's why you don't let your husband move away by hisself," she said, turning to me. Then she turned to Danielle and said, "And you don't keep taking a man after he cheats on you. You will both learn."

"Mom, be quiet with your old-school rules, that don't work anymore. Men are different today."

"Times are not different. The rules don't change. Men are men and only do what you let them get away with."

"Well, I'm going to listen to myself, and I think I have a solution," I announced.

"And what's that?"

"I'm going to let Dwight go. I'm going to give him a taste of freedom."

"A taste of freedom. So your marriage is crumbling now. And your solution is to leave him up there for more time. For how long? Are you crazy, girl?"

"Mama Dee, I'm going to leave him up there as long as it takes. It can take two months, six months. He will miss us and come home," I said, agitated.

"That is kind of dumb, Tracey. You should just move up there," Danielle added. I looked at her like *please don't try to tell me what's dumb.*

I spent the rest of the evening trying to explain my plan, but Mama Dee still didn't get it. She said she wished me luck and Danielle kept redirecting the conversation back to her and Reggie. And it was becoming increasingly an-noying, so it was time for me to leave.

On the ride home I thought long and hard about my op-tions. I wasn't listening to them. I knew my husband better than he knew hisself. I was going to bring Dwight home. I started "Operation Bring Husband Home," and my mission was going to be successful. I realized we got married young and that might have been a mistake. Dwight just needed a taste of life without a family. I wasn't making excuses, but that might be the reason for him acting crazy. Maybe he felt like he missed out on his freedom, being tied down with the same woman since fourteen. So I was going to give him his freedom and let him experience being a single man. I was not going to call him or bother him. I didn't care how long it took. He would be back. I would break him. He would come home. I knew Dwight.

When Dwight called later that evening, I said, "You realize that we're separated."

He hissed, "Tracey, where are the girls?"

"Do you really care?" There was a long silence. I said, "Are you planning to come home this weekend?"

"Of course, Tracey."

"Well, I think you should stay with Mama Dee or Danielle."

I knew that would infuriate him. He wasn't going to be here and there and have everything his way. I planned to make his visits as uncomfortable as possible. That way, he would want to find a solution fast. I was surprised when he sighed. "Okay, Tracey. If that's what you think is best. It's not a problem, as long as the girls are there, too."

CHAPTER 15

Alicia

After weeks of cuddling and pretending I understood why we were waiting to have sex, I was tempted to rape Dwight. I sat at my desk instant messaging my friends about the dilemma. I explained the issues. I wanted Dwight to pressure me, but he assured me that he'd be ready only when he was sure about the destiny of his marriage. Under normal circumstances, I believe it's better to just fuck and get it over with. If the sex isn't good, there's no need for him to stay around, but I felt different about Dwight. I wanted him and I wanted him bad, but considering he'd only had one sex partner in ten years, I was prepared for the worst. And unlike any other man in my past, I didn't plan on leaving him if it wasn't good.

As the girls coaxed me to be the aggressor, Dwight came to my desk and startled me. I quickly shut down my messenger window. He didn't look fazed, as he only came to remind me that we had a meeting in a few minutes. We headed to the third-floor conference rooms and when we stepped into the stairwell, I made sure it was just the two of us. I said, "Babe . . ."

He frowned. I continued, "Do you ever imagine making love to me?"

"All the time."

He put his hand on the door so we could exit into the corridor. I put mine on top of his and prevented him from turning the handle. I said, "I trust you. I trust you with my body. I don't want you to worry about messing things up. It's gonna be what it's gonna be."

His eyes bugged out like he was scared. The space between us got smaller and smaller, my slacks rubbed his pants, and I wrapped my arm around his waist. "I want to make love to you."

My words lingered as I swiftly turned the knob and strutted in front of him to greet our customers sitting in the third-floor lobby. He staggered behind, looking slightly confused. It was clear that he was used to being in charge, but he was moving too slow for me. Everyone gathered in the conference room and I rushed to the bathroom. While in the hallway, I sent Dwight a text message: I WANT TO FEEL YOU INSIDE OF ME. I WANT TO SPILL OUT ALL OVER YOU.

When I entered the room, Dwight looked up at me. His eyebrows wrinkled and then he smiled. I could tell that he was turned on and he wanted to take me right there on the conference table, so I wrapped my thumb and my index finger around my can of Monster and slid them up and down. Sucking my bottom lip, I pretended to be into the meeting, and Dwight was tongue-tied and dumbfounded. I'd thrown him off guard. He tapped the back of his pen on the table nervously, but I kept my composure as I sent more seductive signals. When the meeting was over, everyone stood and Dwight remained seated. I chatted freely with the customers, casually winking at him when no one was looking. Finally, he was in a condition to stand. After we escorted the customers to the door, he said, "Do you want to leave now?"

I'd been ready to make love to him from the day we first lay in bed together, but his holding out forced me to fall for his personality. That scared the shit out of me. I sped behind him down the highway, headed to our destiny; there was no turning back. My adrenaline was racing and by the time we reached my house, my panties were drenched. He got out of his car first and I followed. I walked up to him and began reaching up his shirt and rubbing his mouth. When he tasted my goods on my fingers, he said, "You're nasty. Were you playing with yourself?"

We rushed into my house. At the front door, we began ripping each other's clothes off. We kissed and rubbed all the way to the bedroom. I grabbed a condom from my nightstand and he struggled to open the wrapper. My vagina was yelling for him to hurry up. Still, he fumbled. After seemingly forever, he pulled it out and tried to roll it on, and he tried, and he tried. Before the passion died, I snapped, "Just put it in . . ."

That's exactly what he did and it felt so natural, so right, a perfect fit. Not too big, but not too small. My vaginal walls clamped onto him, holding him tightly as he glided in and out of me. My heart sank deeper and deeper with each stroke. I felt like a virgin all over again . . . not in the physical sense, but in the emotional: pure and free and open. I felt like I was in love, but I couldn't explain how the player had fallen victim to the game. Or maybe I'd fallen for his lack of game, which made him a rare man, and which in turn made me a rare woman. I was the only woman he found worthy enough to stray on his wife with. So many thoughts whirled through my head that I neglected to bring out my A game. I simply moved my hips and submitted to his flow. Shit, I was supposed to be turning him out. Instead, as my heart pounded and I felt like I wanted to cry, for the first time in my life, I think I had been turned out.

Dwight rolled over beside me, and I stared at the ceiling. Tears of joy and satisfaction rolled from the corners of my eyes. He lifted up on his elbow and wiped my face. He said, "What's wrong?"

"I just don't know how I got here. Please don't hurt me," I said, trying to keep a straight face.

I was laughing like hell internally, as he began to speak, "Alicia, I keep telling you that this is real. I like everything about you."

Sniffing, I said, "But you're married."

"But we're definitely on the rocks . . ."

"I just don't want to keep falling for you and have to lose you."

He didn't respond and a strong feeling of anxiety came over me. I was no longer joking or pretending. I didn't want to lose Dwight. He was a keeper.

CHAPTER 16

Alicia

Being the mistress when the wife is in another state makes it more like the wife is the mistress. I never see him talk to her. He talks about his girls, so I'm certain they talk, but I never see. So, in my mind, she really doesn't even exist. His marriage is just a figment of his imagination, considering he had practically moved in with me.

I sat up in bed and watched him sleep. I always wondered what he was dreaming, because he always had a partial smile on his face, which made me smile. I rested my head on his pillow and rubbed his chest. He put his arm on my arm and stretched. "You up?"

"Yes, baby," he said.

We lay in silence, snuggling. It was the way we started our day, the calm before the storm. When the relationship started, we agreed that if it got hot and heavy, I would be the one to change jobs. I'd been on six interviews in less than two weeks. Dwight coached me through them, and I received an offer letter yesterday—more money and a better position. We enjoyed each other and we didn't want to ruin it by working together too long. In less than two hours, I was about to turn in my resignation. I was afraid that I was disrupting my life without a guarantee. But as he caressed me so gently, I knew he was worth it, even if we were temporary.

Finally, I reached for the remote and he kissed me. "You okay?" he asked.

I nodded and turned on the television. During our second phase of morning intimacy, we chatted about everything, from gossip to gospel. This was something I never had. Everyone else was just a man. Dwight was more than a man. He was a damn Transformer; more than meets the eye.

It was always the way a man looked or the way he dressed or how much money he made or how many places he took me, but Dwight was different. It had all to do with his character. Nothing was surface with us. How could it be that all these years, I didn't even know what I was looking for? This was the first relationship I'd been in since my college boyfriend that I could remember feeling so safe with expressing my emotions. The strange part is that I wasn't protective of my feelings even though he had yet to really confirm that he wanted to definitely leave his wife. We were mentally building a life together and totally ignoring the life he left behind. I wanted to be smarter. I wanted to not love a man who belonged to someone else, but I was convinced that he would always honor my love no matter what.

Everyone knew why I was leaving. Optimus countered with more money and a more prestigious position and I declined. Dwight promised me that he was worth it. My mother always said not to play where I work and I never imagined I would. Since I was silly enough to get caught up, and really caught up at that, I had to be the one to leave. On my last day, they threw me a huge potluck luncheon. I was so tired of lying and explaining that I just needed a change, I didn't know what to do. When it came time for my farewell, I was filled with emotions. I kept crying. It was harder than I expected. This is just why I try to avoid becoming emotionally attached. I wasn't ready to leave, but I definitely wasn't prepared to expose to the office that I was in love with a married man either.

Dwight helped me carry the boxes out to my car and he appeared to be skipping. I looked at him. "Are you happy to be getting rid of me?"

"Nah, I'm just tired of all the speculations."

I smirked. "I guess you're right."

After he put everything in the car, I reached out for a hug. We swayed from side to side. I thought it was pretty bold of us and I pulled away. He kidded, "Look, it's all good now. Who cares what they say?"

I shrugged. He was right. I'd been through this before, leaving a job, swearing to keep in contact, and believing my coworkers were my friends. After two weeks, they forget about you and you forget about them. They would eventually forget all about me and my speculated affair.

Later that evening, Dwight and I went out to dinner. We went to Oya on 9th Street in DC. The atmosphere is almost heavenly. White walls, white tables, white chairs. There was just a peaceful spirit swirling around us, joy rising in the smoke from the votive candles. We sipped bubbly as we cuddled in a corner booth. It was our coming-out celebration.

By the time we got home, my stomach had balled into knots. I'd either had too much champagne or my two-day-late period had arrived. When I went into my walk-in closet to grab my Always pads, Dwight hopped in the bed. "Hurry up, baby. You know I have to work in the morning."

I headed to the bathroom. "I don't know why you want me to hurry up. I think the red devil is here."

He pouted and grunted. Sometimes he can be such a baby, but since he tries so hard to spoil me, spoiling him is effortless. When I pulled down my panties, I was surprised that they were clean. Hmm. Oh well, I put on a pad anyway for protection, because I knew the devil would pop up sometime during the night. Dwight rolled over and almost immediately began to snore when I told him that there would be no hanky-panky.

I woke up around seven, forgetting that I had an entire free week before going to work. I sat up in bed trying to decide if I should go back to sleep, or watch TV, or clean up, or make breakfast, or go to my mother's house. Some people always have to have something to do at all times and that is me. The thought of chilling made me anxious. I decided to get up and go to the bathroom. My period still hadn't come. Okay, I'd been taking my pill daily. There was no logical reason why I was late. I attributed it to stress. Maybe I should just learn how to relax. I climbed back into bed and as usual admired Dwight as he slept peacefully. I caressed his chest until he started moving. When he appeared slightly coherent, I said, "Baby, do you know we could have done it last night? I didn't even come on."

"Do you think you're pregnant?"

"Don't play. You know I'm on the pill."

"Man, I'm potent. You never know."

"I hope you're not that potent."

"You should probably get a test."

His recommendation went into one ear and out the other. He had the audacity to call from work a little later and ask me if I was positive that I wasn't pregnant. I told him there was nothing to be concerned about. He said, "Man, as much sex as we have, you better make sure."

My heart skipped a beat. *Make sure.* I am sure. There is no way I could be. A child would complicate an already overly complicated situation. My words came out slow. "What are we going to do if I am?"

"Did you hear me?"

"What?"

"If you're pregnant, you won't have to go through this alone. I promised you I'd be here for you and I will."

"How can you say that when you're still married?"

"I've just been procrastinating, but my plans never changed. It's just a process of sending the papers."

"It's not just a process. What if she wants to fight for her marriage?"

"It's no longer up to her. It's too late."

After Dwight got back to his work, I rushed out of the house and went to the grocery store to get a pregnancy test. When I got back into the house, I ran into the bathroom and ripped the box open. I straddled the toilet and peed on the indicator. *Let's get this shit over before I go crazy.*

I lay balled in a knot in the middle of the highway about to be run over by a car. Suddenly, I didn't know how I transitioned from my bathroom to here. The piercing sound of brakes screeching in my ear shook sense into me. What the hell was I doing? I prayed it wasn't too late. I lay still awaiting the impact of the car. The driver hopped out screaming, "Miss, are you crazy? I could have run you over."

Tears rolled down my cheeks. "Thank you."

"Are you okay, miss?"

She helped me off the ground and cars blew their horns, irritated that I'd held up traffic. I thanked her again. I was happy she didn't kill me or the baby growing inside of me. My mind drew a blank after I saw the positive results. My main focus was changing my situation. I staggered. The lady looked concerned and asked, "Do you need a ride?"

I nodded.

"How far are you going?"

"Just up the road . . ."

Overexpressing my gratitude, I hopped in her car and she dropped me off a block away from my development. I still felt woozy, but I was happy God had spared my life. I kept badgering myself. That was so stupid.

When I got home, I went online to see the rate of pregnancy with my new birth control pills. The damn pills I decided to switch to after seven years. The ones that were supposed to have a double benefit. They supposedly help your skin and help maintain your weight. I should have known that was too good to be true. Would you believe that these damn pills are known for this bullshit? I scrolled through the message board. *I took my pill at the same time, every day, and still got pregnant. These pills don't prevent pregnancy.*

I became angry with all of the women on the website. Why didn't anyone call me and tell me? I went into the kitchen and almost poured a drink. Oh God. This is not good. What do pregnant women do to calm their nerves? Before I could call him, he called me.

I picked up and said, "Oh my God, Dwight, I'm . . ."

"I know."

"You know what?"

"I know you're pregnant."

My nerves danced around in my belly. "What are we going to do?"

"Just calm down. Getting all worked up isn't going to change it." Tears rolled down my face. He sighed. "Wow . . . this is crazy."

The preoccupation in his voice scared me. I wanted him to sound like he did earlier when he was adamant that he was leaving his wife. Now, he sounded as if his world was crumbling rapidly. As he pondered on the line, I said, "Dwight, I hope you don't think this was intentional."

"I know you better than that. I just need to get my head right. A lot of things have to get done now. It's urgent now. Wow . . ."

That was nearly the twentieth "wow." I was confused. I was scared. I was angry. I wasn't sure that I could be a good mother and here I was on the line with a man who belonged to someone else and his voice wasn't reassuring me, either.

He told me that he'd come over after work. But now, I needed to talk to my mother. She wouldn't convict me. She would understand me. I dialed her number, and before I spoke, I sniffed.

"Alicia, is everything okay?"

"No, I'm pregnant."

She was quiet. Then she said, "It's not the worst thing in the world. You make good money. You're independent. You'll be fine."

"What about my relationship situation?"

"That will work itself out, too. Right now, just worry about you."

"But, Ma . . ."

"Don't worry about him. He's going to do what he wants to do regardless. You need to focus on whether or not you're prepared to be a mother. Whether you're married or not, a baby is a woman's responsibility. Marriage does not protect you from that."

"I guess."

"Well, I'm excited to be a grandmother. This is the best Christmas gift I've had in years. I thought it would never happen."

She made me smile for a minute. "Yeah, I never really planned to have kids."

"I think every woman should have one. When can I start telling people?"

I laughed. "Ma, I'm only like two days pregnant. Don't start telling people yet. Let me go to the doctor's first."

"What is Dwight saying?"

"Not a whole lot."

"Let him take it all in. He'll come around in a minute. Just lay back and let him absorb it."

And that's what I did. I decided not to call and find out what time Dwight planned to leave work. Instead, I decided to keep my head straight. I didn't need any more blackouts and near suicides. At least I'd already left the job. It could have been worse.

Several hours of agony passed before he called back. I thought about an abortion, but my mother called two or three times, adding more reasons why this is the right thing at the right time. When he told me that he was on his way, he just didn't sound like himself.

By the time the doorbell rang, I'd thought about all of the outcomes. I was defensive as I swung the door open. His tie hung from his neck and his shirttail was halfway out. He smelled like a barrel of beer. He grabbed me and began kissing me. I was momentarily relieved. Maybe he wasn't as frustrated as he had sounded on the phone. When I yanked away from him, he pulled me back. "Baby, can you believe this shit?"

I took a deep breath, walked away, and plopped down on the couch. He followed and lounged beside me. I stroked his back and asked, "What are we going to do?"

"I called my attorney."

"And?"

"He's drafting up the divorce papers as we speak."

"Did you talk to her?"

"She definitely wants a divorce and I want to be with you."

"How long will it take to be final?"

"If she doesn't contest it, it will be final in thirty days."

I leaned in to kiss him and to thank him for being a man and handling his business. He touched my face as I backed away and I noticed he was no longer wearing his ring. "You know I love you, right?"

"Now I do," I said, still partially insecure. I wanted to know what came next, but I was afraid to ask.

CHAPTER 17

Tracey

If I heard Dwight's voice now, it would send chills through my body. I was irritated with him and our situation. I knew what I had to do. I awoke this morning and looked around my room. I missed Dwight not being here. All I could do was be the best mom and the best Tracey I could possibly be. Months had passed and I guess Dwight thought this arrangement was fine. "Operation Bring Husband Home" was proving to be an uphill battle, but I had to stay the course. I just filled my life with so many things so I wouldn't notice he was gone. I take the girls to the science history museum, we color, and we go to the park. We'd even been hanging out with Sophia and Leah, going to the beach and on lunch dates. I signed up Destiny and Jordan for everything from tennis to modeling. I came home from work, I read books with the girls, prepared and ate dinner, then they went to bed. Once they're asleep I got our clothes ready for the next day, and then I followed up on leads and e-mailed clients. If I wasn't tired I would watch television and then get up and do it all over again. *He doesn't want to call me, fine. I got forever. I'm not budging.*

There was a loud knock on the door. I looked at my watch. Who would be knocking at my door at two in the afternoon? I peeped out of the blinds and noticed a sheriff. I quickly yanked the door open. Before I could ask why he was here, he said, "Tracey Yvette Wilson?"

"Yes."

"You've been served these court-ordered documents as of December sixteenth, 2006." He turned to walk away.

"What is this? What kind of documents?"

"Ma'am, I don't know. I just serve papers."

I ripped open the manila envelope and nearly fainted. Divorce papers. I couldn't believe my eyes. I called Dwight. "I don't believe you."

He responded calmly, "Really. You don't believe that I want to move on with my life?"

"And just forget about your family. Have you lost your mind?"

"I don't plan to forget about my family. Look at the papers, Tracey. I plan to continue to take care of you. I'll come to Jacksonville at least once a month to see the girls. I plan to do what I promised you when I married you. You demanded a divorce months ago and I wasn't sure. I wanted to work things out and all you kept saying is if you can't have it your way then you wanted a divorce. You got what you want."

I breathed heavily on the phone. He wasn't serious. He was just trying to scare me. This was nothing more than another tactic to make me come to Maryland. I wasn't giving up what I was working on to chase my husband. It was time for Tracey to take care of me. And if Dwight loved me the way he claimed, he would understand. Our relationship had become a damn staring match. Who could hold out the longest?

"You're right. I don't want to be married to someone who would leave his family."

"Have a nice day, Tracey. If you're not too busy, please have my princesses call me this evening."

"I'm not going to do shit. I'm going to explain to them that Mommy and Daddy are getting divorced and he doesn't care about them."

"Wow, I never realized you were so juvenile."

The line went dead. I looked at the phone and tried to call him back. It kept going to voice mail. So I called his mother. I cried in the phone, "Mama Dee, Dwight sent me divorce papers."

"Well, you told him you wanted a divorce," she said unsympathetically.

"I know, but I didn't mean it."

"Well, Tracey, if a man can't prioritize family then maybe you do want to divorce him. Is that what you want?"

"I don't know."

"Did y'all think of counseling?"

"No, we just called it quits. I mean, maybe we've been growing apart for a long time, but we just didn't know it until we weren't in the same house."

"If you want your marriage, you better work on it."

I wanted her to call Dwight and tell him to bring his ass home, but she didn't seem to be taking sides. It was moments like this when it was clear that no matter how long she'd known me or how much she loved me, I was her son's wife and not her daughter.

She added, "Ask yourself have you done all you can do."

"Yes, I've done all I can do."

"Oh, well, then you got to make a decision."

I huffed. She just didn't understand. When I hung up, I called Danielle's crazy ass. I hoped she'd give me better advice. As I explained what was going on, she said, "Girl, please. Dwight ain't divorcing you. He just trying to scare you."

"You think so?"

"Yeah, let his ass sweat it out. He know he got a good thing."

"You're right, Danny. I'm not going to worry about it. I'm not signing anything."

"Yeah, rip those papers up and throw them in the trash."

That's exactly what I did. I sent Dwight a text message. AS LONG AS MY BILLS ARE PAID, YOU CAN HAVE YOUR DIVORCE.

CHAPTER 18

Alicia

Dwight's divorce was days from final when we went for the sonogram. He'd let his apartment go and officially moved in with me, until he found the house he wanted. As we dressed for the appointment, he said, "You know what?"

"What?"

His verbal excitement didn't coincide with his droopy chin. "It's a boy."

"You're funny."

"Actually, it's not funny at all."

I didn't respond, because I knew what he was thinking. Some mornings I felt so happy, but then others were sad, because I never knew what was bothering him. I knew he missed his girls and his wife wasn't letting him speak to them. There were times when I wondered if he missed her, if he was sure about us and our family. He always assured me this was what he wanted and I tried my best to assure him that he'd made a smart decision. As I watched him zone out, I knew this was a morning that he questioned us, and his uncertainty hurt.

I never talked too much when he was like this, because I didn't want to say the wrong thing. I just wanted to make sure that everything would proceed as planned. This had to work out and I didn't plan to say anything to change things. I didn't pressure him. I just prayed there would be no hiccups.

There was still a sense of discomfort when we went into the doctor's office. When Dwight reached for my hand, I knew his spirit had returned. Once I was on the table and prepared to discover the sex of our child, he was smiling and gloating that he knew we were having a boy. He was right. I was going to give birth to his son. He kissed me and it made me feel good that I was giving him something that he always wanted and almost had to face the reality of never having. That is, until he met me. Maybe our relationship was destined. He gave me something that I never thought I wanted and I gave him what he always wanted.

The nurse printed the film. "Here you go, Daddy. Here's the first picture of your son."

It made me feel so good to witness the joy on his face as he thanked her. I reached for the picture. "Let me see."

He looked again. "Little Dee."

"Yes, that's Little Dee."

He laid the picture on his chest and then handed it to me. I looked at it and asked him to show me how they knew it was a boy. He was so proud as he pointed to the body parts. He held my hand and helped me off the table when the nurse left.

As I put my clothes on, he said, "I can't believe you put it on me and got me sprung."

I laughed. "Stop being silly."

"I'm not." He continued, "Now you're about to be my baby-mama." I cringed, because I vowed to myself that I would *never* carry that title. It just sounded so inadequate. His paced slowed. " . . . and my wife."

I looked up from putting my leg in my pants and Dwight was dangling a diamond solitaire between his thumb and index fingers. Our whirlwind love affair flashed before my eyes. All the things he promised me were becoming real. He proved to be everything I didn't realize a man could be. As I stood there in amazement, he smiled.

Still, I stood frozen. Although we'd talked in great lengths about the next step in our relationship, I never trusted that he would choose me. I guess a piece of me always feared that the first wife prevails time after time, but not this time. This time I'd won.

"Don't do this to me right now. Say something. Say yes. Say no."

"Yes, yes. Of course, I'll be your wife."

He hugged me and I chuckled to myself. All morning I was sad because I thought he was sad and all the while he was just preoccupied with popping the question, or should I say, with telling me that I would be his wife. Suddenly, all I could do was thank him. I thanked him for being everything my father wasn't. I thanked him for proving all my friends wrong. I thanked him for being man enough to let go of a wife who wasn't meant for him. I held him tightly and thanked him for teaching me how to love.

When we left the doctor's office, I began to cry tears of victory inside the car. Before calling everyone to brag, I tried to get myself together. He rubbed my knee and with every gesture he confirmed he was there for me.

With tears still streaming down my face, I called my mother. "Ma, guess what?"

"What are you having?"

Her excitement about the baby excited me and I said, "I'm having a wedding"—I looked at Dwight—"a small wedding. Dwight asked me to marry him."

Her voice lowered. "Is his divorce final yet?"

My eyes shifted, because while I'd already begun rejoicing, my mother reminded me there was just one semi-hurdle before we could cross the finish line. I was excited about the intent, but my mother wasn't. She was a mother, concerned about my feelings.

"Well, the attorney said she hasn't contested it and she told Dwight she wouldn't. So it will be absolute on the court date, and that's this Friday."

My eyes questioned Dwight if that was correct. He nodded and said, "And we're going to apply for our marriage license on Monday."

She asked me to repeat what he said and I did. Her doubtful sighs scared me. A part of me wondered if she was slightly jealous that this never happened to her or if her concern was valid.

"Okay, Ma. I just wanted to let you know. We're going to lunch. I'll talk to you a little later."

"How do you know I don't want to celebrate with you guys?"

"Ma . . ."

"Okay, just leave me out."

She sounded pitiful, but I couldn't handle her fact-checking. Just let me be in the moment. All the technicalities would be ironed out in due time.

• • •

Dwight and I went out with my girls to break the news together. He was a nearly divorced man and we were facing a future together. By the time the whole crew arrived, we'd told the story in a bunch of little pieces.

Dwight was all of our success. He belonged to the crew and above all, he gave everyone hope again. Dreams do come true. I never imagined actually planning my life with someone and transitioning from me to we.

Dwight got a call from work in the middle of our evening. He looked at me. "Somebody would have to fall in love and now I gotta be up late nights alone."

I laughed. "Well, I apologize. You could have been the one to change jobs. But you wanted me to leave. Right?"

"You're right."

He kissed my cheek. "Gina, will you make sure my baby gets home safely?"

She raised her martini glass. "Sure will."

"That means you need to put that glass down."

"Don't count my drinks."

He laughed and kissed me again. "Baby, let me know if I need to come back and pick you up."

"I will."

Before he hit the door, my girls slapped me fives like we'd won the championship. "You put it on him, girl," Tammy said.

Andrea shook her head. "That's the quickest divorce and remarriage I've seen in my life."

Tammy nodded slowly. "Hell yeah, they all claim they're leaving and none of them ever go through with it."

We all looked at her and shook our heads, because we knew she was speaking from her own hurt. I don't know who laughed first, but then we all began laughing. Not that we were laughing at her. We laughed at the game and why the hell do we actually believe they're leaving. A part of me believed and the other half didn't, but I guess it just confirms what kind of man Dwight actually is. I reverted back to what he told me when we first met. *I'm cut from a different cloth.* And that he is . . . and he would be mine in just about two weeks.

On the ride home, Gina asked, "Is he nervous about jumping out of one marriage and right into a new one?"

I shrugged my shoulders. "I think he's just the settling-down type. He believes that a man needs a woman to reach his full potential."

"I understand, but it just seems so fast."

I thought so, too, but I wasn't going to tell him to be patient and miss my chance at happiness. I wanted it while he wanted it. We wanted to be together and waiting was not an option. I definitely had no desire to be a single mother.

"Does his wife . . ." My eyes shot at her and she reworded it. "Does his ex-wife know about you?"

"I don't know. I try not to talk about her. All I know is that they are practically divorced and we're engaged. That's all that matters to me now."

"I was just asking, because it just seems like she let go really easy."

"Honestly, it seems to me that she wanted this as much as he does."

"How are you guys going to manage with his kids? I mean, he seemed like he was a good father and . . ."

"We haven't really discussed it."

I tried to sound irritated, to let her know that I'd had enough of her interrogation. We'd deal with all of that stuff after I am Mrs. Wilson. My first goal is to get down the aisle and then I'll have jurisdiction.

CHAPTER 19

Tracey

Tracey, I have to get out of this house before I kill somebody," Danielle cried into my ear over the telephone.

"What's wrong now, Danielle?" I sighed.

"Reggie is acting stupid. I need to get away from him, before I kill him."

"What did he do now?"

"Everything. I'm just tired, I can't take it anymore. Because I'm not worrying about him anymore. I'm about to get unmarried to him. Get an annulment! Something!"

"Danielle, shut up," I said.

"Why you telling me to shut up? I'm serious; I'm really done."

"You say that you're done every time."

"No, I'm for real this time. Don't you know, a girl called me and told me she went to dinner with my husband last night."

"How she get your number?" I asked.

Danielle paused and said, "Well, I went through his phone

and dialed all his outgoing numbers and she picked up and I asked her, 'Do you know my husband, Reggie?' She said yes and then she told me everything. I'm coming to your house. Let's just go somewhere and talk. Okay?" she asked.

"Alright."

Wade came over and watched his nieces while I stepped out with Danielle. We went to a little restaurant near my house and the place was almost empty. We sat at a table near the window and looked over our menus. It didn't take any time for Danny to break down and cry. She poured her heart out to me about Reggie as soon as our food came. I had to scoot my chair next to her to keep her from losing it. She said she wanted him to stop cheating and just be happy with her, how she would give him anything he wanted if he was just faithful. I wanted to tell her to leave his ass. But we all told her before so it wasn't worth repeating. As she talked my mind began thinking about Dwight. I was happy he was not a cheat like Reggie. He was a genuine good man and father. When we were on good terms we didn't have those kind of problems. At that moment I was questioning why I was even beefing with Dwight. Our only problem in our marriage was about location. If we had the right location we would be fine. We didn't have all these other issues about cheating and women calling his phone. I wanted to call Dwight. I wanted to call him and tell him to come home. But I shouldn't have to. I came out of my daze and shook my head at Danny a couple of times to let her think I was actually paying attention to her ranting.

"You know what I'm saying. I'm not wrong, am I?" she asked.

"Not at all," I said, not knowing what she was talking

about. Then she stood up, took a deep breath, and wiped her face with her hands to keep the tears back. I patted her back and assured Danny it was going to be okay a couple of more times. I was consoling her about her marriage and I needed someone to console me on mine.

Dwight's morning phone call came in as usual, a little after eight. I called out, "Jordan, your father's on the phone."

I didn't bother to say hello. As I handed the phone to her, I thought I heard him yelling my name through the receiver. I'd been making him stay at Mama Dee's for the past few months. I knew that the thought of me with another man would make him wake up. I'm sure Mama Dee told him I'd been going out with Danielle and her friends. And since he left, he'd been asking the girls to put me on the phone and I've been hanging up.

After he spoke with both of the girls, Destiny handed the phone to me. "Mommy, here. Daddy say it's important."

"I bet," I said as I put the phone on the hook. As I hustled the girls out of the house, my phone kept ringing. Finally, once I sat in the car, I checked my messages. Dwight said, "Tracey, I'm just calling to let you know today is our court date and the divorce will be final if you don't contest it. If this is what you want, you don't have to do anything."

I hung up the phone and rolled my eyes in my head. I sped down the highway to take the girls to school. It seemed as if no one wanted to answer their phone. I called Mama Dee. I called Danielle. I needed to remember why I was about to let my marriage go. Finally, I called Dwight. Maybe we shouldn't be so hasty. He answered, sounding almost desperate.

"Dwight, divorce is final. Are you sure you want this? Don't you think we should stop playing games?"

"I don't know, but I know that I don't want to play games with you, either," Dwight said.

"I'm not playing games, you are. I've told you, pay my bills and you can have your divorce."

"Trace, I'm on my way into a meeting. It's very sad that we can't talk like civilized adults. You have a lot of growing up to do." He hung up the phone.

I slammed on the brakes and made a quick U-turn and headed to the courthouse. I didn't know what time the appointment was, but out of the clear blue sky a sudden urge to stop this divorce came over me. Maybe that's what Dwight wanted me to do. That's why he was calling frantically. Maybe I wasn't doing the right thing about my marriage. Maybe I've been immature and wasn't handling everything properly, but it wasn't too late to stop it. Or maybe it was. I didn't know. As much as I wanted to prove to Dwight that I didn't need him, I couldn't lie to myself. I desperately wanted Dwight to come back home. I was tired of him living the free life in Maryland. I thought about being a real single mom. I thought about having to go out in the world and find another special person like Dwight. And then I came to the conclusion there wasn't anyone else. I didn't know how to tell him right now, but there was no way he was getting a divorce. I walked into that courthouse and contested the entire divorce. I didn't know what I would do afterward exactly, but I knew I couldn't let Dwight go like this. I needed a few more months to take this all in. When I arrived at the hearing, his attorney had already left the courtroom, but the judge still heard my case and withdrew my divorce.

CHAPTER 20

Alicia

Call me ignorant, but I really never knew why people called weddings that occurred because a woman was pregnant *shotgun weddings*. I heard that nearly a hundred times since we got engaged. Even I began to say that I was having a shotgun wedding. When I discovered the origin of the term, that back in the day, a father would make a man marry his daughter or he'd shoot him, I was highly offended. It got to the point that when someone would jokingly say it, I corrected them. This marriage is completely voluntary. It would have happened whether I was pregnant or not.

I was so happy the night before my wedding. Finally, I didn't have to say I was getting married. Now, I was less than twelve hours from being married. I stayed at my mother's house and we sat up until one in the morning discussing my life, her life, and the life we wanted for DJ. We laughed about all the losers I had to encounter before Dwight. She told me that a mother could only hope that her daughter landed someone as sincere as him. It made me proud to make her happy. It was as if all the silly mistakes or choices I'd made in the past were somehow erased with his love.

It was hard to sleep knowing that I was hours away from marrying a great man . . . a rare man. I tossed and turned and tried to block out images that displayed the ceremony not happening. What if he's told his wife everything and she pops up here and barges in on the wedding? What if he doesn't show up? What if I go into false labor? Lord, just get me to this courthouse in one piece.

The alarm clock buzzed and my head popped up, my heart beat rapidly. I couldn't believe it was my wedding day. Wow. After all was said and done, Alicia Dixon found a man she thought was worthy enough to marry. I called Dwight just to verify that he'd be there. He laughed. "Baby, don't worry. I'll see you in a few."

I called the girls and they, too, confirmed that they'd be there. When I got out of bed, I smelled the aroma of turkey bacon and followed the scent to the kitchen. My mother smiled at me and gave me a hug.

"Alicia, girl, I was getting worried. Didn't know if this day would ever come."

"Well, it did and we're here. So, let's get ready."

"Have you talked to Dwight?"

As I plopped eggs on my plate, I began to giggle.

She asked, "What's funny?" Before I could explain, she began laughing, too. Why was she asking in a conniving way if I was sure he would show up? I guess we both weren't sure if this was a prank or not. She wanted to be sure he would show up too.

"Yes, Ma. I talked to him this morning. He's going to meet us at the courthouse at nine."

"Well good, because I've told all my friends and I don't want any change in plans."

"Ma, I don't know why you are so nervous."

She raised her brow and huffed. I chuckled again. Well, I guess I was slightly leery, too.

In my bedroom, tears welled in my eyes before I put on my dress. Though I felt like a balloon in my white baby-doll dress, I was anxious to get there. I pinned my twists up into a spiky ponytail and used a bunch of makeup contouring techniques to slim down the features that had spread on my face. By the time I was done, I felt like a bride, even if I was a makeshift one.

When we arrived at the courthouse, the crew was already there. Momentarily I was excited to see them, and I went to slap fives, but their attire made me gasp. They began chatting, but I covered my mouth.

Gina asked, "Why the hell are you acting crazy? Is everything okay?"

"Is there a reason y'all have on black?"

Everyone laughed. Still, I stood baffled. Tammy said, "Damn it. You're the first in the crew to get married. We figured this might be our only opportunity to be bridesmaids."

Andrea added, "And we all had black in our closets."

"Oh! I thought you guys were trying to say you didn't approve or something."

"Girl, please. You know we would have told you if we had a problem. This is all of our wedding," Gina said.

She slapped five with Tammy, who said, "You ain't lying."

My mother shook her head. "You girls are pitiful."

Everyone's neck unconsciously snapped in her direction

like *please*. No one dared to say anything, but our expressions said everything. We exchanged words with our eyes.

Then someone asked the million-dollar question, "Where is Dwight?"

My heart sank as I gazed up at the clock. My words came out slow and uncertain. "He should be here by now."

Andrea said, "He'll be here."

Tammy joked, "I hope your old boo Ian didn't catch him coming in the courthouse and kidnap him."

Only she would think of something so crazy. My eyes squinted and I wanted to pluck her, because the last thing I wanted to think about today was my past relationships. Especially considering it was one that I regretted. I shook my head. Why did she think that was funny?

Despite my irritation, everyone laughed and added their two cents into the Ian story. Finally, I said, "Can you guys stop?"

Tammy made a face at me and I rolled my eyes and said, "Please."

She slightly frowned. "Damn, I was just joking."

"I understand."

Minutes later, Dwight walked through the metal detectors. The crew clapped as he walked down the hall. He blushed and strolled toward us. After embracing everyone, he stood in front of me. "How do you feel?"

"Like the luckiest woman in the world."

He kissed me, and my mother kidded, "Let's save that until you guys are married."

We laughed and he asked which courtroom we were supposed to go to. We headed to the room for our nine-thirty wedding.

I held his hand tightly when we entered the room. It

disturbed me that his palms were sweaty. My eyes questioned him. He released my grip and ran his hand over his pant leg, but when he held my hand again it was still moist. I asked what I really didn't want the answer to: "Are you sure you want to do this?"

He paused and I stood paralyzed. It seemed like an eternity before he spoke. "Of course."

All of my organs began to function again. The judge entered the room and I looked at Dwight. He laughed. "You are too funny."

The judge called us to order, and in five minutes I was Mrs. Wilson. Can you believe that it happened so fast? We kissed to solidify our union. The ceremony was over and still I felt like I was dreaming. This couldn't be. I touched my husband. He was real. We signed the marriage certificate. It was real. I had snagged an endangered species: a successful black man who loved me. If I wasn't pregnant, I would have jumped in the air and tapped my feet together.

We stayed at the Mandarin Oriental Hotel to consummate our marriage. Seconds after we entered the room, Dwight unzipped my dress. The protruding pouch seemed to arouse him more. He kissed my shoulders as he stood behind me and slowly ran his hands down the silhouette of my body. He said, "I love you, Mrs. Wilson."

Suddenly, I became a little tensed. I really hadn't wanted to think about changing my name before everything was actually final. Didn't want anything to jinx me. In the midst of our passionate moment, I was wondering, *Should I just hyphenate my name? Should I simply drop my last name?*

He turned me around to face him and we kissed. This was more than I dreamed of, he was more than a man who loved me. He knew how to make love to me. We held hands and stared into each other's eyes. I was his future and he was mine. He unbuttoned his pants and let them fall to the floor. As he stepped out of them, he sat on the bed. His erection summoned me to straddle him. I slid down on my husband and I exhaled. While he guided my waist, I escaped into euphoria. Our moist bodies clung together as he became saturated with me. We were united not only by emotion but by law. Legal sex felt safe, secure, and endless. I wanted to carry his name and his name only. That's how much I loved this man.

I dropped my head on his shoulder. "I'm going to drop my last name."

"Drop what?"

"I'm going to drop my last name and just go by Alicia Wilson."

He kissed my arm and said, "Thank you."

"I thought you claimed it didn't matter to you."

"I just wanted to see what you were going to do."

I was so glad that I passed his test, because he'd certainly passed mine. It was okay to be vulnerable with him. There was no need to be over-independent just for the approval of outsiders.

CHAPTER 21

Tracey

Over three months had passed and I had yet to receive my court documents telling me that the divorce was contested or given a new court date. And Dwight hadn't been home, either. Mama Dee always said don't tell everybody everything. I guess that went for her, too. I didn't tell anyone that I'd contested the divorce. I just wanted to see how all of this would play. Would Mama Dee and Danny still treat me like their daughter and sister? So for right now I am family, but you know how people change when you get a divorce. Today Mama Dee is watching the girls. As always, we walked in the house and Mama Dee was in her kitchen, mixing her legendary potato salad. I came into the kitchen and pulled up a seat. The girls gave her kisses and took their bags upstairs. Mama Dee looked me over one time and said, "You look tired."

"I am. I'm real tired."

"Where's my only son? Why hasn't he been home? Y'all still playing games?"

"You should call him and ask him," I answered her with an attitude.

"I don't believe y'all. It's so sad."

I shrugged it off. "I'm happy. He's happy. We can't keep harping on it. Can we?"

"I don't even know why y'all going through all of this. Y'all just stubborn. You ain't going to do nothing but get remarried."

"You need to stop worrying about us because I'm not."

She put her hand on her hip. "You think I ain't. Y'all act like you still fourteen and fifteen years old. Y'all grown," she said as I left her kitchen and walked outside. It was so hard to accept that I'd given all these years to a selfish bastard. I sat on the steps and took in the sun's warmth. Danielle drove up in her Kia Sorento.

"Hey, sister-in-law," she said as she exited her car.

"Hey," I said sadly.

"What's wrong with you? Have you spoken to my brother?"

"No."

"And you are not concerned. He hasn't been home in months."

"No, he will come around. I ain't chased him in all these years. Why would I start now?"

"Because he is your husband and you don't know what's going on with him?"

I didn't want to be having this conversation with Danielle of all people. She knew she didn't have the ideal marriage, either, but I still felt like I had to explain myself to her. "He is still paying all the bills and he talks to the girls," I said.

"What did you do with the divorce papers?"

"I contested the divorce papers. I'll divorce Dwight when I'm ready, not a moment before. If he really wanted a divorce don't you think he would have come down here and handled that instead of trying to mail something to me? Enough about him."

"What are you doing tonight?" Danny asked.

"Nothing, staying in the house. Your mother is keeping the girls, and I'm not going to do anything but rest and enjoy my peace and quiet. "Why, what are you doing?" I asked.

"Going to Nikki's bridal shower."

"Bridal shower? I thought you said she was pregnant."

"Yeah, she is. It's a . . . don't laugh. It is a bridal shower and a baby shower—she's getting married next week."

I tried to control my laughter, but I couldn't. I almost choked with laughter. "Are you serious? Let me get this right—a baby shower and bridal shower in one."

"Stop laughing, it is not funny."

"You and your people. Y'all are too damn funny."

"You should go with me."

"You know I don't like your ghetto friends and they don't like me."

"Yes, they do like you. They just think you're bougie," Danny said.

"Well, I'm not bougie just because I don't have a man doing time or a criminal record."

"News flash, sister-in-law. Your ass is bougie. I'll be there to pick up your bougie ass, so be ready."

I reluctantly accompanied Danielle to Nikki's shower. There was no sense in staying in the house and I knew I was going to get plenty of entertainment. The shower was being

held at Nikki's mother's house in the middle of the proj-
ects. Why did I let Danny bring me out?

We entered Nikki's mom's small, cramped apartment.
Everyone looked us up and down and Nikki came and
checked us for our gift.

"Hey, cousin-in-law," she said, hugging me. Nikki's
stomach was the biggest extra large basketball that was
going to explode at any minute. Her navel was poking out
through her white shirt, which clung to her skin.

"How my cousin doing?" Nikki asked.

"He's doing good."

"Look at my ring," she said. "That's right, I'm getting
married, bitches," she said, showing the tiniest piece of
metal I've ever seen in my life. The ambience of this bridal/
baby shower was pure ghetto. Nikki's mother, Vivian, had
baked brown cupcakes in the shape of a penis. *How nice*, I
thought, shaking my head. And people were of course deep
throating them. We had a seat and sank down almost to the
floor on the battered sofa.

During the middle of the shower, Nikki's baby-daddy/
fiancé came through the door and everyone started clapping
and saying "What's up, Poppa." He had long dreads tied up
into a bun and a white-and-black scarf tied around his neck
covering his chin. His tattoos started at his biceps and
stopped right below the knuckles of his fingers. His shorts
were hanging and long enough to be pants. If I saw him in
the streets I would definitely clutch my purse. He came
over to Nikki and acted like he was play fighting with her
stomach.

"Be careful before one of those punches land," her mother
said. Then she asked him to help her take some things to

the basement. After he went into the basement all of Nik-ki's friends started commenting on how fine her man was.

"You are so lucky. He ain't even been home a year and he working for the sanitation department and he gonna marry you. That is so good."

"Why you looking at my man?" Nikki asked.

"Nobody looking at your man, bitch. You better shut up 'fore you get fucked up." I thought they were for real but they all began to laugh. They were so excited that this convict-looking man, who was not, truth be told, even a good catch, was marrying her. I guess they were just happy with any ole man. I couldn't keep myself from laughing at them. If they only knew what a good man really was. The only person who knew I wasn't laughing with them, but at them, was Danny. And she didn't know I was laughing at her ass, too. Danny poured me more drinks, and everything those people said and did became even more funny.

After the baby shower/bridal shower was over, I stag-gered to the car. We both were laughing about all the ghett-toness that transpired in that house.

"I'm just glad I got a good man," Danny said as she un-locked the car door. *And you know that's wrong*, I thought. She was delusional, too; her man wasn't shit, either. I didn't even bother to comment. Uh-huh, your man is good, too! Whatever. I was just so happy I didn't have to drive home so I could sleep my alcohol off. I giggled until I nodded off.

Danny tapped my shoulder once we were in front of my door. I felt as if I had been asleep forever, but it had been only twenty minutes.

"You okay?"

"Yeah, girl, thanks for asking me to go. I haven't laughed that hard in years."

"You're welcome, but listen, call my brother. I don't want to lose you as my sister-in-law."

"I'll think about it, Danny," I said as I unlocked my door and waved good-bye. I came in and flopped on my sofa. It had been a long time since I was all by myself. The silence was scary. I felt so alone. I don't know what came over me. I guess being a little tipsy had a lot to do with it, but I realized that my house was empty. Not only physically empty but really empty. I no longer had a family. I started asking myself the same questions I had been asking for months: Was I crazy for letting my husband move to another town alone? Was I being too stubborn? Was I bluffing and he called my bluff? I looked over at my alarm clock; it was three a.m. *I should call him and try to talk to him*, I thought, but I didn't want him to hear desperation in my voice. I'll call him in the morning when I have a clear head.

CHAPTER 22

Alicia

God knows what you can bear. Dwight always claims he is proactive instead of reactive. Although it wasn't intentional, my job change was definitely proactive. There is no way I could have worked this far into the pregnancy otherwise. My feet had started to swell and I felt wiped out at all times. My new job was laid back. There were no surprises. For the first time in five years, I actually had a forty-hour workweek. I was even able to work out up until a month ago, when I was told I had a slight case of toxemia. I argued with the doctor. What did I do wrong that would cause me to have high blood pressure? I ate right. I exercised. I wasn't stressed. Turns out that my pregnancy-induced addiction to V8 may have been a factor. He explained that a cup a day was fine, but I'd been drinking two liters. That was too much sodium for anyone. So I had to be extremely diet-conscious to protect the little guy growing inside of me.

Dwight had taken a couple of days off of work so we

could pack up my condo. He'd surprised me and put a contract on a five-bedroom home in Hanover. It was a little farther from my mother than I preferred, but it was cool. I had a property manager screening possible tenants for my place. It looked like there wouldn't be a long lapse in occupancy. After we moved out, I was going to have it professionally cleaned, and the tenants could move right in.

My mother had been the one attending all my doctor's appointments with me, but since Dwight was off, he decided to go with me to my thirty-third-week appointment. We planned to shop for furniture when we left and schedule delivery for all the major appliances.

Dwight massaged my neck while we sat in the waiting area. I was so at peace and in my own world that I hadn't noticed a young lady sitting across from me. She was pregnant, too, but she looked lonely. She wasn't wearing a ring. There was a melancholy vibe surrounding her. Watching her made me appreciate Dwight more. I reached up and pulled his arm away. He frowned. He didn't understand what was wrong, but I didn't want us to make her feel bad.

When it was time for me to go back, the nurse sent me in for a urine sample. I handed her the sample when I came from the bathroom and she told me to get on the scale. Her neck snapped back. She flipped through the chart. "Mrs. Wilson, you've gained more weight than we like to see you gain since your last visit."

We followed her into the exam room. "How's your diet?" she asked.

Dwight answered, "She's been really good with her diet."

I said, "Well, I stopped working out."

"That shouldn't matter."

I'd definitely been feeling like a fat slob and I attributed it to my lack of activity. She wrapped the blood pressure band around my arm and tightened it. When it released, her eyes popped out. She scribbled it down and said, "Your pressure is really high. Dr. Griffin will be with you in a minute."

She whisked out of the room. My heart drummed. "I don't understand. I've been doing everything right."

Dwight held my hand. "You just never know what causes stuff like this."

I wanted to ask if his ex-wife ever experienced this. Instead, I said, "When did you last speak with Tracey?"

He frowned and shook his head. He obviously didn't want to discuss it, but it had been bothering me. I wondered if she knew he was remarried. I wondered if she knew we had a baby on the way. I wondered if she knew that we were buying a new home. And just possible, all the wondering could have brought on the stress-induced hypertension. I couldn't think of any other reason.

The doctor came in and explained that I had high levels of protein in my urine and I was in jeopardy of a stroke. I literally almost had one just hearing those words. Why me? What did I do to deserve this? He instructed me to immediately check in to the hospital.

We went straight to the maternity ward. They put me in a room and laid me on my side, hoping that would lower my pressure. Dwight stroked my back as I tried to calm down. He called my mother and I could hear her. She was hysterical. I told him to call my friends, but he didn't think it was a good idea. He thought they'd excite me.

They decided to keep me there, on bed rest, indefinitely.

I asked the nurse, "Are you telling me I'm going to be here for the next five weeks?"

"We hope so."

"You hope so?"

"Yeah, we do our best to delay delivery until about thirty-eight weeks. Sometimes we're successful. Sometimes we're not."

Hell, success to me is getting out of here. I'll die lying in bed for the next five weeks. "So I can't do anything?"

"Not if you want to deliver a healthy baby."

I huffed. "What about going to the bathroom?"

She held up a bedpan and tapped Dwight. "Mr. Wilson, you'll have to make sure your wife goes in here."

My mouth hung open. "What about number two?"

She raised her eyebrow, confirming that I was to use the damn bedpan for that, too. This was disgusting. I wanted my mother to hurry. Damn if I wanted my man holding a pan under my ass while I shit. This is completely unacceptable. I was determined to hold everything until my mother arrived.

Six hours later, Dwight, my mother, and I had discussed every current event, every conceivable topic, watched a bunch of reality shows, and I wanted to get out of bed. I was tired of talking to them, so I called Gina. While I chatted on the phone, Dwight and my mother had come up with an overnight schedule. She'd stay over during the middle of the week and Dwight would stay from Thursday to Sunday. I was already depressed. Dwight knew it, so he tried not to leave my side for the next two days.

The only time he left was to go to settlement. Ironically, the doctor came in to do the normal check. This time of course, my pressure had skyrocketed and there was still too much protein in my urine. He told my mother to call and let Dwight know they were going to do an emergency C-section. Dwight Wilson Jr. was coming five weeks before expected. I was emotional, because I'd yet to get furniture for the new house. I didn't have enough clothes for the baby. I was so preoccupied with what I didn't have that I couldn't focus on what I was having. A baby was coming out of me and coming fast.

I was so concerned that Dwight wouldn't make it to the hospital that I think I stressed the baby more. Just when the doctor said they couldn't wait any longer, Dwight rushed into the room. By the time they put scrub tops and masks on my mother and Dwight, I was feeling no pain. Dwight rubbed my arm. I'm not certain if it was his touch sedating me but I felt as if I were floating. Everyone in the room was a blur. I heard people talking, but mainly I heard his voice and I could see his smile. I read his lips.

"He's a big boy."

A big boy? Is he here? Shouldn't I feel something? I didn't feel anything. But I finally heard my son cry. Dwight rubbed my hair and kissed my forehead. "You were great."

It was like I wanted to ask questions, but I didn't have the motor skills. I wanted to go back to sleep, but I had to see my baby. My eyes rolled and I fought to stay awake, but I lost the battle. Seemingly hours later, I woke up alone in a room in severe pain. Where did everyone go? Help me!

There was a button in my hand and I pressed it. I needed a nurse to come help me, but Nurse Nasty stormed in yelling at me, "Stop pressing the pain medicine. It's only gonna dispense a certain amount every hour. No matter how many times you press it."

Damn lady, do you really have to talk to sick people like

that? I didn't have the energy to tell this hooker that all I wanted was someone to help me find my family. Hell with the damn pain medication! She obviously understood my slurring, because shortly after, my mother and Dwight entered the room.

I said, "Where's the baby?"

Dwight smiled and kissed me. "He's in the nursery making those other boys look bad."

"Huh?"

"He's a heavyweight. Seven pounds, four ounces."

My mother chimed in, "Can you imagine how big he would have been if you'd gone full term?"

I felt cheated. Why hadn't I seen him yet? My eyes shifted from Dwight to my mother as they explained what happened when he came out. *He has your eyes. He's Dwight's complexion. He smiled. It took a minute for him to cry.*

When the hell are they going to bring him in here? Dwight must have read the frustration on my face. He said, "I'm going to get him right now."

"Thank you, Boo."

He walked out, and my mother began to explain how wonderful he was in the delivery room. "He's such a sweet guy. I hope you know how blessed you are."

"I do."

As I acknowledged my blessings, he returned with our baby. My eyes watered as I reached for DJ. "Can I hold him?"

Dwight cautiously laid him on my breast. I moaned and he lay peacefully. His eyes closed tightly like he was getting the best sleep in the world. I stroked him and Dwight stroked my hair. He looked so proud and it made me happy that I gave him what he wanted. He tugged on his little cap. "C'mon, man. Wake up for Mommy."

I was just in awe of what we had created. Not to mention, I never thought I wanted this experience. I'd been a mother all of an hour and I was convinced that it was the best job a woman could have. This little boy had my heart and I wanted to give him the world.

My mother asked, "How do you feel?"

"I'm just . . ." I paused. "I'm just so happy."

She said, "Me, too. I'm so glad you made me a grandmother."

As we oohed and ahed, I suddenly recalled that we were in a transition. Where was I going when I left the hospital? I said, "Dwight, how did settlement go?"

"Good. I went for the inspection right before settlement, but I didn't get a chance to go back."

"When are you going to move everything in?"

He smirked. My mother laughed. "He said you'd be worried about that, but I told him you guys should stay with me for a couple of weeks. That way you won't be tempted to get everything organized and I can be there to help you."

"But . . ."

"There are no beds at the new house and the condo is all packed up. So we concluded it was the best decision." I pouted and he continued, "So I'm going to take our clothes over there tonight."

I nodded, but I wasn't sure if I wanted to stay in my old full-size bed and cram DJ's bassinet in the tiny space with me. Just as they were telling me the plans they made for me, my nurse came in to ask if I planned to breast-feed. I looked at Dwight. It wasn't my preference, but he demanded that I at least do it for three months. He said, "Yeah. She's breast-feeding. Is anyone going to help her get started?"

"I read all the literature. I know what I'm doing," I said. I wanted to be resistant just because. I needed to at least make one decision for myself.

Dwight smirked at the nurse and she smiled back. "Mr. Wilson. The midwife will be in momentarily to discuss everything."

My mother said, "It's helpful to have someone refresh your memory."

I looked at her as if to say *how many kids have you had?* Shortly after, I got my lesson in lactation. We had to interrupt DJ's nap, and attempt to get him to latch on, which he refused to do.

We tried and tried and I wanted to quit. My bossy husband insisted that all babies do that initially. The midwife looked impressed with his knowledge. She asked, "Do you have other kids or have you been studying?"

"Yeah, I have two girls. Four and seven."

She looked at me and suddenly despite him being my husband, I felt slighted. She said, "This is your first, right?"

I nodded and glanced at my mother. She noticed my discomfort and moved closer to the bed. "You'll get it, honey. Don't get stressed."

"I don't think I'm the one that has to get it. DJ does."

Everyone laughed, but suddenly the pain I felt wasn't funny anymore. I looked around for the button that was taped to my hand. "I need medicine."

I pushed the button and prayed that I hadn't exceeded my fix for the hour. Just as I drugged myself, my mother let me know that the girls were on their way. I'd given birth to the first legitimate kid in the crew and this was a celebration.

When the girls arrived, I was so sedated that I barely participated in the conversation. Mainly, they talked to my mother and Dwight. I floated in and out. It had been way too long and I was ready to escape the confines of the hospital walls.

CHAPTER 23

Tracey

Forty-eight hours later I was debating my next action, but it was obvious. Dwight had asked me to move and I said no and that was crazy. I don't need anyone to tell me I was silly. I loved this house. But I can have another house. "Operation Bring Husband Home" is officially a failure. I am abandoning all plans. Fuck it, he had won. My white flag was raised high and I was waving it. All that my husband was trying to do was take care of his family and I wanted to act stupid like a child. I am so damn foolish. I have to make things right. I have to go and get my man. If Dwight wanted me to move I would move. I picked up my phone to let him know enough is enough. I dialed his number; I couldn't wait to hear his voice. But I didn't get a chance to hear his voice, because his voice mail picked up. I need to see my man now. Something came over me, like this intense need to be with him. I was going to go to Maryland right now, this moment. I was going to book a plane ticket online and get on the earliest flight they have. I turned the lights on and grabbed my suitcase and began packing. When I went online I didn't see any available flights. No flights being available didn't deter me at all. I would just have to make that eleven-hour journey. The girls had school the next day, but it was the end of the school year. Jordan wouldn't be missing anything anyway. I had to go up there and convince Dwight to come home. I had to do something. I just wanted to be where Dwight was, whether it was here in Jacksonville or in Maryland.

I showered and began packing our clothes. I'd let Wade check the mail and watch Raven and the house. Jen can cover all my deals. I walked into Jordan's room. She was asleep. I didn't really want to wake her, but I had to. I patted her on the shoulder.

"Jordan, wake up. Go get in the shower."

"Mommy, where we go? It's still dark outside," she asked.

"I know, just get dressed, baby. Mommy wants to take you somewhere."

"Where we going? Is today a school day?"

"Just get dressed," I instructed her as I went back into my bedroom and continued to pack. I filled the suitcase to the top and zipped it up. I flipped it over and dragged it down the steps. *It's going to be cold up north*, I thought to myself as I went and grabbed our jackets.

Jordan came out of the bathroom as Destiny went in. Des was not happy that I interrupted her sleep. She was whining during her entire shower. Even after her shower, she went back to sleep on the floor in the hallway. I picked her up and put her on my bed. I dressed her limp body and placed her on the sofa. I looked around the house to see if there was anything I was forgetting. I couldn't think of anything so I packed my girls and luggage in the car.

I drove into a dark gas station. I stepped out of the car and inserted my credit card into the slot. I looked around; there wasn't anyone else around. As I pumped my gas I made sure the attendant saw me. At least if someone attacked me he could call the cops. I inspected my tires to make sure they had air in them. The pump clicked, letting me know my tank was full. I got back in my car. I looked back at the girls sleeping. I put my seat belt over my body. I inserted my cell phone into the charger. I typed Dwight's address into the navigation system. It estimated it was 742 miles and was going to take eleven and a half hours to get there.

I have a great man and I'm letting him live in abandon. Once we figure out everything, I promise I'm going to treat him the way he is supposed to be treated.

On my journey north, green trees passed my windows on both sides of the highway. I drove past trucks with MACK stamped on the front of them, and sped past motorists going too slow. I was on a mission. The only thing that kept me up was my CD collection and thoughts about what I was going to say to Dwight. I was going to tell him how stupid I had been all these months. I was going to plead with him to please take me back and tell him how it was my fault for not moving with him. My thoughts were my company as I traveled up Interstate 95 trying to stay aware and awake. I wiped my brow, hoping to clear the sleep that was creeping up on me and trying not to sway into other cars that passed. I was so tired, but I couldn't rest. I couldn't rest until I knew everything is okay with Dwight.

• • •

The sun was rising as I crossed the North Carolina border and entered Virginia. Construction was slowing my flow. I became frustrated and kept beeping my horn and switching lanes. The closer I got to him the more anxious I became. I did an eleven-hour trip in less then ten, with three stops for gas and food. My navigational system said I was only forty miles away. The car was on a quarter tank, but I didn't want to stop for gas. The closer I got the faster my heart raced. I was so nervous. I guess it is just hard to say I'm sorry. I know my baby will understand. He'll probably want to know why it took so long. He won't be mad at me. I'll probably have to kiss his ass for a little while. The navigational system interrupted my mind's rambling. The system instructed me to exit in a quarter mile. I turned off the exit. I turned onto his block and parked the car. I pulled the address out of my pocket. I looked to see what brick housed my husband, and Dwight's Nissan Maxima was shined up and sitting across from his address. I stretched my legs and took in a sigh. *Here goes nothing*, I thought. I knocked on the door. I couldn't wait to see his reaction.

When Dwight opened the door, his mouth opened so wide. He was obviously speechless. He had lost about twenty pounds since I'd seen him last. Destiny and Jordan saw him and ran up to him. Dwight's body was more muscular, his face was clean-shaven and looked smooth. He looked so good. Before he could get a word in, I grabbed him and started crying. At first he didn't hold me back, but I took his hands and placed them in the center of my back and cried. The girls hugged Dwight's legs and arms. He wiped away my tears and picked the girls up into his arms. And we all walked into the house.

His place was sparsely furnished. One love seat and a grandfather chair.

"Oh my God, Daddy, we missed you so much," Jordan said.

"I missed you, too, girls," he said, sitting on his love seat. I was so happy we had come. I had made the best decision. I was so relieved. I walked outside and brought our bags in. All I wanted to do was go to sleep. I went upstairs and put my belongings up. The middle two rooms were completely empty. After a few moments Dwight came up the steps and said, "We really need to talk."

"I know, but I just drove for almost eleven hours and I just want to relax. Let's not talk tonight."

"What about our divorce? This is serious, Tracey—you can't just march into my house months later like there is nothing wrong after we got a divorce."

I grabbed his hand and said, "No, it's okay. We are not divorced yet. I contested the divorce. We were never divorced."

"What do you mean you contested the divorce?"

"When you sent the papers I was very upset with you and I couldn't decide what I wanted to do. So the day of the proceedings I just filed the paperwork to contest everything."

"Listen, Tracey, this is not going to work—"

Before Dwight could get the rest of the sentence out, Destiny ran upstairs and said, "Daddy, come downstairs! I have so much to tell you. Me and Jordan have been doing everything." Dwight knelt down and picked up Destiny. As he turned around, he whispered to me, "We really need to talk."

I said okay and shook my head.

• • •

The next morning I called Wade to tell him that I was going to let him house-sit.

"Wade, I need you to go to my house and keep an eye on it. I left a key to the house for you in the back under the flowerpot."

"Are you for real? So I get to house-sit."

"Yes, take care of my house. Don't bring any trash to my house."

"I won't. I promise to bring the most upscale loose women I can find. They going to think I'm ballin'. How long you going to be up there?"

"I don't know yet. I'm going to try to make Dwight move back home. But if he won't come then we are going to stay up here."

CHAPTER 24

Alicia

It was three more days of being helpless, lying in bed, and watching DJ's every move before the hospital released me. I just wanted to smell fresh air, eat my mother's food, and watch DVDs. If I could, I would have escaped.

As the doctor discussed all the restrictions for the next couple of weeks, I felt like I wanted to cry. No driving. No up and down the stairs. No drinking while breast-feeding. Motherhood was quickly becoming as undesirable as I always imagined.

I called Dwight to find out why he hadn't come to the hospital yet. When he picked up, he sounded distracted. He stuttered when he greeted me, "Hey . . . hey . . . what's up?"

I looked at the phone. *What's up* is that I'm at the hospital waiting for my husband to come and get me. I took the milder approach. "I'm ready, baby. When are you coming?"

"Ah. I'll be there in a minute."

"Did you go into work?"

"Yeah . . . let me get off this phone. I'm in traffic."

Before I could ask where he was, I was listening to the operator telling me to hang up and dial the number again. I considered taking her advice, but suddenly I began negotiating with my conscience. Maybe he's going through a little postpartum depression. Or it could be me feeling slightly neglected. I tried to shake the feeling as I dressed DJ and prepared to leave.

When Dwight rushed through the door an hour later, I was livid.

"Where have you been?"

"I've been moving some things to the new house and the traffic from there was hell."

"You're telling me that it took you an hour to get here?"

He hung his head. "Alicia, don't start harassing me. Like, do you have somewhere you have to be?"

"Outta here."

"What's the rush?"

"I just want to go home. What's the rush with you trying to move into the new house and I just had the baby? I can't move for at least three weeks."

"Shoot me for trying to get things together for my wife and son."

I felt bad for throwing a tantrum. "I'm sorry, honey. Give me a hug." He smirked and raised his brow. "Dwight! Give me a hug."

He came over to the bed and rested his head on my shoulder. "Baby, I'm just trying to do the best I can."

"I know. I think I'm just claustrophobic now."

"I know." He chuckled. "And a little depressed, too. It happens after having a baby."

I pushed him away. "Yeah, I was wondering if you had some depression yourself."

As he held the baby in his hands, he said, "Not at all. Not at all. I have everything I ever wanted."

His words were honest, but his expression was confused. I studied him, but decided to be silent. Maybe a piece of him felt guilty for feeling so happy. I decided not to stress him and trust his words until further notice.

When I got to my mother's house, Dwight helped me upstairs and into bed. He put DJ in his bassinet and sat on the side of the bed.

"What do you want from the grocery store? I put a small refrigerator over there."

"Thanks, baby. Get me some fruit. Something sweet, and I don't mean any harm, I think I need a glass of wine."

"You can't drink and breast-feed."

I took a deep breath. "Baby, I'm not sure that I'm cut out for the breast-feeding thing. Plus, he just doesn't seem to be getting enough."

"So you're a quitter."

I shrugged. He stood up and bent over the bassinet. "Little man, Mommy doesn't want to take care of you. I wish I could feed you."

His remarks made me feel like a loser, and out of nowhere, I began to cry. "I'm not a bad mother."

He hugged me. "Girl, I was just playing with you. I'm sorry."

My wailing forced my mother to rush into the room. "Alicia, is everything okay?"

I nodded and Dwight said, "I was joking with her and she got a little emotional."

My mother began to fuss at him. "Dwight, why would you purposely upset her? You know she has to be careful. She had a C-section. You can't stress her out."

My shock met his irritation. "Ms. Emma, do you really think I intentionally upset her?"

"I don't know. The point is you upset her and . . ."

I yelled, "Just stop it. Please, everyone. Just leave me alone."

Obviously, I didn't mean physically leave me alone. Dwight told me that he needed to go out for a while to get his head together. My mother stood in the room like security. Before walking out, Dwight looked at her as if he had something against her. Though I couldn't, I wanted to chase him and ask, why did it seem that I came home to a different man? My fairy tale seemed to be unraveling right before my eyes. Then I reflected on things I read that told me women sometimes feel unwarranted emotions during this period. Maybe this was all unwarranted.

I looked at my mother and she sat on the bed with me. "Do you still need the pain medicine?"

Maybe my feelings were just hurt, but I wanted the medicine. I nodded. She found the bottle and gave me a Vicodin pill. Just as I was about to doze off, DJ began to squirm. My mother told me that she would take care of him, so I lay back on my bed and tried to suppress the emotions raging in me.

When I woke up, Dwight still hadn't returned and my mother was in the rocking chair at the foot of my bed singing to DJ.

"Did Dwight ever come back?"

My mother shook her head.

"He didn't call?"

She shook her head again.

"Does he seem to be acting strange?"

She nodded and I winced. Damn, I prayed that maybe I was just delusional, but obviously not. "How long has he been gone?"

She took a deep breath. "Dwight hasn't stayed here since you've been in the hospital."

"Ma, turn around and look at me when you talk."

She turned slowly and her eyes told me that she felt what I felt. My heart plummeted. "Do you think guilt is getting to him?"

She took a deep breath. "It's like déjà vu."

Every gesture I made begged for an explanation. We were different. He wasn't my father. He took care of his responsibility. He married me. Why didn't I feel like his wife at this moment?

CHAPTER 25

Tracey

Dwight hadn't totally given in to me yet, but I knew it was going to take more than a week for him to forgive me. He'd go back out and claim he had to think. I had Wade send us more clothes. The girls were so happy to be with him that I knew he couldn't bring himself to say it wasn't going to work. I cooked all of his favorite meals and tried to play the sweet wife role, but he hadn't touched me. He was just acting weird and strange. Maybe all these months had changed him, but all I knew is that I wasn't going anywhere. I planned to love him back to himself.

Each time I thought about being single or about Danielle and her crazy marriage I knew I was doing the right thing. I wasn't equipped to be out there on the singles scene. I've always been with Dwight and that was just the way it was going to be. While Dwight was at work, the girls and I would drive around the neighborhood. He lived in a town called Hanover, just thirty minutes from both Baltimore and DC. It was a really nice place to live and I was impressed that we were surrounded by so many wealthy black people. The girls and I had gone down to DC and went to the Washington Monument and walked on the Mall. They didn't understand what they were experiencing, but I was glad I could expose them to it anyway.

One morning, after Dwight went to work, I called Mama Dee to let her know what was going on. She listened closely but didn't offer much advice. So I asked, "How can I get him to start acting like himself?"

"Be confident. Be Tracey. He'll come around."

I felt better after I spoke with her and I decided to really settle in. I started looking into getting my Maryland real estate license, because I was getting bored with sitting home and entertaining these little girls. While I was in the grocery store, it was as if the free magazine wall called my name. There was a children's magazine listing camps and summer activities for kids.

Before I put the groceries away, I called several of the camps to check for availability. I registered both girls in a dance camp not too far from the house. Thankfully, they would start on Monday morning. When I called Dwight to let him know, he didn't sound as excited as me. He didn't know what it felt like to be home with nothing to do.

CHAPTER 26

Alicia

Seven whole days later, I still didn't even feel like Dwight's son's mother. Though initially I thought it made sense for Dwight to stay at the new house, I began to wonder. Was it just my insecurities bothering me? What could he possibly be doing? Shouldn't he be here more?

It's hard to really feel what you feel when there is another woman in the house already questioning your man. I fronted around my mother like his absence didn't bother me, but it was killing me. Here I was with a two-week-old, trapped upstairs in a room, and his damn work phone kept going to voice mail.

I tried the work phone. I tried the cell phone. I called Desiree. I asked her if Dwight was there and she hesitated. Finally, she said, "Alicia, I don't want to get into it."

"What?"

"Didn't you call him?"

"He didn't answer and I'm just asking you if he's there."

She paused. "He's here, but he's with a client."

"That's all you had to say."

She chuckled a little. "How's DJ?"

"He's fine. He cries a lot, but he's the sweetest little angel."

"That's so good."

She seemed to be rushing me off the phone. So I ended the call first. Then I returned to stalking my husband, who had been MIA for way too long. The nice, patient bitch disappeared as I yelled into his voice mail, "Where the hell are you?"

I pushed the OFF button as hard as I could, wishing it were one of the old-school phones that could be slammed. With each message, I got angrier and angrier. The confidence I used to have was gone as my body began to shake. I rocked the baby and jumped every time the phone rang. I just couldn't understand how everything had changed overnight.

My mind began to play tricks on me. Maybe he was seeing Desiree. Why did she seem so strange? We were better than this. I trusted him and I trusted her. How could they do this to me?

I walked into my mother's room and asked her if she would keep the baby while I took a walk. Of course, she didn't want me to leave, but I was tired. I needed air. I needed to think about my life and how something so right seemingly took a wrong turn.

After nearly ten minutes of convincing, she willingly agreed to let me stroll the neighborhood. I put on my sweat suit, but prior to leaving the house, I called him again. His cell phone went straight to voice mail. I called Desiree again and she didn't answer. My breathing got heavy and I felt like I should rush out before the tears started.

I stood at the front door and suddenly I had a plan. Damn it! I had to get to the bottom of this. I don't care what anyone has to say. My purse sat in the closet and I debated. Am I crazy for fighting for my marriage?

I grabbed my purse and rummaged through it to find my keys. They weren't in there. As I snuck into the kitchen, my mother's footsteps creaked in the hallway over me. It was just a matter of seconds before . . .

"Alicia, what are you doing?"

While I slowly pulled out the kitchen junk drawer, I said, "I just wanted to drink some water before I go out."

Just as I noticed the keys, she started down the steps. I balled the keys in my fist to silence the jingling. By the time she hit the bottom step, I'd put them behind my back. Caught! Her eyes questioned what I was doing. I took a deep breath and camouflaged my insanity with a smile.

"Ma, what are you doing?"

"What are *you* doing?"

"I was trying to see if you had bottled water."

"You know I don't have bottled water. Get yourself a water bottle and put some regular water in it."

My fist was still balled as I swung open the cabinet to find a water bottle. I prayed her away and God granted my wish as she headed back up the stairs.

"Alicia, don't stay out there too long. Make sure you take your cell phone."

I chuckled to myself. Damn right, I'm taking my cell phone, because I have shit to take care of. Just as I headed to the door, it rang. My hands shook as I pulled it out of my jacket pocket. It was Dwight's work phone. I exhaled, but immediately tensed back up when I heard his voice.

"Hey . . ."

I looked at the phone. Could I at least get some sort of apology? How about *I've been calling you all day, punk?* Everything I wanted to say would probably come out wrong. Instead, I just asked, "What time are you coming over?"

He hesitated and I snapped, "Where have you been?"

"Working! Where the hell do you think I've been?"

I opened the door and rushed out before my mother heard me. I sighed. "Dwight, I really have no clue where you've been."

He sighed. "This is just really a rough time right now. Please . . ."

"Please, what? This is a rough time for me, too. I just had a baby and my husband is nowhere to be found."

"I'm working!"

"You're not working that fucking much!"

He huffed. "Wow. You know how much work I have to do."

"Do you realize that having a newborn is hard work, too? I need you. If I knew you weren't going to be here for me, I . . ."

"You what?"

"Dwight, I need you."

"I know."

I bit my lip. If he knew, why was he making me suffer?

"Talk to me, Dwight. Tell me what's going on."

"Alicia, having a son was one of the best times in my life, but I'm struggling with it, too."

I sniffed. "Why now?"

He took a deep breath and I heard an interruption on the line. He asked me to hold. Shortly after, he returned and before I could speak, he said, "Lemme hit you back."

He hung up and I rushed to my car. I didn't know where

I was going, but I planned to find him and figure out what was going on. Hell, with this sudden change, it could be drugs. I just needed to see where he was going after work.

When I pulled up to his work parking lot, I found his car and parked my car in an inconspicuous space that would allow me to see him. My mother started calling my cell phone just minutes after I got there. She left frantic messages, swearing that I wasn't healed yet and that I should come home.

I beat on the steering wheel, praying that I wouldn't have to act a fool in the work parking lot. If there was any evidence that he was sleeping with Desiree, I'd have no choice. After an hour of being drowned with anxiety, I saw him walk out of the building. Keeping my eye on him, I watched the building, looking for Desiree.

He talked on his cell phone. Why did he appear so intense? I let him start his car before starting mine. My hands clamped tightly on the steering wheel and my eyes were glued to the windshield. I followed a few cars behind. It was pertinent that I didn't lose him. After a few obvious turns, it was clear that he was headed to our new home. Trying to avoid being spotted, I pulled over on the main highway just blocks prior to the turn on our street. The few seconds that I sat gave me a moment to breathe. In my pursuit, I don't remember thinking. Getting to the bottom of this bullshit was the only thing on my mind.

My mother called as I was counting to one hundred, trying to space the time he arrived and when I popped up. Could she really punish me for driving when I shouldn't be? I decided to answer. She immediately began shouting and asking where I'd gone and why I hadn't answered my phone.

I tried to stay calm and pretend that I wasn't out here stalking my husband. I snickered, "Ma, I had to get out. I'm at the new house. I'll be home soon."

"What? Why are you trying to kill yourself?"

"I'm not going to kill myself. Lemme go. I'll be home in a minute."

I closed my phone and pulled off. Butterflies filled my stomach as I turned the corner. Why was I afraid? Showing up here is just going to let him know that I will not stand for an absentee father.

CHAPTER 27

Tracey

Dwight, what the hell is going on? Why the fuck haven't you been there for me?" I peeped out the blinds. I saw a woman screaming and an older woman with a baby in a navy blue and white striped car seat standing in front of the door. Dwight ran out the door.

"Dwight, what the hell is this?" I asked as I followed him onto the porch.

"Go into the house," Dwight demanded.

"I'm not going anywhere." I turned my attention from Dwight to the woman who was crying. "What's going on?" What the hell was the woman talking about? Why was she crying and why the hell was she out here screaming at nine in the morning?

"Go into the house. I have this," Dwight yelled at me again.

"No, Dwight! Whatever business she has with you, she has with me."

"So this is what this is about. Your ex-wife is paying you

a visit," the woman yelled with authority. Did she say ex-wife? I didn't know who this woman was but I knew I needed to correct her.

"Ex-wife, honey? I'm still his wife," I said, turning my attention to him.

"You mean your ex-husband. I'm his wife now."

"We are not divorced, so that's impossible," I said as things still were not making sense.

"He is married to me now and this is his son!" she screamed. I almost passed out. By now the girls had run outside. I didn't want them to hear the nonsense the woman was speaking about their father. I grabbed my daughters and ushered them in the house. I took them into Dwight's bedroom, turned on *Hannah Montana*, and turned up the volume. I ran back downstairs and to the front door.

"Dwight, come in this house right now."

Dwight looked at me standing in the door and then at the woman crying. He didn't move for what seemed like ten minutes and finally he said, "Alicia, take the baby and your mother home. I'll call you." Then he walked back toward the house.

The older woman who was holding the baby screamed, "Dwight, you are not going to do this to my daughter. Oh, hell no. You gotta be out of your damn mind. I will come and slap you up myself."

Dwight and I went into the house and closed the door. My body started trembling. He walked me to the sofa. With my voice and body shaking, I said, "What does she mean that is your baby?"

"I was trying to tell you. You didn't give me a chance. You just walked in here. I was trying to tell you a lot of things have changed since you stopped taking my calls and hung up on me and screamed that you wanted a divorce almost four months ago."

"How could you, Dwight? That baby is a newborn. We were only supposed to be divorced a few months ago. You do the math—you started this relationship well before our marriage ended. Soon as you got down here you started cheating on me," I said as I stood up and started flailing on him. My arms hit him so fast all over his body. He stopped my raging arms by grabbing my wrists and holding me down.

"Please stop. Please stop. We have to talk about this."

"Talk! There is nothing to talk about. I don't know you anymore. You fucked up everything." He grabbed my waist. "Do you love her?" Dwight didn't say anything. I thought maybe he didn't hear me. "Clearly we have a problem."

"I don't know what to say. You left me up here by myself."

"How could you? You have a little baby? You married somebody else? I feel like I don't even know you," I yelled. I was so disgusted. I couldn't even look at him. I felt like I was about to kill him. Rage was creeping in my bloodstream. How could it be that he had another family?

I looked out the front window and saw the woman still out there. My heart beat fast and emotions took over. She had my husband's son. I was jealous. I was mad. Before Dwight could stop me, I ran out the front door, reached out and grabbed the woman's hair, and tried to wrestle her to the ground. The next thing I knew I was busting her all in her face. I had blood all over my knuckles. Then her mother yelled, "Get off my daughter!" I didn't mean to hit the old lady. She just got knocked down in the process. But she was in the way of me beating her daughter's ass. I don't know what came over me. It's just like I wanted to kill her, pay her back for making my life hard. He would have come back to Florida if she hadn't given him any options. She gave him options and I gave her head a beat down with a right and a left combination. As soon as one punch landed, another one was coming. My fists just kept crushing into her skull. Who did this bitch think she was, you have a baby by my husband and you think you gonna come up here and talk your mess on my front door? Oh, hell no. I had the woman in a headlock and I was trying to catch my breath. Then her mother and Dwight were able to pull us apart. She called me bitch and I called her every husband-stealing slut name in the book. Finally, her mother held her and Dwight held me. She shouted, "Bitch, I didn't steal your husband. You gave him away."

Her mother helped her to her car and Dwight escorted me back into the house. He yelled, "What the fuck is wrong with you?"

"You cheated on me!"

"You told me you wanted a divorce."

I broke down and started crying. "Dwight, I just wanted you to come back home. That's all, and if she wasn't here, you might have, but you made a baby as soon as you got here."

For the first time since I got there, he held me with sincerity and stroked my hair. "The baby was premature, Trace."

"I know you, Dwight. If she wasn't so willing to fuck a married man, you would have come home."

He kissed my forehead. "Maybe you're right. Who knows?"

After he calmed me down he told me he was taking a

drive and he would be back. While he was gone I contemplated my next move. Should I go? Should I leave? I couldn't believe this was happening to me. I swore Dwight was different. I thought I had an exception to the rule. I guess there is no such thing. Other people's husbands cheated on them. Things like this weren't supposed to happen to me. Dwight had never cheated on me. My heart and head felt so heavy. Why would he risk it all? Why would he jeopardize it all and have a damn baby? I didn't know what to think. This was so hard to digest. I had thought I had my man on lock. Maybe I took advantage of that for too many years. Maybe he had been cheating on me all along and I just didn't know.

The next day I dropped off Destiny and Jordan at camp. I did not want them to see me cry and that's what I had been doing. Dwight asked me if I wanted him to stay home, but I told him to go to work. I needed to be alone and sort things out. Every few minutes I felt like I wanted to cry. I wanted to stay and work things out with Dwight. But then I would think about Dwight and his new family and I became nauseated. I felt sad. I decided that although I wanted to be married to Dwight I couldn't stay in Maryland. I began packing my and the girls' things back into my car. I called Dwight and told him I was going back to Florida. He told me to wait until he got home to talk, but there wasn't anything to talk about. As soon as I had everything in the car, Dwight came speeding down the street.

"What are you doing?" he asked.

"I'm leaving you. I will not be disrespected." I already had it in my mind that I was leaving. I was going to pick up Destiny and Jordan from camp and get on the highway and go home. "Dwight, I can't deal with all this. You know what, this time I'll sign the divorce papers. And you can go get married for real and have a happy life. I don't care about you, Dwight. And obviously you don't care about me or your daughters. You need to get yourself out of this shit and you need to do it on your own. Trifling ass. Have a nice damn life."

I got in the car and pulled off. Dwight got in his car and followed me, chasing me down the street. He sped up to me demanding that I pull over. I tried to concentrate on the road and keep my eyes focused, but I could see his hand motions out of the corner of my eye. I looked over to see Dwight yelling, "Stop! Where are you going? Pull over!" He was driving erratically down the street and was about to make me crash. I pulled over just so we wouldn't crash. He ran over and tried to get in my car with me. I wouldn't open the door.

"Open the door, Tracey," he said, trying to unlock the door.

"No! What! What can you possibly say to me?" I said as I cracked the window.

"What do you want me to do? I'll do anything, Tracey, just don't leave me again. I didn't mean for this to happen," he said as tears flowed down his face.

I didn't want to see him cry. I didn't want him to hurt and I didn't want to hurt. But I couldn't stop being upset with him. I began screaming, "Dwight, stop crying. Stop acting like you care. If you did, you would never have done this. Your tears don't mean anything to me. We were perfect. We had the perfect life. And look what you did."

Dwight looked directly in my eyes through the window and said, "What about me? Look how you left me! Look how you left me, Tracey. You left me, Trace."

I sat and looked at him for a moment and my eyes filled with tears. Every time I blinked another tear fell. I stared at my husband, the love of my life, who was crying, hurting, and staring at me. I couldn't run; I had to listen to what he had to say. I opened my car door. Dwight came in and hugged me, and we sat in the car and talked. Dwight told me that he never planned to hurt anyone. I was convinced that I did want to be with him. I still blame her.

"I wish we could have communicated better."

"I know, Dwight, but I thought if I gave you space you would just come home."

He nodded. "We handled everything like this shit wasn't real life. I feel bad for trying to do the right thing."

"The right thing? Dwight, you didn't even know that girl. Why did you feel like you owed her?"

"Maybe because I'd lost you and our marriage."

My eyes watered. This was one big ugly misunderstanding. But now what were we going to do? I asked, "So, what's next?"

"We work it out."

I nodded but didn't respond. I didn't want to lose him more now than ever.

For the first time since I arrived in Maryland, Dwight and I slept in the same bed. Dwight held me closely. He kissed me all over my body and I stroked his back, and he touched between my legs, making me squirm. He made love to me like he loved me. Every stroke was apologetic and sincere.

CHAPTER 28

Alicia

I'd never fought over a man in my entire life. I had relationships down to a science. Knowing when to leave is the first formula to success. How had I missed all the warning signs? I should have known it was too good to be true. He'd portrayed her to be a selfish woman who didn't care about him. The woman who just attacked me loved Dwight as much as I did. It was crazy for me to believe that she could let him go so easily.

Initially I was angry when my mother popped up. I was sitting in my car, stunned, when she tapped on the window. She told me to get out and get to the bottom of it. I really didn't want to, because I knew what had happened. I'd been played. She had DJ's car seat looped on her arm. She said, "Let's go. You didn't come here to sit in the car."

My mother was like a woman with a vengeance. This was not only my battle it was hers, too. It all happened so fast, but it was clear that Dwight was a fraud. Please, someone erase this nightmare. My heart felt as if it had been ripped from my chest. His wife had settled in the house that I helped him select. My mother didn't say anything as she helped me into my car. She just rubbed my back. Really, there was nothing to say. My rare man had turned out to be just another man. They will all do what feels good for the time being. Why don't they consider everything before satisfying their own selfish needs? I hated Dwight. No, I loved Dwight. Or was I in love with his representative? My Dwight would never be so careless. He would know about any technicality in the divorce. He would know that our marriage wasn't legal. Is he just a con artist? So many questions filled my brain. But still my heart wouldn't let me hate him. I still believed in him.

My mother and DJ followed me back to her house. When we got there, I went to the bathroom and began to throw up blood. My mother heard me gagging and rushed in.

"Alicia!" She knelt down and hovered over me. I heard her sniffle. This was as painful to her as it was to me. She rubbed my back. "Baby, do you want to go to the hospital? Your stitches may have ripped."

"No, just leave me alone. I'm okay."

"Alicia, you're not supposed to have any strenuous activity for weeks. You just got into a fight. Let's go to the hospital."

"I don't want to go. Just leave me alone." I curled up on the bathroom floor and tears rolled from the corners of my eyes. My mother lay beside me and put her hand around my waist. I sniffed. "Why me, Mommy? Why me?"

"Baby, don't be the victim. Don't be the victim."

"But I am. I just had his baby. He had to know he wasn't divorced. He had to have known she was coming here. I just don't understand."

I wanted my mother to say something profound, something that would justify Dwight's actions. Instead, she said, "I don't either."

My baby's cries took precedence over mine as my mother hopped up to attend to him. The excruciating abdominal pain overpowered the pain in my chest, so I closed my eyes. Just as I attempted to drift away and convince myself this was a dream, my mother's piercing scream forced me to jump up. She rushed toward me and blood dripped from her hand. I shouted, "What happened?"

She shouted back, "You're bleeding! You have to go to the hospital."

I looked down and my shirt was drenched with blood. My knees weakened and I suddenly felt faint. DJ screamed at the top of his lungs. My mother yelled into the phone, "My daughter is bleeding! Yes! Yes! Please send an ambulance."

I wobbled from the bathroom to get a towel from the linen closet. My mother yelled at me, "Sit down! Just sit down!"

I held the towel over my stomach. I needed to get DJ. He shouldn't suffer, just because we were messed up. His poor little lungs couldn't handle that much crying. I panted, "Get the baby, Ma. Get the baby."

Maybe I was just moving my mouth, because she simply held me and ignored my baby. "Ma, please. Get the baby."

When we heard the ambulance sirens, she rushed to the door. I was so embarrassed. How could I explain that this was all a result of a fight with my baby's father's wife? This was some ghetto shit. I was disgusted with myself. I was even more disgusted with my situation. The paramedics rushed in and began ambushing me with questions. *Damn it, I just had a baby. My incision is bleeding. Who gives a damn what I did to make me bleed? Just take me to the damn hospital.*

Nearly twenty minutes elapsed before they put me on the stretcher. My mother told me she'd follow the ambulance. I gasped. "Don't bring the baby. Call . . ."

My mother huffed. "Call who? Don't worry about it. I'll be there."

When I got to the hospital, I was treated immediately. I didn't even know what was occurring and the drama in my life wouldn't allow me the chance to worry about it. I had popped several stitches. The female doctor asked the inevitable, "What were you doing?"

I said, "I fell down the steps."

"Really?"

Her sarcastic tone made me feel like she knew I was lying, so I changed the subject. "So how many did I pop?"

"Quite a few, Mrs. Wilson." That name made me cringe. My marriage was bogus. She continued, "You have to be careful. This could have been worse. You're actually lucky that you bled externally. If your stitches busted internally, depending on your pain tolerance, you may not have known. You could have died."

You mean to tell me that love really does kill? Suddenly, all I wanted was to be alive and take care of myself and my son. Dwight didn't matter. His lies didn't matter. I nodded at the doctor. She smiled at me and repeated, "You're so lucky."

After she restitched me, my mother came into the room. I asked, "Where's DJ?"

"Dwight's here."

I was furious. "Why is he here?"

"I called him."

"Why did you call him? He doesn't belong here! This is all his fault."

She rubbed my hair. "Baby, you don't mean that. Dwight is just confused right now. Be patient."

"I can't be patient. Why did he lie?"

"Calm down, Alicia. Maybe he didn't."

Maybe that was all I needed, someone to validate what I wanted to believe. Dwight couldn't have done this intentionally. The anxiety boiling in me simmered down and I told her to send him in.

He stood at the curtain opening. I stared at him and he stared apologetically at me. The only thing I could say was, "What happened? Why? Why? Why is she here? Why didn't you tell me?"

He hung his head. "She popped up here and I just didn't know what to do. I'm just trying to figure this all out."

"But if she told you she wanted a divorce, why is she here now?"

He took a deep breath. "Like she said, the divorce was never final." He paused. "Which means . . ."

My voice intensified. "Dwight, how could you not know? You're lying to me!"

"I'm not lying, baby, and I feel like shit."

I turned my head away from him. "You should feel like shit."

"I'm so sorry about everything. I'm sorry that I hurt you. I'm sorry about you being here. I'm just sorry."

"A sorry fucking excuse for a man."

He hovered and tried to hug me. His face rested on mine and he wiped my tears. "I'm so sorry."

"But she just can't come back and say that she wants the marriage after all this time."

"I know."

"When is she going back?"

"I don't know. I'm working on that."

"Working on it? She can't just move into my house."

He released a long hesitant sigh. "I can't just put my girls out. What am I supposed to do?"

"You're supposed to be with me."

"I am."

"You're not."

"I'm working this out. I promised I'd be there for you and I won't let you down now."

"Are you sure?" I asked.

"Yes, I'm sure. She won't be here long. It's all a show. Let me work this out and we'll be happy again."

He came back to the house and helped me get settled. I needed him to hold me and guarantee that it would all be okay. Instead, he told me that to keep the peace, he had to go home. I closed my eyes to hold back the tears. He kissed my forehead before leaving, and crowned me the other woman again.

CHAPTER 29

Alicia

I still didn't know the status of my relationship. Tracey hadn't left and she guaranteed me that she was in for the fight. I don't know if it was looking at DJ every day, but I'd never felt like I needed anyone before, and I needed Dwight. A plethora of emotions consumed me as I sat up in the room where I grew up, now with a baby. Just ten months ago, I had it all. Why the hell did I have to fall in love?

The baby cried in the bassinet and I just wanted him to be quiet. My mother was at bingo and I was alone. What gave Tracey more right to my husband than me? And DJ just wouldn't stop. Why couldn't I rationalize with this baby that I was having an emotional breakdown and I needed him to be quiet?

Dwight's occasional visits and vows of love just weren't enough. I needed him here with this baby and me. I needed to be in my own home, not here with my mother telling me that I don't know how to be a mother.

I had to get out. When I hopped out of bed and scooped DJ into my arms, I didn't really have a plan. I just wanted to run away. This new life was for the birds, and how did I let this man convince me that it was what I wanted? I wanted my single, childless life back. As I sat Indian-style in the middle of my mother's living room floor, having a screaming competition with DJ, my mother walked in.

She yelled, "Alicia! Alicia!"

I cried, "I just want it to go away . . ."

She immediately grabbed the baby and began shouting at me, "You got to get it together."

My hands clamped onto my hair and I rocked back and forth. "I didn't know it would be like this."

She tended to the baby while she talked to me. "Life is never like it's planned. You got to roll with the punches."

Vulnerability is a bitch. How did I let this happen? Why did I let my guard down? I thought he was so different. It's just not fair.

Her words didn't make sense as tears fell rapidly from my eyes. She tried to help me from the floor, but I struggled to stay there. I'd reached an all-time low and I needed to just deal with it.

My emotional state scared her and I heard her on the phone. She said, "I don't know if she took something or what, but she was lying here in the middle of the floor looking like a crazy woman. I need you to come over here as soon as possible."

After about ten minutes, Dwight walked into the house. He looked down at me and I tried to wipe my face. He took a deep breath and tears welled up in his eyes.

"I'm sorry. I never meant to hurt you."

I rocked back and forth. I couldn't speak. It hurt too bad.

He knelt down beside me. "It shouldn't be like this. I'm going to make it right."

Suddenly, I began wailing, "Dwight, why would you do this to me? I didn't deserve this."

He wrapped his arms around me. "You don't. You're such a good woman. You don't deserve this. I'm going to make it right."

"Why can't you make it right, right now? Why?"

He rocked me. "I wish I could. I wish I could. This is killing me."

"Where do you want to be?"

"I want to be with my kids." He paused. "All of them."

"What about us?"

"I want to be with you, too."

"Why aren't you? Why is she living in the house?"

He hung his head. "I love you, but I owe her."

"What? Why do you owe her? You don't owe anything. She let you go. She handed you right over to me. How can she just come back and say she changed her mind?"

He helped me up from the floor. "C'mon. Let's go upstairs."

"Just answer me."

He grabbed my hand and led the way to my bedroom. When we sat on my bed, he said, "I think I let go too soon."

"But what about me? I didn't ask for this. You told me you were leaving before I ever started dealing with you."

I sobbed pathetically. In all my life, I've never cried over a man this way. Maybe like my mother always said, it's different when you make life with someone. After creating a miracle, it's hard to let go.

My head lay on his chest and he stroked my hair. "You don't deserve this."

I beat his chest. "You keep saying that, but why are you doing this to me?"

"I don't know."

"Don't say that anymore. You're a smart man. You can find the words to explain this to me."

He lay back on the bed and pulled me with him. We faced each other and began to talk. "I've always been a one-woman man and when we got together, I knew this is where I wanted to be. It was over between Tracey and me. But what I didn't realize, being up here and away from reality, is that it's not that simple when kids are involved."

"We have a baby now."

"So it's twice as complicated now."

"What are we going to do?"

"I'm not leaving my son and I'm not living without my girls."

"You can't have that."

"Tracey is going to stay here with the girls and I'm going to be a father to my son."

I felt like he had suffocated me. What about me? I gagged. I wept harder.

He said, "I know it's hard, but right is right. I love you to death, but we're not legally married. And Tracey is still my wife."

The next morning, I woke up and called my attorney and began proceedings for an annulment. My marriage was a joke and this parenting shit was real, so I had to make sure my mind was right. What was I holding on to? He was confused and in my heart I knew he still loved me, too, but I couldn't live in disarray any longer. As much as I hate quitting, I threw in the towel. Tracey won. All my nightmares had come back to haunt me.

CHAPTER 30

Tracey

Mama Dee had been calling me and asking me why I didn't call her back. On her last message she said, "Don't make me come up there." I laughed at her message. She was right; I so didn't want her to come up here. At least not until this mess was straightened out. I already promised Dwight that I wouldn't tell anyone about his love child. I am so ashamed. I still don't know what we are going to do about us. I'm just taking it day by day. Coming up here is like starting all over. I don't know anyone and I don't even have a job. But I'm making the best of it.

Dwight was late for dinner again. He blamed it on working late. I tried to go along with the idea that everything was just great and we were still a happy family. I've been acting like his son doesn't exist, like Dwight wasn't in a new relationship, much less a marriage. But deep down I knew when he was late he was probably with that other woman. Every time I feel a little upset I take Dwight's credit card and go shopping. And the shopping is really good here. I probably did a good six thousand on his AMEX card so far. I don't even hide the receipts or bags anymore. I spent three hundred in Bath & Body Works alone. I bought all types of ginger and lemon lotions and cherry blossom body washes. I bought the girls clothes from Limited Too and Children's Place.

Dwight tiptoed into the house wearing a white cotton work shirt and black slacks. His shirt was hanging out of his pants and he looked like he'd just awoke.

"Where are you coming from?" I asked.

"Just driving around thinking."

"Dwight, were you with that woman?" I asked, looking him in his eyes to see if I could detect if he was lying.

"No," he said, trying not to make eye contact with me.

"Where were you at?" I asked, following him into the kitchen.

"The office."

"Be honest."

"I am being honest."

I couldn't continue to act like anything normal was happening. "What are you going to do? How are you going to fix this?"

"Fix what?"

"*Fix what?* That woman, that boy."

"I don't know."

"Dwight, let me ask you a question. Do you want to lose us? Just leave her alone. What is she doing for you? Huh? We've been together since— I can't believe you can ruin my life like this. I love you, I want to be with you, but I'm not going to share you!"

"I don't want you to share me."

"Obviously you do. 'Cause that's what I'm doing now. You coming home late or waking up early. I'm sacrificing my life to be with you. And you're having the best of both worlds."

CHAPTER 31

Tracey

Some nights Dwight would come home at a reasonable hour and others he'd be late. It was like I was sharing him and I didn't like it. I wanted Alicia and her son to just disappear. One day, I found myself praying they'd have a car accident and then I realized that was just mean and evil. Nobody deserved that, even if she was a home-wrecking slut.

The girls and I headed upstairs around nine and I let them lie in bed with me for a minute. They were knocked out by the time I heard the garage door opening. I carried them one by one into their rooms. When Dwight came upstairs, he looked worn out. I knew when he visited his other family, but he never admitted it. I said, "How was your day?"

"It was good."

He walked into the walk-in closet and began to undress. I leaned on the doorjamb, watching him move slowly. I said, "You okay?"

"I'm fine. Give me a minute."

He was irritated and I didn't know why. I wanted to help him, but his expression demanded that I leave him alone. When he finally walked out of the closet wearing pajama pants and a wife beater, he asked if I still needed the light. I glanced down at the book in my hand, thinking, *What the hell do you think?*

He shook his head. "You know what, never mind."

He climbed in bed and rolled over with his back facing me. I continued reading until I fell asleep. A few hours later, I was awakened by whimpering. I popped up, assuming it was one of the girls. I looked around and Dwight wasn't in bed. Following the sound, I headed into the bathroom. Dwight was kneeling on the side of the tub, crying like a baby. Tears fell from his eyes like from a wounded child. I said, "Baby, what's wrong?"

"I never wanted things to be this way."

"It's okay. We're working through it. It's going to be okay."

He looked me in the eye and said, "You and I are working through this. I've abandoned another woman and my son. My life was never supposed to be like this. We fucked everything up. All I wanted to do was take care of you. Now I feel like I should take care of her. She's over there with my son, doing the best she can, and she has to go right back to work, because I can't afford to take care of her and you, too. She's living with her mother, 'cause she planned to move in here with me."

I'd known Dwight nearly twenty years and I'd never seen him so weak and so helpless. I felt there had to be something I could do to make this right. Other men make the same mistake and could care less about how a child and another woman are going to make it. His tears proved that he was the man I married. I'd sent him off into the wild, and there had to be something I could do to make it all better, to make him stop hurting. I'd been praying. I mean praying hard, asking God to send me a solution to my predicament. I kept asking myself: What is going to make me happy? What is going to make him happy? What is going to make the children happy and keep us a family? The only conclusion I came up with was to accept her. Dwight has always wanted a son. He is not going to leave her alone, and my daughters need their father. There were so many angles of looking at this situation. Allowing that woman and her son to be a part of my husband's life could be the best or worst thing ever. How many women are adult enough to know that their man is involved with someone else and accept it? I mean really accept it? Danny was sharing her man unwillingly and she was always upset and hurt. He loves her, but all his love couldn't keep him away from other women. She was constantly finding earrings, hair in her car, smelling perfume on him. I don't want that for my life, and besides, it is my fault. I was the one who pushed Dwight away. He is a good guy, he is a good father. He was respectful enough to marry this other woman so she wouldn't have to be a single mom. Maybe I could possibly not share, but know that she exists. But only if she respects me and is kept out of my face. Maybe I could look the other way. It could work for us. If I did agree with this situation, I would never have to worry about where he was because I would know.

My thoughts kept racing by—one part of me saying I'll never knowingly share my man. The other says it is better than losing him. I made up my mind. I was going to take action.

• • •

The next morning while Dwight showered, I grabbed his phone and wrote down Alicia's phone number. Around twelve, I got up the courage to call. I didn't fully know what I wanted to propose, but I knew something had to be done. She answered cautiously, "Hello."

"Alicia. This is Tracey." She huffed and I continued, "I know I'm the last person you expected to hear from, but I didn't call to start any drama."

"Uh-huh."

"Can we meet for lunch?"

"To discuss what?"

"How we can deal with the situation we're in like adults."

"That sounds like a plan. Where do you want to meet?"

"I don't know. I'm still getting familiar with the area."

"You're right off of Arundel Mills Boulevard. Meet me at the food court of the mall around the corner."

My heart beat rapidly as I sat waiting for my husband's other wife to come. Finally, she arrived, strolling the cutest baby boy. His head was full of curly black hair. Alicia had on gym clothes and her stomach looked as if it was flat again. I was envious of her body. For a minute, I reconsidered my plan. I walked over to her and greeted her. She said hello and walked toward a table. We sat across from each other and I looked down at her baby and saw a miniature Dwight.

"Hello, how are you? And what's your name, handsome?" I said as I reached for the smiling baby's hand.

"This is DJ."

"DJ."

"Yes, Dwight Junior."

Her saying Dwight Junior crushed my heart. I took a deep breath. This was going to be harder than I expected. "Um, I'm going to get some coffee. Would you like some?" I said, getting up from the table.

"Yeah, I'll take a latte with two creams and two Sweet'n Lows."

I walked over to the counter and I turned back and looked at her holding my husband's son. What was I going to do?

We sat in the food court for two hours. I didn't even get up to go to the restroom. She explained her side of the story and I explained mine. She seemed like a nice person. She even showed me her wedding ring. It was bigger than mine. There were moments throughout our conversation when I wanted to run out of that mall and go kill Dwight. I mean, she knew about me, our girls, and our family. She seemed like she was real confident in her relationship with him, but I wasn't.

By the end of our conversation, I knew there was only one thing to do, and that was allow her and her child access to my husband. What I was about to say didn't even make sense to me. But the words came out of my mouth. I slowly said, "I don't know how this is going to work. I can't even tell you I'll agree with it tomorrow. But I'm going to allow you to be a part of my husband's life."

"You are?" she asked, surprised.

"It is best for everyone. Especially our children, and I don't believe in raising kids differently and I think children should grow up with their father. My parents are no longer here. And I believe Dwight made a mistake and we're going to have to deal with it right now."

"You're right. I can't wait for the girls to meet their brother."

"Oh no, I hope you will respect that I don't want to tell my children that your son is their brother. I want them to have a relationship. I want them to meet him and get to know him. And when they are a little older we can tell them."

Finally, she said, "Does Dwight know about this?"

"I wanted to speak to you first and then I'll go to him with it."

"So how will all this work?"

"I'll give you a call this evening."

"I'll be waiting."

CHAPTER 32

Alicia

When Tracey asked me to meet her, I thought about not going, but I felt something in her voice. She seemed sincere and as if she really wanted to find a solution to our problem. I walked out of the mall, thinking how right she was. Whether it was sexual or not, we were sharing Dwight. After I locked DJ in his car seat, I sat in the parking lot for a minute. It was strange that I was really considering this. Did this mean that he would be my man and hers, too?

I called the girls and told them I was in need of an impromptu girls night out. Andrea couldn't make it, but Gina and Tammy said they'd be damned if they couldn't make it. Before going back to the house, I took DJ on the BWI bike trail and did a light jog. The smooth tree-lined trail helped bring clarity to what I was feeling. Why would I do this? What did I have to gain from this?

When we got back into the car, I drove around in the Odenton and Arundel Mills area looking at new townhouses. Everything was in the low four hundreds. I began to feel overwhelmed and headed back to my mother's house. When we walked in, she was watching her soaps. She looked up and scooted to the edge of her seat. "So what did she want?"

"She suggested we start being more open, doing things as a family."

"After she attacked you? Is she crazy?"

I slouched down on the couch beside her and lay DJ across my lap. "Ma, she's just a woman trying to right her wrongs."

"She sure didn't seem like that when I met her."

"I mean, I don't know where she had this sudden change of heart, but I really think she meant it."

She shrugged. "I don't know. I don't trust her."

"Ma, a woman knows her man. She knows that Dwight and I have a special connection."

"That's the same thing I used to say about your father's wife. But I knew he loved her, too. Whatchu think?"

"I know he loves her. I never questioned that. So, what if Yvonne would have come to you and asked you to share my father. Would you have done it?"

She chuckled. "Maybe your father would still be alive."

"Whatchu mean?"

"I guess I never thought openly sharing him was an option. But I think the running back and forth, living two lives for so long, killed him." Her head dropped. "And maybe you would have had a better relationship with him."

We both reflected on that. I thought about how hard she cried on my sixteenth birthday that I felt like my dad's mistress. I was second to his children by his wife. I never felt like I mattered. It was his wife, their kids, my mother, and I was nothing more than the remainder. She wailed for hours and I didn't understand why, but as DJ rested on his stomach on my lap, I finally understood. It must be hard wanting your child to have something that you know they deserve, but not being in control of giving it to them. There wasn't really a whole lot more to think about. It wasn't about what I was gaining, rather what DJ was gaining. By the time I met my friends for drinks, I had already called Tracey and told her that I wanted to work this out.

CHAPTER 33

Tracey

Mama Dee would kill me for this, but I had to do what I had to do to make everyone happy again. I couldn't help but feel burdened with the guilt that I somehow caused all this drama with my stubbornness. When Dwight came home from work, he looked sad. The girls ran up to him, hugging his leg. He kissed me on the cheek. I sent the girls upstairs and talked to Dwight about my solution to our big problem.

Alicia came over the next day. She had the baby in her arms. I told her to come in and have a seat. I introduced her to the girls and went back to the kitchen and finished dinner. As I set the plates on the table and was acting like nothing, I was thinking: *Am I crazy? Is she crazy? Is Dwight getting over?* But she was there and I had agreed.

Dwight's two families were all sitting at the table. He looked at me and I looked at Alicia. I looked over at my kids. I bowed my head. I said grace. This was for my family.

This was for my children. I had to find a way to deal with it. The girls talked about their camp and their new friends. Dwight kept his head down the entire meal and barely ate his food. We finished dinner almost in silence.

Dwight walked Alicia to her car. I stood at the window and watched as Dwight bent over to give her a kiss. My heart dropped. *I don't think I can tolerate this. But I have to*, I thought as she pulled off.

Dwight came back in the house and asked me to come upstairs. I followed him into our bedroom and closed the door. He grabbed me by my waist and said, "Tracey, are you really okay with this? My other family coming over for dinner?"

"Yes, I want everyone to be happy."

"I don't think it is fair to you. Although I'm happy you're woman enough to do this for me. I'm not sure it's right for you. You don't have to do this."

"I love you and I don't want you to be apart from your son."

"I admire you, Tracey. I know most women couldn't do it. Being a part of my son's life is so important to me." Him saying that made me feel that I did the right thing. If this was going to make Dwight happy, I would have to learn to love it.

CHAPTER 34

Alicia

We were doing what was in the best interest of our kids. Most people would probably consider the agreement insane, but what was the better option? Fight over Dwight forever? Watch him die of heartbreak like my father died? I loved him and Tracey loved him and we were going to be together, despite what anyone thought.

Humans are one of the few species where the male is expected to have only one mate. So are we all really fighting against the laws of nature? Maybe Tracey and I had found the solution to the epidemic of infidelity. My only preoccupation with the entire agreement was the rules she wanted to impose. Initially, I was offended with her request, but once I came to know her, it made sense. We needed those guidelines to make the transition work for everyone. In addition, I knew in my heart that if he could, Dwight would probably just be with me. We had something special, and as long as I kept that in the forefront of my mind, I could swallow any of the insecurities.

Where else would I find a man like him? I wasn't searching for him, either.

By the time I went back to work, the storage bins were empty. I slowly left more and more stuff at *our* home until everything I needed was there.

Visiting was one thing, but my first full night in the house was the weirdest. I was irritated by the way Tracey moseyed around the house as if she was the lead wife. *Do you want something to drink? Do you need anything? Are you getting comfortable?* After a while I felt the need to snap at her and explain that I was no longer a guest. This house belonged to *our* husband.

I walked into the kitchen and Tracey was making dinner. Dwight sat in the family room with the kids and I felt out of place. I argued with my insecurities, demanding of myself to get with the program.

I asked, "Do you need any help in here?"

"No, no. I don't let anyone in my kitchen."

My kitchen? Okay, shake it off, Alicia. You don't like being in the kitchen anyway. Wag your tail and walk away. I folded my arms and walked into the family room with Dwight. The girls sat on each side of him and played with DJ, who was sitting in his lap. I sat on the sofa across from them.

Dwight said, "Sit over here."

Why did I look in the kitchen to see Tracey's reaction first? Just as I suspected, her eyes shot in our direction, but she didn't say anything.

Destiny said, "Are you okay?"

I nodded. What made her ask me that? I sat down beside her because she seemed the most friendly. She was young enough to be open, but old enough to make me feel at ease.

She said, "He's a happy baby."

I smiled. "Yeah, he is quite happy."

"Mommy says that happy babies are made from love."

She put the entire house on freeze. I laughed it off. "Yeah, they are. Love is very important."

"Do you love Daddy?"

I took a deep breath and nodded. *Little girl, just shut the hell up!* She continued, "Do you love Mommy?"

I nodded. Her bright eyes stared into mine as if she sincerely trusted me. She put her index finger on her cheek. "Um, do you love DJ?"

By this time, I was relaxed. "Yes, I love DJ."

She climbed up and folded her hands on my shoulder. "Do you love me?"

"Yes, I love you."

She giggled. "You don't know me. Mommy said strangers can't say they love you."

Dwight pinched her leg. "What did Mommy tell you? She's the housekeeper and she'll be living with us now. So she's not a stranger."

Jordan smirked and said, "Yeah, Destiny, do you remember that?"

Jordan didn't believe that bullshit. Tracey called for the girls to come help her set the table. When they left the room, I looked at Dwight. He smiled at me. "They're a trip. Aren't they?"

"Yeah, talk about the third degree."

He shrugged. "Hey, everyone has to get used to this. It's not your everyday situation."

We laughed and DJ appeared to be listening intently. His attentiveness made us giggle more. A plate slammed on the table. Our heads spun toward the kitchen. Jordan said, "Sorry, Daddy."

Jordan smirked at me like the apology was meant only for her father and not me. When would these feelings go away? What could I do to make this *my* home, too? I stood up and walked into the kitchen and began helping the girls set the table.

I said, "Tracey, why did you say you didn't need any help?"

She half-smiled. "The girls look forward to setting the table."

I returned her half-smile. "Well, I'll just pour us some wine."

She interrupted my fake chuckle. "Oh no. We don't drink in front of the girls."

Who the hell is *we*? *We* are now three and, damn it, I planned on having my wine with dinner. The more sensible side of me decided this wasn't the time for debate. "Oh, I'm sorry. I didn't know."

Shit! That wasn't the way I meant for it to come out. It was pertinent that I lay my rules down, too. This is not going to be one-sided.

She obviously noticed the preoccupation all over my face. "We'll have a glass when I put them to bed."

It seemed to me that she thought I was here to keep her company. I wasn't certain if she understood that we were both the lady of the house. It bothered me that not only was she the first wife, she was fortunate enough to move in first. Everything in the kitchen was how she wanted it. I was in her house. This had to change.

When dinner was ready, she fixed the plates and everyone sat down at the table. I couldn't help thinking about how to balance out this relationship. Dwight said grace, and when I looked up, the girls and Tracey were staring at me.

My eyes shot back at them. I wasn't going anywhere. We are going to make this work one way or another. Their aggression seemed to relent. I felt good about my stance. I had to let them know that I, too, was the boss around here.

When dinner was over, I started removing the dirty plates from the table. Tracey rested her back in the chair. "Be my guest."

I didn't respond to her comment. She obviously hadn't accepted our situation. I was no guest. I was here to stay, whether she liked it or not.

She played with DJ while I loaded the dishwasher. It seemed to come so natural for her. He babbled at her. She tickled him. They seemed to be bonding well. She had the advantage of starting out with him as a baby. I, on the other hand, had to befriend two little girls who were only used to their parents. It hit in a hard way that the biggest issue here would not be how Tracey and I dealt with each other but how these two little girls would grow to accept me as more than just a permanent houseguest.

They asked if we could watch a movie and I thought maybe I should let them watch it as a family. Maybe I should just go to my room and give them their time. As I stood and headed to the in-law suite, Dwight said, "Baby . . ."

Everyone cringed, but I said, "Yes."

"Where are you going? You don't want to watch a movie with us?"

"It's been a long day. I want to finish getting settled. DJ needs a bath."

"I'll give him a bath."

"Okay. But I still have things I need to do."

When I was alone, I called my mother. As I whined in

the phone, she said, "Alicia, you're strong enough to make your presence known in that house."

I sniffed. "I know. I don't know."

"Well, you have a nice house now and . . ."

"They have a nice house."

"Everyone just has to get used to you being there. You've never struggled with fitting in before. This is no different. You said that she seems open and cool. Right?"

"I mean she is, but I . . ."

"What? I'm sure she has to get used to this, too. Talk to her, Alicia."

"It's just so hard."

"I'm sure you both will have a lot to share. Be a big girl and talk to her like a woman."

After I got off the phone, I sat on my bed wondering what the hell I was supposed to talk to her about. How could I express my insecurities to the competition? Just as the thought crossed my mind, it hit me. I had to retrain my mind-set. We were in this fight together.

I held my head in my hands and rocked back and forth. Was I losing my mind? I knew all these things, but why did I feel so unsure? Why did I want to run away? I stared in the mirror and pepped myself up.

I stood up and walked around the room, feeding positive thoughts to myself. I was inspired. Hours passed before I opened the door. I walked into the kitchen and noticed Dwight and Tracey sitting on the floor in the family room playing with DJ.

Unconsciously, I walked over and sat down with them. Tracey seemed to enjoy all aspects of motherhood. She let him beat on her face and she laughed. I apologized. She said, "Girl, please. He is so good."

"Thanks."

"No problem."

Dwight stood up and walked into the kitchen. He grabbed a beer from the refrigerator and said, "I'm going up. Y'all can sit down here and chat."

He came and grabbed the baby. I looked up at him and then across at Tracey. I guess if he was going up, that obviously meant he was sleeping with her tonight. Although I wanted to scream, I smiled. "Okay. You can put him in the crib after you give him a bath."

"That's if we don't fall asleep in the big bed. Right, man?"

I prayed they did, because that would mean there would be no hanky-panky tonight. I was slightly relieved at the thought. Tracey shrugged. "Yeah, he can sleep with us if you want him to."

He headed upstairs and there was a moment of silence. Finally, I spoke, "So, how are you feeling about this?"

She chuckled. "Girl, this shit is crazy."

"I know."

"I guess I keep thinking that I can't believe I'm doing this for Dwight."

"I think it's just hard for me, because I'm like the outside coming in on a ready-made family."

She nodded. "I understand. And in reality, I guess we're both doing it for our kids and we have to remember that."

"Do you think the girls understand?"

She shrugged. "I don't know. Kids just accept things as-is. We'll try to figure everything out. They'll warm up to you."

"I don't even know what to say to them."

"They're kids. Just talk to them. You don't have any nieces or nephews?"

I hung my head. "Well, sorta, but I don't see them."

"Why?"

"Well they're my half sisters' kids. And we're not close at all."

She nodded slowly. "Oh. I understand."

I could tell that she was confused and I wasn't sure I was ready to explain that I had become part of a vicious cycle of adultery. As far as Dwight and Tracey were concerned, I was an innocent single girl who'd gotten herself into this situation for the first time.

"So I haven't really been around a lot of kids. You know?"

"They're just little people. They are good to anyone who's good to them."

It seemed that she was making it clear that she hoped I would treat them well. I listened intently because I wanted it to work.

I walked into the kitchen and opened the wine cooler that I'd filled up when I moved in. "Tracey, you like red, right?"

"I would just like a drink."

I laughed as I grabbed a bottle of Syrah and two wine-glasses. After I took them into the family room, I returned to the kitchen to get cheese and crackers.

She asked, "Do you want to watch a movie?"

"You love movies, don't you?"

"Yeah, girl. I'm a Lifetime fiend."

I laughed. "Are you?"

"Yes. This shit here"—she pointed to me and her—"this is a damn Lifetime movie."

We popped in a movie, but it watched us get to know each other. I respected her, as a woman, as a mother, and more important, as a wife. She was as willing as me to make this work.

I would have probably picked her to be a friend anyway. She laughed and chatted and I felt great about our decision. Sure, it wasn't typical, but we both seemed happy. I was a little bothered when Dwight brought DJ down and they went upstairs to go to sleep, but it seemed easy to just suppress the thought that my man was having sex with her. He was just sleeping in another room. I fell asleep without the slightest hint of jealousy. Tracey was all right with me.

CHAPTER 35

Tracey

Every day, I pondered whether it was easier to share Dwight blindly or openly. I found benefits in both. The largest benefit in being blind is that you don't have to witness your man's feelings for another woman. Somewhere along the line, we decided to go on group dates. When we did things with the kids, it was easier. No one looked at us strange. But when it was the three of us, people seemed to look at us like we were bizarre. I'm not sure if people could just feel that he belonged to both of us, or if I just felt self-conscious. If I said I wasn't still in competition with Alicia, I would be lying. I make sure Dwight was always sitting next to me when we went out. I usually sat in the front seat of the car, and I always tried to dominate all of our conversations. Sometimes I felt like a child trying to get attention when she was around. Probably out of respect, she never was overly affectionate when I was around and I appreciated it. When they had quality time together, whether they were in the house or out, I stayed busy. Between taking care of my baby—because DJ had become more mine than hers almost immediately—and teaching Destiny to read and staying on top of Jordan in school, I had plenty to do to keep me from thinking about what they were doing. I was becoming a better mother because I wasn't worried about where Dwight was. I didn't have to run to cook or make sure he ate. It seemed that he was taking better care of the children and me. Since all of this started, Dwight made sure everyone was okay. Although we were coming along okay I still kept a distance away from Mama Dee and Danny. Me and Dwight agreed that we didn't need them all up in our business. The same can't be said for Alicia's mother, Ms. Dixon. She was a regular at the house. She bought the girls Barbies and dresses. She came over uninvited all the time. I tolerated her pop-up visits because she was a very nice woman and supportive of whatever Alicia did.

Four months in, and Alicia had become a part of our family and she practically had moved in. She was living on the first floor in the in-law suite. I stayed in our bedroom, the girls had their rooms, and Dwight and DJ occupied the back bedroom. Alicia was a nice woman and she was very persistent. She literally made herself my friend. She would call me during the day, like she was my man. And then she would say, "I just wanted to say hi." Jordan and Destiny really took to her, mainly because she bribed them with candy and toys. She braided their hair and even took them to the movies and the aquarium to give me and Dwight alone time. Every now and then we got into little verbal spats when she crossed her boundary. Like, she tried to tell me I eat too much fried food and red meat. She made suggestions on our dinner menu, but I always ignored them. She knew that although she is tolerated, I am number one and the only queen bee.

CHAPTER 36

Tracey

There were only about twelve people in the real estate class and they all seemed rather friendly. There were six parts to the test and one night, someone suggested we meet for a study session. I was the anxious one saying, "Yes, we really all should get together."

That is until someone suggested meeting at my house. *No, ma'am. Not at my house.* The thought of Alicia being there and me having to explain her existence was unthinkable. So I quietly said never mind and went home.

When I walked into the house, Alicia was resting her head on Dwight's lap. She quickly jumped up. "What's going on, lady?" Alicia yawned.

"Don't get up," I said.

I was exhausted and it was nights like this that I was glad he had someone else to hump on and not bother me.

"How was class?" Dwight asked.

"It was good. I'll talk to you about it tomorrow. I'm really tired."

I headed upstairs because I didn't want to bother them on their night. I knew that during my time, I wanted no interruption. I turned the shower on and closed my door. I reviewed my notes from class. It wasn't going to be as easy as I imagined.

"How was class?" Dwight came into the bathroom behind me and I nearly jumped out of my skin.

"Good. It was all right."

"That's cool. I just want to remind you that we're going out tomorrow."

"Yeah, I mean we've all been so busy that it's just been easier to stay home."

"Alright, baby girl. Have a good night," he said as he kissed my cheek.

"Good night, Dwight."

We ate at an Italian restaurant in Georgetown named Filomena. We were seated and I just grabbed Dwight's hand and kissed it. It felt as if it had been forever since we had been together by ourselves. It felt like someone was always home. If it wasn't Alicia, it was the girls and DJ. At dinner I had the best seafood linguine I'd ever tasted, but more than that, I just enjoyed being with Dwight all alone. It felt good, like old times.

Our dinner date night ended in a hotel room a few blocks away. He called Alicia to tell her we wouldn't be in. I heard her say, "Okay, good night." It always bothered me leaving the kids at home with her. She was a complete wreck when it came to parenting skills. So that meant we'd have to be home bright and early in the morning.

Dwight murmured, "I love you, too." As soon as he hung up, I began to absorb every moment I was with my man. I attacked Dwight's body with sloppy kisses while undressing him. He took my hair and pulled it up as I knelt down and looked up at him seductively. His eyes were closed, anticipating my next lick. He leaned his hips closer to my mouth. I slowly circled the tip of his brown, pulsating, vein-engorged dick with my tongue. Then I went in faster, swallowing his entire manhood into the depth of my throat for several moments. He then laid flat on the bed as I rode him in reverse, my back facing his chest, with his body still in full strength. He grabbed and cuddled my breasts, and held on tightly. Moments later, his body released all its energy into me. When it was all over, I realized how much I missed his undivided attention.

CHAPTER 37

Alicia

We had it down to a science. Everyone was happy. We had practically isolated ourselves from the outside world. My mother had something to say here and there, but I told her to keep her thoughts to herself. I don't know why I thought I could hide from my friends, but I did. I ignored their e-mails and phone calls, because I needed to sift through this mess with a clear head filled with only my personal thoughts. They gave me a few months of freedom before they called me out. I logged on to my computer at work and there was a message from Gina and everyone else was carbon copied. It was titled: BITCH, STOP PLAYING. The message read: "We've been through too much for you not to trust us. We love you no matter what your crazy ass is doing. You don't have to call me, but call somebody."

Maybe I had been waiting for them to reach out to me and tell me they understood, because I was anxious to dial Gina's number. She picked up. "Ho, don't you ever just go

MIA and not tell us what the hell is going on. The last time we didn't hear from you, your ass was in jail."

I laughed. "Stop playing. Speaking of jail, why did Deshaun call my mother's house collect?"

"You know he's going to be on your doorstep when he gets out, but don't try to get on another topic."

"I need to write him and tell him I'm married."

"So, are you still married? What the hell is going on? The last you shared with us was that Dwight was confused."

I took a deep breath. "Well, he's not confused anymore, because . . ."

"Did she go back?"

"No . . ."

"Well, what happened? Are y'all back together?"

I snickered. "Well, Tracey and I agreed to share him."

"Bitch, don't play with me."

"I'm not. I've been living in the same house with them for months."

She linked Tammy and Andrea in on the line. I had to explain everything to them. I was missing steps and they sat on the line stunned. They couldn't believe that I'd stooped so low. It had been wise of me not to discuss it with them until it was carved in stone, because they weren't half as judgmental as they would have been had it been in the deciding stage. They missed me and despite being in tri-marital bliss, I missed them.

We agreed to meet for drinks after work. They needed to see me and make sure I hadn't been drugged. On my way to meet them, I called Tracey and pretended it was a last-minute decision, since she'd picked DJ up from my mother's house early.

"Hey, you."

"Where are you?"

"I was on my way home, but I think I'm going to have drinks with my friends. Is that cool?"

"Go ahead, Dwight came home early."

My eyebrows wrinkled. When I spoke to him last, he said he was working late. I paused. She said, "Yeah, he said he was stressed and decided to fight fires in the morning."

"Oh."

Suddenly, I felt like I wanted to go home, but I resisted the urge. She said, "Well, we'll see you when you get home."

"Okay. I should be there no later than ten."

"You know I'll be up."

As soon as I hung up with her, I called Gina. I could tell she was already feeling nice. "It's our long lost girlfriend."

I could hear everyone in the background shouting, *"Where is she? Is she coming? Tell her to c'mon. We still love her."*

"I'll be there in a minute."

I was speeding and it became immediately apparent that I hadn't been true to me. I'd been so caught up in this relationship that I forgot what used to make me happy.

When I walked into the restaurant, they cheered me on. By the time I reached the table, I was giggling. "Y'all are crazy."

"Ho, I can't believe you didn't return any of our phone calls in a month of Sundays."

I took a deep breath. "I just didn't feel like being judged."

"Now that you're living the polygamous shit, what can we say?"

I pouted. "It's not polygamy."

In unison, they said, "Bitch, please."

"Y'all make me sick. It's not polygamy. It's . . ."

Tammy passed me a drink. "Here, have a drink, 'cause your ass is in a polygamous relationship."

Andrea said, "Who gives a damn? Are you happy?"

"Actually, I am."

Tammy asked, "Well, how is his wife handling it?"

"His other wife."

She waved her head as if to say *whatever, just tell us about her*. "She's actually really cool. She's been very helpful with teaching me how to be a mother. She likes to have wine in the evening. It's like having a homegirl living with you. It's kinda like living in a dorm."

They all seemed to momentarily imagine how fun that could be. I added, "She cooks her ass off."

Gina said, "I was going to say you look like you're having a hard time getting that baby weight off."

"Forget you. Shit! I'm trying. I still run three miles a day."

"If she's cooking every day, you better start running five miles."

"Well, if she does all of that, what the hell do you do?"

"Shit, I work. I pay for extracurricular activities."

Andrea said, "You got it made."

"Well, what can I say? Shit. I recommend everyone try it."

"So when are we going to meet her?" Gina asked.

My eyes shifted from side to side. "Uh . . . um . . . y'all are too rough."

"Nah, we want to meet her," Tammy said.

"Okay, I'll invite her out on another night."

"Isn't Dwight home tonight?"

"Yeah, but—"

"Tell her to come up here tonight."

After a drink and more coaxing, I called home. Dwight answered, "Hey, Alicia."

"Hey, where's Tracey?"

He said, "You don't want to talk to me?"

"Yes, but the girls want to meet Tracey."

"Oh, no. Y'all not corrupting her."

I frowned. "What?"

"I'm just joking. Here, Trace, Alicia wants you."

She picked up. "Hey . . ."

"I'm out with my friends and they all want to meet you."

She hesitated and finally she said, "Are you serious?"

"Yeah."

"I thought you said they—"

"They're over it. Let me give you directions here."

"But—"

"Dwight can keep the kids. C'mon."

She made it to the restaurant in about thirty minutes. Tracey was practically family to me so I paid little attention to her country-fresh attire. I'd given her style that label because she was always shopping, new clothes every day, name brand and all, but she was still country. As soon as she walked in, Gina said, "Is that her?"

I smiled and nodded. Tammy laughed. "She's a straight bama."

I waved at her and she headed to the table. It was clear that all my girls were shocked. She came over to the table and spoke to everyone. She had that outgoing country swagger that made everyone like her. It appeared that she was innocently naïve, but it dawned on me . . . now *I* was in *my* element. The home was hers.

I was surprised that my friends didn't interrogate her. They actually were extremely nice and open. They asked questions about our situation and we tag-teamed them. By the end of the night, our arrangement seemed ten times more desirable than being single. The big question remained: How many other women would be down for this type of relationship? Tracey defeated all the skepticism with her final comment.

"It's not about the women. It's about the man. I know my husband is a good man." She looked at me. "And Alicia obviously knew as well. I could spend the rest of my life searching for him again or I could be with him"—she paused—" . . . and her."

Tammy leaned in and said, "So do y'all get down? Like, have y'all had a ménage à trois?"

My eyes nearly popped out of my head. "Hell no, it ain't that kind of party."

Tammy laughed. "Bitch, don't act like you've never had a girl before."

As drunk as I was, I could read Tracey's expression. She was shocked. I could have jumped across the table and choked Tammy. That wasn't necessary. Didn't she realize that, despite how good our situation was, there were things that I wasn't ready for Tracey to know about me? My stomach balled in knots and the only thing I could do to make me feel better was to keep the drinks coming. In less than thirty minutes, I'd gulped down three martinis. They continued to ask Tracey inappropriate questions, but I felt so good that it didn't matter what they said.

CHAPTER 38

Tracey

When Alicia asked me to come out with her friends, I didn't know how to react. On the way there I thought were they inviting me out to beat me up or see if I really exist? Before I could sit down her friends hit me with questions: "How do you like Maryland?" "Girl, why'd you leave that good-looking man up here and alone?" they asked in unison.

Alicia introduced them to me as I looked them over one by one, like *mind your business*.

I wasn't as intoxicated as they were. I just smiled and they couldn't detect what I was thinking or how I felt. An hour in, their questions began to rub me the wrong way. They were very loud, but were treating me like they really knew me.

"So let me ask you two! Are all of you having sex?" one shouted.

"Of course not," I said, wondering why her friend would ask such a disgusting question.

"So y'all don't be having a threesome?"

"We don't have sex together at all," Alicia answered before I could.

"Oh, don't act like it wouldn't have been the first time."

As we were leaving Sea Blue I noticed Alicia was too intoxicated to drive herself home.

"Alicia, ride with me. You're too drunk to drive," I said, noticing her slow, lopsided walking.

"Okay," Alicia said, stumbling into my passenger seat.

"Put your seat belt on," I said as I started the car. She drunkenly put the seat belt over herself. I put the car in reverse and looked out the rearview mirror. I began the drive home.

"It's nice to see that you care about me. That's so sweet," Alicia slurred. I looked over at her as she continued, "I'm so glad me and you are getting along. Because Lord knows I didn't want to end up like my mother. You know, my mother was a mistress her entire life. I never wanted to be like her. My father was a married man that never married my mother, and the other day she tried to tell me the same thing is going to happen to me. I told her we are different. Right, Tracey?"

"Yeah, you're right, we are different. So your mother never married your father?" I asked, probing her for more details about her upbringing.

"No, she waited for my father to leave his wife and he never did. And she just sat back and watched her life slip away. I looked at her my whole life like I'm not going to be like her."

"Wow."

"Yeah, so I promised myself I wouldn't have ever let my

son go without his father. I'm glad we both have Dwight and you realized how much he loves me."

"How much he loves you," I repeated, staring at her and ignoring the highway in front of me.

"Yup, 'cause if you didn't I would have still been with Dwight. No matter what you thought or did. And I probably wouldn't have stopped until he was all mine. Well, I did take him from you already." She laughed. Something in her choice of words made my skin crawl. I was about to pull the car over and put her out. She squirmed in the passenger seat. There were a few times I wanted to just knock her head into the window. Instead, I used the time to ask her questions I normally wouldn't ask her if she was sober.

"What did your friend mean when she said it wouldn't be the first time with a woman?"

"Oh, that. She was only playing. I kissed this girl in college and I let her eat me out at a party." She laughed.

"Did you like it?" I asked as I studied her face.

"A little, but all that shit about a woman knowing another woman's body makes no sense to me. 'Cause a woman can't do anything for me. I love dick, girl. I love dick so much, when I can't get any I use my dildos and vibrators. And I love for a man to fuck me. I love pornography, just watching a man's motion as he pumps himself into a woman. It's just beautiful. Like Dwight's dick isn't the biggest, but he works it right. You know, like he hits every angle," she said as she went to high-five me. I pulled the car over and began to vomit.

"What's wrong?" she asked, springing up from her drunkenness.

"Nothing," I said as I bent over my door, throwing everything up.

"Probably that lemon shot you had," she said as she fell back.

"Yeah, that's probably it," I said.

"I wish it was my night with Dwight. I need some bad. I guess the vibrator will be working tonight." She giggled. I looked over at her in disgust. I didn't even bother to tell her when we made it home. I opened the car door and began walking to the house. She could sleep her drunk ass in the car. I didn't want to say good night to her. I wasn't even sure I liked her anymore. By the time she got out of the car I was already at the top of the steps. I pushed all thoughts out of my head. I felt happy that it wasn't her turn with Dwight. I blocked out the thought that a drunk woman was downstairs in my house, lusting for my husband.

CHAPTER 39

Alicia

Dwight sprung up at five-thirty in the morning to creep upstairs when he stayed with me. That often made me feel empty, like a random one-night stand. Mornings were our bonding periods. We used to make plans, share dreams, and just gaze outside at the rise of a new day. I woke up shortly after he left the room and put on my workout clothes, made DJ a bottle, and called for Dwight to come and get him. He slouched down the stairs and reached for the baby.

"I'll be back in about forty minutes."

He nodded, but still he stared at me. "You look so good in those tights."

"Tights; baby, these are spandex."

Holding the baby in one arm, he tugged at my Under Armour pants. "I want you."

I looked in the open foyer. "Not while the detective is around."

We giggled, and sure enough, I heard Tracey moving around. It was as if she could smell our affection. He shrugged.

And I didn't wallow in the moment. I opened the door and headed out for my run. This would probably drive most women wild, but it was the lesser of two evils. I'd come to realize we had to pacify Tracey. It was simply a matter of us being creative. I found other ways to steal my quality time.

Tracey got in a habit of dropping DJ off at my mother's house in the morning so that I could work nine-hour days. Since I get paid the same salary for working nine hours as I did working eight, she didn't realize I was taking longer lunches. Sometimes I'd sneak off with one of my coworkers, but most days I went with Dwight if he was free.

Our anonymous lunch dates were so we could do things that prissy Tracey didn't like. So, in addition to sneaking off, we got the opportunity to do our own thing. It was slightly as if we were cheating on her, but the way she had it designed, she got more at-home time than me. So I had to do what I had to do. Working does have its advantages.

When I called to let Dwight know that I was outside of his job, he said he'd be down momentarily. It just so happened that Desiree walked out of the building. I hadn't seen or spoken to her since that day that I harassed her. She smiled and I beeped just to be courteous. She came over to the car and said, "What's up, stranger?"

"Nothing, what's up with you?"

"Picking up your slack. I'm sure Dwight told you."

Why did that make me uncomfortable? I didn't like her working so closely with my man, but I nodded although he really hadn't mentioned it. She smiled. "I wasn't sure if you guys were still together."

I frowned. "Why?"

"Because he never mentions you."

Ain't this the damn devil. I was happy and content when

I pulled up and this depressed whore transferred her unhappiness to me. "So what made you feel you should tell me that?"

"I was just shocked to see you, and he doesn't talk about his relationship at all, but he will say a thing or two about the kids, and I got the sense they were living with him and . . ."

Dwight walked out of the building and she said, "All right then, girl."

He noticed me shaking my head when he jumped in the car. I took a deep breath and he said, "What's up?"

"Nothing."

I refused to talk about Desiree, because I knew it was probably uncomfortable for him to talk about me *or* Tracey. But I guess for some strange reason, I thought I was the work wife, since all of his coworkers knew we'd gotten married. Of course, they were all shocked by our whirlwind love affair, but nonetheless they knew we were together. And it was just strange that Desiree wondered if we were even together.

We drove to Wendy's before heading to the movies. I still hadn't said a lot to him. He kissed my cheek and I pulled away. "What's wrong?"

"Nothing."

"Something is wrong."

"It's not," I snapped.

He grabbed my chin and began kissing me. It's funny that a kiss makes it all better. Maybe it released some happy hormones in me. When the loud horn of the car behind us in the drive-thru interrupted us, I smirk-smiled at him.

"Now that's my baby."

"Am I really your baby?" I asked.

I couldn't hear Dwight because the drive-thru attendant shouted through the speaker, "May I help you?"

We ordered our food, and as we drove to the first window, I asked again, "Am I really your baby?"

"What do you think?"

"I don't know."

He stared deep into my eyes and said, "You know you're my baby."

His words were sincere and suddenly I was secure again. By the time we inhaled our lunch, it was time to stand in line for the movie. I looked around and wondered if anyone even worked. How do people have time to wait hours to see a movie? Luckily, we'd purchased our tickets online. At least we didn't have two lines to stand in.

He wrapped his arms around me and rested his chin on my shoulders. "I love that you like the same stuff I like." We swayed together as I rubbed his forearm. He continued, "That's why we have so much fun."

When they let people enter the movie theater, Dwight laughed at me running to grab middle seats in the middle row. He shook his head as I nearly tackled the young kids to get it.

After we were settled, we laughed at the hysteria surrounding us. It seemed as if we sat in the theater for nearly an hour before the previews started. I looked at my watch. It was after one and I imagined we probably wouldn't get out until around four. "Are you going back to work?"

He shrugged. "It depends."

As he massaged my leg, I wanted to climb on him and make love to him in front of everyone in the theater. I stroked his upper thigh and leaned in for a kiss. We rubbed and kissed like two horny teenagers. Oblivious to the people around us, I unbuttoned my pants and guided his hand down. He played with me and thrust his middle finger in and out. I moaned and he started laughing, interrupting my moment. I stopped. "What?"

He whispered in my ear, "You can't be making all that damn noise in the theater."

"So what do you want to do?"

The movie had been playing way too long anyway and it hadn't exactly got my attention, so I said, "Let's get out of here."

After I buttoned my pants, we rushed out of the theater. When we got into the car, I leaned over for him to kiss me. He grabbed my hair and pulled me to him. I struggled to unbutton his pants. Then I unbuttoned mine. I yanked his penis out and began toying with it, while he fondled me. He begged, "Kiss it, baby. Kiss it."

He didn't even have to ask because that had been my plan all along. I bent over and slowly put my mouth on it. His scent. His touch. The way he massaged my neck. Everything about the moment made me yearn to taste him. I wanted to swallow his erection. I wanted us to be one. My head slowly lowered and rose on him. His tip poked at my throat. He thrust his fingers aggressively in me and expressed his undying love for me as he spilled out into my mouth. And I took it all in. I looked up into his face. His eyes remained closed and a look of exhilaration spread across his face. He was motionless, but moved by the way only I knew how to love him. *Bet she can't do it like me.*

I took him back to work and decided I would call Tracey and let her know that I'd pick up DJ, because I was leaving work early. Maybe she received subliminal messages when Dwight and I crept off, because I sensed some irritation in her voice. When I got off the phone with her, I called Dwight and told him how she sounded. He said he'd noticed she'd been tense over the past couple of days.

I suggested, "Maybe we need a vacation."

He asked me to research a trip to Jamaica. There were couple resorts and family resorts, but where does a threesome go? I decided to call Half Moon, a resort that I used to frequent with another married man, and asked if they could offer me a package for three. The Imperial Suite would be ideal because there was a bedroom and a plush living room. And the additional adult was only eighty dollars extra per night. I asked my mother if she'd be willing to keep DJ if we booked the trip. She agreed and I clicked BOOK IT.

CHAPTER 40

Tracey

When Dwight first mentioned that we were going away to Jamaica, I was so excited about me and him having alone time. That was until he mentioned that Alicia was coming, too! I should have known better. All this sharing is becoming old. She is starting to annoy, irritate, and all the above. But at least on this trip I would be sharing him with only one person and not four. There would be no children and seven days of adult conversation and half of it will be spent alone with the man I love.

The day before the trip I flew with the girls to Jacksonville. I spent an extra three hundred eighty-nine dollars just to take them to Jacksonville. Dwight told me to let the girls fly alone, but I just couldn't imagine it, although the airline guaranteed they would be safe. After getting them there securely, I just wanted to hurry home to finish packing. Mama Dee was at the airport gates waiting for them. I gave them hugs and kisses and went to go catch my next plane.

• • •

I traveled fourteen hundred plus miles by plane in less than ten hours and I was tired and had a bad case of jet lag. Dwight was supposed to meet me when I returned, but he wasn't there so I took a cab home. His and Alicia's cars were parked outside. I walked in the house and saw DJ sitting alone downstairs. I didn't know what was going on. But I knew they better have a good excuse for not picking me up from the airport.

"Where's everybody at, huh?" I asked as I picked DJ out of his high chair. I jogged up the steps and saw Alicia sitting on the floor crying.

"What's wrong with you, girl?" I asked.

"Nothing," she said between sniffles as she held her knees.

"You sure?" I asked as I looked over at Dwight, who was standing over her.

"Yeah, I'm okay. It's nothing . . . I just wish that DJ could know the other side of his family. I wanted him to go to Jacksonville, too! I don't know my dad's family. It's just I feel like I'm repeating the cycle. You know."

I gave Dwight another look like *you got to be kidding me.* There was no nice way to tell her she was overreacting. Dwight backed away from her and stood against the opposite wall of the hallway with his arms folded. I walked over to her and sat down next to her with DJ still in my arms.

"Um, I understand how ya feel. But come on, nobody is going to understand this. You know that, right?"

"We need to make them understand," she cried.

"Alicia, listen. DJ will meet the rest of the family, but not right now. We are about to go on this vacation. Let's have fun and discuss this when we get back." I pulled her slouched body up off the ground.

"Come on, let's go pack for the trip. We all need this vacation, alright?"

"You're right," she said as she wiped away her tears with her fingers.

"Now go pack."

By the next morning Alicia was still playing the I-am-so-upset card. I was through with it and her. This was her idea to go on vacation and now she was about to ruin it. Her mother came and picked up DJ and gave us all a judgmental look. *Whatever*, I thought. The only thing that mattered was my husband right now.

The bright sun was absent from the beautiful Jamaican skyline. It wasn't exactly dreary outside but the sky was grayish with trails of white in between. The shuttle pulled up in front of our hotel. The hotel was peach and white with gold trimming going up the woodwork. Palm trees and tropical pink and yellow flowers were on both sides of the entrance. Dwight got out of the van first. He helped me and then Alicia. The driver handed our luggage to the bellhop, who was wearing all white with gold buttons running straight down the center of his coat. His dark brown skin had deep dark cherry tones.

"Welcome to Jamaica," he said with a heavy accent as he began pushing our luggage to the lobby. We stood in the lobby, and there was beautiful artwork on the ceiling.

Another woman welcomed us again. Alicia checked us in as Dwight held my hand and walked to get a better look at the ocean. The infinity pool was right by the beach. It was very breezy and it definitely was going to rain. Alicia came and tapped us to let us know our room was ready. We entered our adjoining rooms. They were mostly white with island colorful decor.

"This was a great idea, Miss Alicia," I said.

"You're welcome, Miss Tracey."

"So what do you want to do first?"

"I'm going to get in the pool," she said as she pulled her indigo blue bikini out of her bag. As soon as she went into the bathroom Dwight kissed me on my neck and pulled me into my room.

"Go to the beach, Alicia; we will be up here getting some rest," I said as I giggled and shut the door.

"Dwight, I miss us spending time together," I said as he slowly kissed the back of my calves and thighs. He carefully took my panties off with his mouth.

"I know. I'm so glad Alicia planned this trip for us. She is so considerate." Why did Alicia's name have to come up when we were spending time alone and he was kissing on me? I wasn't going to worry about that right now. Because my man was about to pleasure me. I could feel the heat from his breath approaching my spot. And then he was there— his tongue began to dip up and down between the opening of my legs. I moaned loudly. I moaned because it felt so good and I moaned because I wanted Alicia to hear me. And me screaming made his tongue enter deeper and penetrate harder. I was screaming and saying, "Oh my God, Dwight." I wanted her to know that he made me feel like this and she would never ever be able to replace me. Our trip was seven days long. I was going to enjoy every minute of it.

First thing in the morning, Alicia came and knocked on the door. I answered. I had that all-night-sex glow that I wanted to show her.

"I was seeing if Dwight was ready to go snorkeling."

"He is not up yet, Alicia. Give him a little bit. When he wakes up I will tell him to knock on the door." At least I had thought Dwight was asleep. But he came up from behind me, wiping his eyes and yawning, and told Alicia to give him a minute.

I knew I was being selfish, but I wanted to have breakfast with Dwight. I wasn't ready to turn him over just yet. But it was her turn to do an activity with him. I sulked in the bathroom as Dwight showered and dressed quickly, leaving to go snorkeling with her.

I had nothing planned for the day. I wanted to get a good look at the island and maybe pick up my souvenirs. I dialed Mama Dee and checked on my girls.

"They are fine. You're not going to call here every day are you?"

"Of course not."

"Good, well, we just came in from getting some groceries. How is Jamaica?" Mama Dee asked, out of breath.

"Beautiful."

"Where is my son?"

"He is at the pool."

"Don't leave him alone with those island women." She laughed.

"I'm not. I just came up to change my clothes."

"Where are you going today?"

"Sightseeing and snorkeling." I said the first thing that came to mind.

"Well, have fun."

"I will." Truth be told, I didn't know what I was going to do with my day. I was in this beautiful place and all alone. I couldn't wait until tomorrow when it would be my turn again. I came downstairs and sat by the pool in a yellow lounge chair all day. The rays of the sun put me to sleep. I felt so relaxed. A waiter came up in white shorts and a white shirt, and asked me if there was anything he could get me from the bar.

"What do you suggest?" I asked the Caribbean man with long locks flowing down his muscular shoulders.

"Our special is the Islander. It has a splash of pineapple juice, coconut, and rum."

"Okay, I'll take that."

After a few drinks I was ready to party, but there was no one to party with. I went back up to the room to see if they had returned. I wrote them a note telling them to come down to the pool area. After a few hours of making small talk with other guests and drinking by myself, I walked down to the beach. The sun was setting and there were white gazebos on the beach. Couples and wedding parties were everywhere. They all looked so happy and excited. I smiled as one bride in an ivory dress kissed her husband after he dipped her back over his arm. They appeared to be so in love, like me and Dwight used to be. I then began to wonder where and what Alicia was doing with my husband.

Eleven in the evening and I was still by myself. They didn't call or come back to the room. I know last night me and Dwight stayed in without her, but it wasn't the whole day. I didn't want to call their cell phones, but I did anyway, only to hear them ring in the room. I was getting upset thinking about how much fun they were having.

I attempted to watch television, but there was nothing on but old movies I had already seen. And then I heard the door opening. It was Dwight. I jumped up and said, "Hey, baby." As soon as he came in my entire mood changed.

"Hey."

"What y'all do all day?"

"We went to the other side of the island. This place is beautiful," he said as he undressed and turned the shower on. I undressed and followed him. As I stepped in, he turned the shower off.

"What are you doing?" he asked as he reached for a towel to dry off.

"I'm getting in with you," I said, looking up at him and wondering why he was showering so quickly.

"I was just coming up to change my clothes. Me and Alicia are going on the beach to talk. I'll be right back. I just have to calm her down. She is having a rough time still about DJ not meeting Mama Dee. Then from there we'll probably hang out at the bar. You can come if you like."

"No, I'm okay. I'm tired. I'll get ready for our day tomorrow."

Dwight didn't come right back. I waited up and listened out. Then at four-fifteen I heard them enter the room. I turned the volume down on my remote. There was all this groaning and thumping. I could envision what they were doing by the way the bed was moving and the sound of Dwight panting. What I was hearing was making my body sick. I turned the volume up and placed the pillows over my head to silence their noise.

One day with me, the next with her, and it should have been my turn again. But those two decided it was group date day. We went Jet Skiing and sightseeing. It was an okay day. Dwight was showing me a lot of attention and I didn't feel left out. We took so many pictures of all the scenery.

At night we all got dressed up and went to a club. An island man approached us and asked if we wanted any weed. I didn't know what the hell he was talking about. But Alicia did. He looked kind of scary to me. His dreads were all the way down his back. And he wasn't wearing a shirt. The white part of his eyes were yellow, surrounded with red lines. She walked over to him unafraid, even though he could have been a cop or anything. She said yes and gave him money, and he gave her a little bag of marijuana. I thought for sure Dwight would look at her like she was crazy. But he asked him if he had any paper. Dwight hadn't smoked weed since college and now he was with it. I was speechless. Alicia grabbed Dwight's hand and said, "Let's smoke this on the beach."

The waves came crashing in, giving us a gentle breeze each time. It was so dark you couldn't even see the water, but you could hear it. Alicia rolled and lit up the weed like a professional. She inhaled it long and hard until the tip turned a bright orange with traces of black. Silly Alicia even had Dwight take a picture of her smoking. I laughed at her dumb ass. Then she passed it to Dwight. He took a couple of tokes and he placed it in my mouth. I inhaled and began to cough. My chest was burning a little.

"What is in this?" I said, coughing again and turning the joint sideways.

"That is only the best weed in the world." Alicia chuckled as she patted my back a few times. Dwight lay on his back, blowing rings of smoke out of his mouth. Alicia scooted over to him and took the joint and did something I told her not to ever do. She kissed my husband in front of my face. I just sat there with my knees up, looking into the ocean, thinking. I wasn't supposed to but I was becoming jealous.

They kissed for a few moments and then she passed the weed back to me. I took a few tokes and inhaled it all in. It began mellowing me out. I turned my head, ignoring them both and thought about all that was going on.

Dwight tapped me, *Come on, babe.* I stood up and held his hand. His other hand was locked with Alicia's. He stopped, turned to me and then to her, and said, "I don't care what the world says about us. I have everything I need. I'll never need another woman. Our children, our family is what matters to me. I am so lucky to have y'all in my life." He kissed me then he kissed her again.

"I am committed to us, to our life. Dwight, I love you, and I love your family, and I will do whatever it takes to keep our family together," Alicia said.

It was my turn. I couldn't say anything. They both looked at me.

"Go ahead."

"I don't know what to say. We are a family and I am committed to my family. No matter what anyone thinks."

"You okay?" Dwight asked as he noticed I wasn't into this little declaration-of-love commitment ceremony.

"Yeah, I'm fine."

CHAPTER 41

Tracey

They were so into each other, even on the ride home on the plane. They didn't notice that I hadn't opened my mouth the entire flight. This was the first vacation in my life that I couldn't wait to get home. The days Dwight spent with Alicia I was mad. And the days he spent with me I was thinking about why he couldn't be satisfied with just me. As soon as our plane touched the tarmac I immediately opened my phone to dial Mama Dee to tell her I would be there tomorrow to pick up the girls.

"Mama Dee, we're home."

"How was your trip?" she asked.

"It was good."

"Great, well, don't worry about coming to get the girls. We are already here."

"You're already where?" I asked as I sat up in my chair.

"In Maryland. I knew you were tired so I drove them home. I'll bring them past in the morning."

"In the morning . . . um. No, I'll meet you, Mama Dee,"

I said as I looked over at Dwight. He was still asleep. I tapped him and woke him.

"Dwight, your mother is in Maryland," I whispered. His eyes popped open.

"Oh my God."

"What are you going to tell her?" Dwight asked.

"I don't know." I just knew that Mama Dee was not going to know about Alicia or DJ, not right now. The time was not right.

He woke Alicia and she still looked at him like he was a god. As we exited the plane, Alicia announced she had to go to the bathroom. She could judge by the expression on my face that something was wrong, so she asked me, "Are you okay?" I said yes, then she turned to Dwight and asked him the same question.

"She's fine, Alicia," he said, snapping at her. "We will meet you at baggage claim."

Dwight tried to get our luggage off the ramp. I walked over to him to act like I was helping him.

"What are you going to do with her?"

"We are going to drop her off at her mother's. Go get us a taxi."

I walked away and went out and got in the taxi line. Dwight entered the cab and gave Alicia's mom's address. Alicia entered last, still oblivious to what was going on. She was still on cloud nine, saying she couldn't wait to get the pictures printed and talking about how much fun she had. I remained quiet, looking out the window.

"We can leave DJ there until the morning—he is probably asleep anyway," she said as the cab pulled in front of her mother's house.

"No, um, we have to talk. Pop the trunk," Dwight said, instructing the cab driver. He pulled Alicia's luggage out.

"My mom is in town and you can't be there when she comes over." The look on her face was priceless. She was so taken by surprise she couldn't get what she wanted to say out of her mouth.

"What? Why not? I'm your wife, too! Your son is a Wilson. This is not right, Dwight. So you want me to just stay away? Your son doesn't get to meet your mother?"

"Alicia, there is no discussion. That's not going to happen," Dwight said. I turned my head in the other direction. They could duke it out. I don't know what he told her, but she ran in the house and began crying. I felt a little bit of satisfaction seeing her in tears.

When I arrived home I went into her room and took down her pictures, and I moved all of DJ's belongings to the basement. I looked in every room to make sure there wasn't a trace of another woman. I felt like I erased all evidence of Alicia.

Mama Dee was at the door bright and early. Jordan ran up to me and held my legs.

"I missed you, Mommy," Destiny said.

"I missed you, too, Des."

"Where is DJ? I missed him so much!" Jordan asked.

"He went to his house. They will be back. Take your things upstairs," Dwight said sternly, probably mad that she had mentioned her brother's name in the presence of her grandmother.

"Mom, thank you for bringing them home. I have to get out of here and get to work," he said as he gave her a kiss on the cheek. She damn near wiped his kiss off. Mama Dee was looking all around.

"Have a seat. You want me to make you some coffee?"

"No, because I'm not staying that long."

"Where are you in a rush to?" I asked.

"Nowhere, I'm just not staying here. Not with all this foolishness going on."

"What foolishness?" I asked, perplexed.

"You know what I'm talking about, Tracey. I've known you since you were a girl and I want to tell you that I have never been more disappointed in you in my life."

"What are you talking about, Mama Dee?" I said as if I were clueless and she was a senile old lady.

"All I have to say is, you need to clean house and close the back door you open, and don't ever let it swing open again."

"Mama Dee, I don't know what impression you got. But there is nothing going on."

Mama Dee stood up and looked me directly in my face and said, "Your children know that Daddy kisses Alicia like he kisses Mommy. They also told me that Auntie Alicia went on vacation with you, too! Tracey, one thing about children is that they are very perceptive and notice everything you don't. Your secret is not secret. Besides, how does the housekeeper work and you watch her baby? The only winner is Dwight—he is getting over big time. And your children. I can't believe you with this Auntie Alicia business. Wait until they are old enough to realize what's going on. They probably will say my mother was a weak-ass woman. She'd rather let her man walk over her than leave him. I pray you get yourself together, Tracey," she said as she left me on the sofa, stunned. How did she know? How did Jordan and Destiny know? Her words crept in my mind all day. I lay in my bed alone. Alicia had been calling Dwight all morning and I didn't feel like talking to her.

Mama Dee is right—if I don't stop this soon, my children won't have respect for me. In the past few weeks I've been losing control. Alicia has us going on a vacation that I didn't plan. This is insanity and I can't take it anymore. What if Dwight wakes up one day and we are not enough and he wants to add to the stable? And he asks for a third and fourth wife? One minute I was happily married. The next my husband has a son by this random woman who I didn't know anything about. I sat and looked at the girls swinging back and forth on the swings in the backyard. How much did my girls know? What did they see? I had to talk to someone. Mama Dee already said she was disgusted with me, but I still called her. Before she picked up, I was hysterically crying.

"Stop crying."

"I don't know what to do. I'm ready to leave him. But I don't want to leave him, I want to leave her. How do I get him to leave her? Mama Dee I didn't want to lose him. I wanted to tell him to choose me or her, but I was so scared. . . ."

"And you thought he would pick her, huh?"

"I wasn't sure, Mama Dee. I just wanted him to be happy and us to be a family again. I caught him in the bathroom one night, crying like a baby, and I thought it would be best if we had an open marriage."

"Tracey Yvette Wilson, I would have never thought you would stoop so low."

"I know it was wrong. I was dumb, but how can I get out of it now? I mean, I just wanna be back home and have a normal life."

"I don't know what to tell you. You got to plan this one out. Get that hussy out of your house, by any means necessary. If you got to, lie on the bitch and say she stole some money from you."

"You're right, I got to think of something. I'll do my best."

"Now, I taught you better than that. All good women know how to plot and scheme."

Mama Dee was right. Alicia had to go, and I had to get her out of my house. My mind began to wander and I thought of a bunch of things. I knew the job situation would be a problem. Dwight was making a lot more money in Maryland. Not only that, what would make him hate her as much as I did? And what could I do to make sure he never wanted to see her again?

I wanted a normal family. Me and my husband and my two children. I couldn't even remember what normal family life is like. It wasn't this arrangement that had my neighbors looking at me sideways. I was getting my man back— this sharing shit was not working out. We were good before her and we would be good after her. I had to prove to Dwight that this was not going to work out.

CHAPTER 42

Alicia

You better become an active participant in your son's life. I thought somehow those words were just my imagination running away from me. But when I glanced at my mother, her expression confirmed they came directly from her mouth. Why did she feel the need to ridicule me on my son's first birthday? I said, "What did you say?"

She didn't back down. In fact, she appeared irritated with me and ready for war. She repeated, "You better become an active participant in your son's life."

"Ma, I know what I'm doing!"

I scurried around the house getting things together for the party. Tracey had gone out to pick up the cake. The girls and Dwight were in the yard decorating. The moon bounce would be delivered any minute. Why did she pick this moment to start a fight?

"You have no clue. Do you hear him?"

DJ was whining for no reason in his playpen. In fact, he

was driving me up a wall. Now, because he was crying in vain, I'm not an active participant.

I put the baked beans in the oven and said, "Why don't you get him?"

She chuckled. "I should get him?"

"Yes, you get him. It's not going to kill him to cry a little. I have to finish getting things together. I fed him. I changed him. He's fine."

She slammed her cup on the island. "Girl, he's crying for his mother."

"I had him on my hip all morning. And he's still crying. What am I supposed to do?"

She shook her head. "Alicia, he thinks Tracey is his mother."

She took a deep breath and her eyes dimmed. She pitied me. My heart sank and I thought for a second before I spoke, "Ma, I work. Tracey is with him more than I am. What can I say?"

"It doesn't even bother you."

"You're not here every day. He knows I'm his mother."

She huffed. "You're just a hardhead. Why did I think you'd start listening now?"

I sucked my teeth and continued getting things together. When she noticed my irritation, she sighed. "I'm not trying to hurt you. You're my baby and I only want the best for you."

"What are you trying to do? You pick his birthday to tell me I'm a bad mother."

"I never said you were a bad mother—"

She was interrupted by Tracey coming through the entrance from the garage. We stopped abruptly. It was obvious that we were discussing something we didn't want her to know about. She looked offended. I tried to play it off.

"Is it hot out there?"

"Yeah."

She dropped the cake on the table and didn't say much to my mother or me. DJ babbled with excitement as she entered the family room. She stood in front of his playpen. "What are you talking about?"

He laughed hard. She asked again, "I didn't hear you. What did you say?"

He bounced his knees and screamed with joy. I suddenly hated how she related to the child that I gave birth to. My eyes connected with my mother's. Her smirk was slightly arrogant, insinuating that she told me so.

What could I do now? Why did it matter? We were in a different situation. DJ was lucky enough to have two mothers. As I tried to rationalize my emotions in my mind, my mother got up and said, "I'm going outside for a smoke."

Tracey came back into the kitchen. She seemed to be responding with one-word answers. There was an unspoken dispute between us. Unfortunately, we fought over two separate things. She thought my mother and I were talking about her. And I wondered if she was strategically being a better mother to my son than me.

When the moon bounce guy arrived, my mother came in to let me know. "He's on his way to the backyard. One of you needs to let him know where to put it."

We spoke at the same time. "Dwight is out there."

She shrugged. "Okay."

Her smoke break lightened her mood. Why was I pissed at her for forcing me to recognize the truth? I smirked at her and she knew I'd forgiven her. She gave me a quick hug and said, "You okay, baby. Everything's coming together."

Tracey said, "Did you give the girls something to eat?"

"Shit! I forgot."

She didn't acknowledge my negligence and walked out on the deck. She called the girls into the house. They came reluctantly. After they finished eating, they all went upstairs to get ready for the party.

My mother took DJ to get ready and I finished the goody bags. I stepped out on the deck and watched Dwight in the yard. He obviously felt me staring at him and waved for me to come closer.

I slouched toward him. He smiled. "What's wrong, baby?"

"Do you think I'm a good mother?"

"Of course you're a good mother."

"Who do you think is a better mother?"

His chin sagged. "Don't do that. You know we keep competition out of this relationship."

I curled my lips. "You're right. Don't you have to get ready?"

"Yeah. When are you getting ready?"

He intertwined his fingers with mine. It was a blessing that I didn't doubt his love. I looked into his eyes. He asked, "What's wrong?"

"Nothing."

"You still look sad."

"I'm not sad. C'mon, let's get ready."

He smiled. "Let's play in the moon bounce first."

I guess my huge smile said okay. He started running to the moon bounce and I felt that was a summons to race. I chased him and finally caught up. He was really trying to win. He reached his hand out like he was crashing through a finish line. We wheezed as we attempted to catch our breath. I laughed and he laughed harder. "I won."

As I slipped my shoes off, I looked up at him. "I thought there was no competition in this family."

He tilted his head. "What's on your mind?"

"Nothing. Take your shoes off."

He kicked his shoes off and jumped in. I dove in behind him. We rolled around and jumped up and down like this was our party. We giggled uncontrollably until Tracey's voice pierced through us. He looked at me. I looked at him. It was as if we'd been caught stealing money from our mother's purse. He peeped out first.

"What's up?"

"People will be here in thirty minutes. What are you guys doing?"

"Just making sure everything is fine."

She stormed back into the house and we laughed. I said, "C'mon. Let's go."

"Give me a kiss first."

I rolled over and kissed him. He said, "I'm going to get dressed in your room."

I smiled and slid out of the tent. He climbed out and began to jog. "I was trying to give you a head start."

I began to sprint. The slight slope heading to the house propelled me ahead of him. I reached the deck seconds before he did. My hands pumped in the air. "I won! I won!"

He tried to grab my shirt and I fought him away. We shared love taps all the way through the sliding glass doors. Our giggling came to an abrupt halt when everyone including the kids looked at us as if we were having more fun than we should be while everyone else was preparing for the party.

I smirked and sashayed into my bedroom. Dwight followed. He closed the door behind him. "Baby, let's take a shower together."

I laughed. "Dwight, we can't."

"Why not?"

"We only have thirty minutes to get ready."

"We can do two things at once, shower and make love."

I rushed into the bathroom and turned on the shower. "C'mon, we got to hurry up. Lock the door."

He pulled off his shirt. "I already did."

"I should have known."

We hopped in the shower together, both facing the front. He wrapped his arms around me and began kissing my neck. I put my hands on the back of his head. The water ran down our bodies and we clung to each other. Finally, he turned me around and lifted my thighs so my legs could wrap around him. We grinded slowly before he penetrated. I rested my head on his shoulder. We were alone, long before DJ, long before the arrival of Tracey. Nothing outside of our bedroom mattered. That is until our climax was interrupted with loud banging outside the door. I was distracted, but he held me tightly and pumped aggressively until he released inside of me. Suddenly, I was in a rush to get clean and get out of the bathroom. Company was coming and we didn't need any tension among us. Not that it wasn't already there.

I rushed out of the bathroom. "Who's there?"

No one answered. I rushed to get ready, tossing Dwight a pair of jeans and a polo shirt. "Here, baby, hurry up."

I rushed out of the room half wrinkled, half made up. My mother and Tracey had all of the food out on the picnic table. I grabbed some serving bowls and poured pretzels and chips in them. Tracey came through the sliding glass door. "So glad you decided to join us."

I smiled slightly, but didn't feed into it. Dwight rushed out of the bedroom. We had that post-sex connection. He winked at me. I winked at him. We were smiling for no reason as we greeted incoming guests.

The crew pretty much came one after the other. Andrea brought three kids from her church, Gina brought her two nieces, and Tammy brought her daughter. And that was pretty much the entire party.

Tammy decided to make some spiked punch for the adults. We sipped and chatted and got more joy out of the kids than necessary. Dwight and I both drank, but of course Tracey stayed sober.

Unconsciously, we shared love taps throughout the day. It wasn't until after we sang "Happy Birthday" and Dwight stood behind me with his arm wrapped around me while I bent over DJ that Gina made me realize it. She helped me hand out the ice cream and cake. I cut small pieces of cake and she put a dollop of ice cream on the side. Tracey settled the kids as we handed down the small plates. Gina said, "She's a better woman than me."

"You mean we're both better women than you."

She covered her mouth as she spoke softly to me, "You and Dwight touch and feel all the time. I couldn't handle that."

"Whatever. She's not thinking about me and Dwight. Her main focus is the kids."

"Hmmm. Don't sleep. She's a woman before she's a mother."

I looked down the table at Tracey so effortlessly handling all of the kids and said, "Nah, not Tracey. She's a mother first."

CHAPTER 43

Tracey

DJ was sitting in his high chair. I was feeding him applesauce and scrambled eggs. Alicia sat across from me, drinking coffee. She had no idea I hated her. I hated her being in my house. She was waiting for me to finish feeding DJ so she could go to work.

"Why don't you go ahead to the office? I'll drop DJ off at day care."

"You sure?"

"Yeah, girl, I'm sure."

"I don't know what I would do without you," she said as she hugged DJ then me. *I know what I would do without you.*

I said, "Oh, yeah. I forgot to tell you. Dwight wanted you to sign this insurance form. It's for his life insurance." Just as I thought, she trusted me. She didn't even look at the paper. She walked out of the house and I peeled the bogus page off. I had the document I needed to prove she was unfit and I refused to share Dwight any longer.

• • •

As soon as she left for work, I tore her room apart. I found letters from someone named Deshaun, a jailbird pledging his undying love for her and asking when she was coming to see him again. That was a bit of information that I wasn't expecting, but I was damn sure happy to find. I got her laptop, looked through her pictures, her e-mails, and her drawers. In her drawers I found all types of dildos, questionable pornography, and a prescription for Zoloft. She was really a mess. I collected all the incriminating information and proceeded to check her criminal record online. Alicia was making this easier than I thought it would be. Turns out, she admitted to drug use in a court case nearly ten years ago.

The plan was simple: to expose her past and have Dwight doubt her stability. I was going to prove to Dwight that she was a crazy felon who had jailbird and lesbian lovers, was an unfit mother, and who had signed over her parental rights. I typed up a fake letter from Alicia's crazy lover and e-mailed it from a bogus Yahoo account I made up. Then I opened it up from her e-mail address and printed it out.

Dear Alicia,

I have waited long enough for you to break up with him. You said you needed time. I gave you that. You need to start taking your medicine and stop worrying about what the world thinks about you. I don't know why you are ashamed of what you are. Tell him the truth. You are not bisexual, you are a lesbian. I know you, girl. I love you, girl. You have to tell him. I want you back, girl, but don't come back to me with that baby. Leave that baby with him. Alicia, I love you but you got to do something NOW!! If you don't make a decision soon, then I'm going to have to hurt you, him, and his family.

> *Love,*
> *Erica*

I acted normal, but I plotted daily toward the demise of Alicia Dixon. When all my data was in order, I waited for Alicia's regular Thursday night out. That way, I'd have all evening to drill it in. Around one, I called Dwight frantically.

"Baby, I need you to come home."

"Why, what's up?"

"It's an emergency."

Dwight was home in a matter of minutes. I was crying when he got there. His chest sunk, because he knew me long enough to know it was bad news. I covered my face and sniffled. "Dwight, how long did you know her before you started fucking her? What kind of tricks did she do on you?"

He looked away and then back at me. "Tracey, what's going on?" I told him to have a seat and placed the jail letters, the bottle of Zoloft, the sex toys, pornography, the fake letter, and her criminal record all over the table.

"What's all this?"

"You don't even really know the trash you brought into our life. Into our family! Dwight, how could you? Did you know she was a part-time lesbian and full-time drug addict? Huh? Did you know that, Dwight?" I asked as I pointed to the letters.

"What are you talking about? Where did you get these letters from?" he asked as he began reading.

"I was folding clothes and I put her clothes in her room and she had everything all in her room in plain sight. Like she doesn't care."

"I can't believe this," he said in disbelief.

"Neither can I, Dwight, how could you? She told me she had sex with a woman before, but I didn't think it was a big deal when her friends mentioned it to me. But this woman in the letter says she wants her back and to leave DJ. It just doesn't make sense. I was still trying not to believe until she gave me these custody papers, Dwight. I mean, is she really crazy? Do we really have a crazy lady living in our house?" Dwight didn't know what to say. He just stood examining everything, especially the signed custody form. And to add one more blow, I added, "And did you read the part of the letter where she said she is going to hurt us? I mean come on, what do I have to do with it? Better yet, what do our daughters have to do with them? It is not right. She is a liar and just unfit. Baby, I'm sorry. I know you trusted her, but I think she tricked us." I took a deep breath.

He ran his hands down his face. "Tracey, I'm so sorry. I didn't know about any of this. I'm so sorry. What have I done?"

Rubbing the side of his face, I said, "Nothing that we can't fix."

"Man, I don't believe this." He sprang up and headed toward her room. "She has to go. She has to move out today and she is not taking DJ with her."

"No, baby. We've got to get the hell out of here. Maryland. This house. That job. These fast women here. We have to go back home, but we gotta be smart. We can't just throw her out. She'll get vindictive. We gotta make sure everything is right before we confront."

He stomped around. "How the hell do you think I can wait to confront her?"

"Look, we don't want her to do nothing crazy like disappear with DJ, and lawd knows she is a terrible mother."

He huffed and puffed. "So, you're telling me not to say anything."

"Baby, we have to protect DJ and make sure this transition is smooth. I think she'll retract on the custody agreement if she thinks we're coming up against her."

He sat back down and took a few more breaths. "You're right. We gotta be smart about this." He opened his arms for me to come hug him. I smiled, because I'd done it and he had fallen right into the trap, no questions asked.

"So, what are you going to do about this house?"

He huffed, "I don't know. I'm not saying we're moving back today. I guess I'll sell it. I have to find a job. It's just so much to think about. Maybe I need to just rest for a while."

CHAPTER 44

Alicia

Maybe it was my mother's warnings, but I'd begun to feel like the outsider. I walked in the house after my evening jog and the smell of brownies greeted me at the door. Tracey knew they were my weakness and I was curious if she made them so that my ass could spread as wide as hers. I pulled my earphones off and the girls giggled. "DJ, say 'stop.'"

He repeated, "Op!"

Tracey and Dwight laughed, but when I entered the family room all the happiness ceased. Even Jordan and Destiny glared at me. I smirked. "Hey, y'all."

Tracey said, "That was a long run. I thought you got lost."

You could use a damn long run yourself. I gulped down some water. "Yeah, sometimes when I get in my own world I just run until I get lost."

Dwight stood up. "Good thing we're here to take care of your son."

My neck snapped back as he walked out of the family room and headed toward me. I took another sip from my water bottle to wash down the insult. "Yeah, I guess it is a good thing," I said, rolling my eyes.

"The least you can do is speak to him." I felt like I should bang him in his mouth, but I didn't know where all this anger was coming from. He continued, "I mean, I did pick him up from day care."

I ignored him and headed into the family room. "DJ. How's Mommy's boy?" He cracked up laughing. I sang his name again, "DJ. Hey, boo-boo!"

I reached for him and he clung to Tracey, so I pulled him from her. Jordan and Destiny started telling me everything he'd been doing. Then Destiny said, "Something stinks."

Tracey smirked at me. I said, "Well, when you work out, your body sweats and when it's warm out you can smell bad. I'm getting into the shower in a minute."

I played with DJ for a few more minutes and left the room in search of Dwight. When I walked in the room, he was there. "Do you still regret getting pregnant with DJ?"

"Dwight, what kind of question is that?"

"I just wonder sometimes."

I huffed and walked into my bathroom to turn the shower on. "Maybe Tracey is better at it than me, but yes, I am happy being a mother."

I tossed my smelly workout clothes on him. He looked like he wanted to say more, but he dropped his head. I walked back out of the bathroom with no clothes on. "Dwight, what's wrong?" He rubbed my butt as I stood in front of him. I cupped his chin in my hand. "Why have you been acting strange? We don't talk like we used to. I miss you."

He nodded. "I know."

"Come take a shower with me."

He took a deep breath. He'd slept on the couch for the past few nights, not giving me or Tracey our quality time. I'd narrowed it down to him being overwhelmed at work. "Nah, go ahead."

I kissed his forehead and massaged his neck. "You know, we were friends first."

"Yeah, I know."

I stepped in the shower, frustrated. The added amenity of our situation was the babysitting assistance, and now I was being judged for taking advantage of it. A part of me wanted to cry, but then the other part knew that I was contributing greatly to the household. She had yet to sell a home, so I was picking up everybody's slack. Shit, I deserved to have twenty-four-hour day-care services. When I got out of the shower, I got dressed and walked into the room to tell Tracey I'd be right back.

She said, "Where you going, girl?"

"I just need to get my mind together."

"Well, if you need a designated driver, call me," she said, smiling. At least she gave a damn, because Dwight just sat there, staring at the fan, aimlessly bouncing DJ on his knee.

I walked over and kissed DJ. Dwight said, "Have fun."

It seemed sarcastic, but I didn't feed into it. Maybe he was going through his quarterly male PMS. I shrugged. "I will."

When I left the house, I sat in my car without a destination in mind. I called Tammy, because she lived the closest. Inside Tammy's place, I poured my heart out about how I felt that they were insinuating that I was a bad mother. She laughed. "Shit, you're not a good mother."

I pouted. "Don't say that."

"Well, you're not. You're just doing the best that can be expected of you. You can't be a great mother and bring home the bacon, too. Shit, lucky for you, you got a chick living with you that fries that shit in a pan when you get off."

Suddenly, I was laughing and back in good spirits again. I didn't drink too much because I didn't want anyone to *have* to come and get me.

When I walked in the house, Tracey and the kids had gone upstairs. I stood in the kitchen, staring at Dwight while he stared at the television. I sat at the kitchen table in the dark. "Dwight."

"Yes," he said without turning to face me.

"Are you sleeping out here again?"

"Nah, I'm sleeping upstairs."

I rationalized there would be periods where one wife would get more attention than the other. I began to feel sorry for Tracey, for all the times when I was so confident and content, knowing he was more connected to me than to her. I didn't like the way I felt. It was empty and lonely in a house full of people.

CHAPTER 45

Tracey

The day had come. Alicia awoke to my man for what would be the last time. I got up and got dressed. I was feeding DJ breakfast when she came down the steps smiling at her son. I was acting too normal, even told him to say bye-bye to Mommy. I probably missed my calling, because I should be in Hollywood for my acting skills. Alicia didn't suspect a thing. We talked as usual and I even offered to make her breakfast. She had no clue that I'd put the girls on a plane an hour ago. Danielle would meet them at the airport.

Dwight had turned in his resignation nearly two weeks ago. He was waiting for me to call and let him know when she left. We were on our way home, back to our normal life. And most important, she had no clue that the "life insurance" document granted full custody of DJ to Dwight and me.

The minute she walked out the door I started bringing bags out of the basement and dialed Dwight. "She's gone."

"I'll be right there," he said.

The movers would be here in two hours, so I started throwing things in big garbage bags, in the same hasty fashion that I left Jacksonville to come here.

The movers came in wearing blue jumpsuits and moved all our belongings in a matter of hours. Our house was empty and echoed as I walked through it to make sure we didn't leave anything. All that was left was Alicia's bedroom furniture and a bunch of her other random belongings. I looked around and couldn't believe it had been an entire year and I was finally doing what I intended on doing when I first arrived: take my man home. Dwight looked around and then at me and said, "I'm so sorry I took you through this. I don't ever want to look at another woman." He took my hand and we walked out of the hellhole together.

CHAPTER 46

Alicia

It seemed awfully weird that I hadn't spoken to Tracey or Dwight all day. I called his office phone and it kept going to voice mail. I tried the house and the phone just rang. Around five, I got concerned. When I called the day-care center to find out if Tracey had picked up DJ, they told me that he hadn't come in. My heart dropped.

I hoped everything was okay. In a frenzy, I ran out of work and flew in and out of traffic. I was reluctant to do so, but I called my mother. I didn't want to alarm her. It was primarily an attempt to calm myself down. Why did the tremble in her voice frighten me more?

"Ma, why aren't they answering the phone?"

"Baby, maybe they took the day to spend time alone. I don't know. I wish I had the answer."

My heartbeat was in my ears because I couldn't hear anything else as she attempted to rationalize my hysteria. My high speed slowed as I approached the house. I bit my lips. Calm down. These emotions are uncalled for. I peeled from my car. Huge tire tracks were in the lawn and my stomach began to bubble.

I opened the front door and the echo slapped me in my face. Empty! I rushed into the kitchen. Empty! I ran upstairs. Empty! I screamed for Dwight. I cursed at Tracey. "Somebody answer me! Where are you?" I ran into my bedroom. Everything that belonged to DJ, gone. I yelled, "No! No!"

I wanted to fight. I rushed into the kitchen searching for a knife. Everything in all of the drawers was gone. I wanted to run her over with my car. They all had smiled in my face this morning and everything now was gone. What did I do to deserve this?

I called and I called. My legs eventually couldn't bear the pain, and I found myself lying on the kitchen floor, crying. "Please, Lord. Please. Tell me this is all a dream."

Still, I hadn't absorbed everything. They had stolen my baby. Suddenly, my strength reappeared. I hopped up from the floor. I dialed 911.

In between sniffles, I said, "I would like to report a missing child."

I was hysterical as I tried to explain that my son's father and his wife kidnapped my son. The police came and interrogated me. *Just find my damn son!* I paced back and forth. The officers kept asking if they had left any notes or messages. Finally, we discovered a short note on my dresser explaining that they had gone back to Jacksonville. And the only explanation for this irrational stunt was that they no longer wanted to be a part of this arrangement. They wanted to go back to a normal life. In so many words, they were saying that I was the only eccentric one in the relationship and they were tired of living a lie. What prevented them from just talking to me? Why couldn't they just tell me? While I tried to explain the letters and our arrangement to the cops, I broke down. I thought we'd found the solution to an age-old problem, but everything had blown up in my face. The cops kidded about how cool they imagined our life to be. Did this shit look happy? This was stupid. I was stupid. At the end of the day, I was a mother trying to make things work with the father of her child. Did anybody see that I was in pain? My son could be anywhere on the road to Jacksonville and I was being questioned. After seemingly hours, they granted an AMBER Alert.

DJ's picture and name was posted on news stations from Maryland to Florida. I sat on my mother's couch and it flashed across the screen. I finally wanted to be a mother. I needed to be the best mother I could be. Just as I basked in believing I could get over, I got played. I'd treated Tracey like a live-in nanny. I failed to recognize the obvious love between her and Dwight. I cried because he was gone. I cried because I had convinced myself that he loved me more. I muffled my anguish with one of my mother's accent pillows. She rubbed my back and repeatedly apologized. She swore this was her fault.

It wasn't her fault that I'd grown to trust Tracey. It wasn't her fault that Dwight made me believe that I was the treasured wife. And most of all, it wasn't her fault that I had settled for this type of relationship.

We held each other and cried. All she ever had was me and I was the most important thing in the world to her. What would I do without her? What will I do without my son?

CHAPTER 47

Tracey

The moon was following me down the same highway I came up. We had Dwight's car in tow. I had accomplished what I had set out to do. It didn't work out exactly how I'd planned, but it didn't even matter anymore. I was so blessed I had gotten away from that stupid bitch. She didn't deserve Dwight. I was tickled just thinking about her coming home to an empty house. She probably called her mother and they sat on the steps and cried with each other.

Once we were back in Jacksonville, everything would fall right back into place. I missed my house. This ordeal was over, thanks to Mama Dee's ingenuity. We still hadn't decided how we were going to explain DJ to everyone. I guess we were just going to have to tell the truth. *It is what it is.*

The darkness of the winding road was making me tired. We had just crossed the South Carolina state line. We had been on the road for the past seven hours. Two hundred fifty miles from home. I'd had been doing eighty since I started driving. I began to search for a radio station to listen to. Country music stations seemed like the only stations I could pick up, then I heard an oldies station playing Diana Ross—"I'm Coming Out." Oldies were better than country music. The loud beat pumped me up more than I already was. As I sang along with Ms. Ross, I noticed police headlights behind us, so I slowed down. A ticket was the last thing I wanted to get. The cop raced up to the car as if he were going to crash into us. I pulled over to the side to let him go around. But instead of going around, the cop car flagged us over to the side of the road. Why was he stopping me? I woke Dwight.

"Dwight, wake up. The cops pulled me over," I said, as I nudged Dwight and the cop got out of his car. I hated these little racist towns. They didn't have anything better to do than to harass us. I heard the police officer's radio going off and he answered back, "I stopped them. I'm at marker 452." Before he reached the car, two other police cars pulled up in front of us.

"What's going on?" Dwight asked as he looked around at all the commotion.

"I don't know."

The police officer came to the window and asked me for my license. I handed it to him. He just looked down at the license and then asked Dwight for his.

"Can you tell me what I did, officer?"

He didn't respond to my question.

"What do you need his license for? You still didn't tell me why you even pulled me over."

He flashed his light on DJ in the backseat.

"Ma'am, can you get out of the car?"

"For what?"

"Get out of the car!" The officers came over to Dwight's window and asked him to get out of the car also.

"For what? I didn't do anything," I said.

"Ma'am, this is the last time I'm going to say it. Get out of the car with your hands up," the officer yelled.

I looked over at Dwight.

"Just listen to him." DJ was still asleep as the police officer instructed me to place my hands behind my back and place my fingers between each other. Then he put handcuffs on me.

"What are you arresting us for?"

"For the kidnapping of Dwight Wilson Junior."

"What?"

"There is a National AMBER Alert. For you, and this child."

"That's our son. We didn't kidnap him. We have custody of him. Please look in the glove compartment—you can see all of our paperwork." The officer went to the car and pulled everything out. He studied the paperwork. "We still have to take you in."

"You see the evidence right here."

"Yeah, but this all can be fraudulent. If this is real and you are telling the truth, then we will have to let you go," the officer said.

Maybe I did the wrong thing. Maybe I was wrong and about to get caught, I thought as I was whisked away to the police station.

A few hours later an older white man who identified himself as Lieutenant Mitchell came to my cell and said, "Ma'am, I am sorry. But when an AMBER Alert comes across we have to take them very seriously. We had to bring you into custody to verify everything was legitimate."

CHAPTER 48

Alicia

When the investigator called, he said, "Ms. Dixon."

I nodded at my mother because his voice sounded positive. I crossed my fingers. "Yes."

"We found DJ."

I mouthed, "They found him."

I said, "Where is he?"

"We found him in South Carolina." I was relaying all the messages to my mother. She raised her thumbs.

I asked, "What do I have to do?"

While we rejoiced, his tone changed. "We have a problem. Mr. Wilson had his birth certificate with him. He also has a court document where you granted him sole custody."

"Hell no! I never gave him custody. Why the hell would I do that?"

"Well, Ms. Dixon, you're going to have to explain it to a judge."

"What are you saying?" I yelled.

My mother looked at me. She yearned to know what was

being said on the other end. "They're trying to say that I gave him custody."

"Did you?"

I snapped at her. "Hell no! I wouldn't give anyone custody of my baby."

There was a suspicious look on her face. "Ma, I swear I didn't! I swear!"

The investigator seemed to be growing impatient with my ranting. Finally, he said, "Ms. Dixon, I do apologize if there is some misunderstanding, but he had the information ready for us."

"They forged my signature. There is no way in the world I would sign over my baby."

"I hate to tell you this, but I have to close this case. You're going to have to take this to a judge. Let me know if there is anything I can do for you."

I yelled, "Bring my fucking baby home!"

"I'm sorry. I won't be able to do that. You can give me a call tomorrow when you calm down and I'll help you proceed with filing a case."

"You can't help me if you can't bring my son home."

I slammed the phone down and wept in my mother's arms. We were both stunned. Who planned this out so well? How could they just disregard my feelings? I spent an entire year in a house with imposters. I thought he loved me. I thought she loved our arrangement. How could they be so heartless?

I almost allowed defeat to settle in when it dawned on me that I had to get to Jacksonville and I had to get there fast. My mother asked if we should drive. Hell no! I booked us one-way tickets on the first available flight, despite the $700-per-person price tag. What we didn't have packed, we wouldn't. We both had the necessities and the will to find our baby. I sat up and rocked until it was time to leave at four in the morning. My heart ached. I felt betrayed. My mind couldn't rest because I kept replaying my entire relationship with Dwight. How had I let everything go? I thought he was so innocent and I assumed that Tracey was naïve. Now, I was sitting here trying to solve the complicated problem they'd created. I hated them. I hated what they represented. They didn't deserve to be in DJ's life.

When we arrived in Jacksonville, all I had was a Zaba Search.com list of all of their previous addresses. My mother wanted to check in to a hotel before we began our hunt, but I didn't. I offered her the option of checking in and letting me go alone. She refused. So, with no sleep and a bunch of anxiety, we drove around Jacksonville.

My first stop was where I assumed Dwight's sister lived. My mother stayed in the car when I went to knock. My heart raced as I prepared to explain this long story to a woman who was clueless. I had gone along with Dwight and Tracey and had not told their family here about our arrangement because, as they claimed, they wouldn't understand. Tracey would always say we were socially forward and Jacksonville just wasn't ready. A slightly ghetto-looking girl with rollers and a scarf opened up.

"Hi, my name is Alicia Dixon. I mean, Alicia Wilson."

She frowned at me. "Ah-huh."

"I was married to your brother."

"What brother?"

"Dwight." I paused for her to absorb it. "We met in Maryland and—"

"I think you have the wrong Dwight. My brother has been married to the same woman for ten years."

"I know. Dwight and I had a baby and they brought my baby back here and I'm just trying to find him. Can you find them? Can you help me?"

"Do you think I'm fucking crazy? I'm not helping you. For all I know, you're crazy."

She closed the door in my face. Her eyes told me that she didn't believe a word I said. I rang the doorbell again and this time she spoke through the door.

"Get off my damn property!"

I kicked her door like she was in cahoots with them. I yelled to release my frustration and stormed to my car. My mother looked at me. "Alicia, look at you."

I snapped. "What!"

"We need to check in first, clean up, and present you as someone to be believed."

I beat on the steering wheel and yelled, "I gotta find my baby."

She spoke calmly. "If you don't clean yourself up, they are going to make you the crazy woman."

Momentarily, I considered it, but I decided to go to another address. I assumed it was Dwight's mother's house. When no one answered, I crept to the back of the house. I was convinced someone was there. As I tried to peep in the kitchen window, my mother came around to get me. "Let's get out of here before you get yourself arrested."

We walked back to the car. Finally, I said, "Maybe we should head back to the hotel and get cleaned up."

"Yes. You can't fight fire with fire. Make yourself look worthy. These people don't know you. You're some stranger claiming their family members stole your baby. Who do you think they'll believe?"

I nodded and entered the hotel address into my GPS. Tears rolled from my eyes as I silenced my anger with the navigator's voice. When we got to the hotel, my mother made a brilliant suggestion. She decided we should make flyers claiming they had kidnapped my son. I downloaded pictures from the Internet of me holding DJ, pictures of Tracey and Dwight, pictures of me and Dwight, and put them on a flyer. The heading read, KIDNAPPED: HAVE YOU SEEN THIS CHILD? I added: THESE PEOPLE HAVE MY SON. HELP ME FIND HIM. IF YOU SEE THESE PEOPLE, PLEASE CALL ME. And I left my cell phone number.

I took a shower and changed my clothes. We printed up hundreds of flyers. I drove back to the two neighborhoods and I put them everywhere. I was sure neighbors would be shocked to know they were kidnappers. We posted the flyer on every pole or light post in the development and we put them on people's doors. We went to the house and knocked on the door and no one answered. We parked the car in the driveway and waited and waited. We left twice to grab a bite to eat. Finally, around ten o'clock, an officer drove up and parked behind me. I got out to explain the situation. He flashed a light in my eyes.

"Alicia Dixon."

I blocked the light with my hands. "Yeah."

"This is private property and you have to leave."

I pointed to the house. "These people, who own this house, they stole my son."

"Ma'am, I'm sorry. The neighbors are complaining. They say the owners are concerned that you are harassing them. If you don't leave quietly, I'll have to arrest you."

My mother stepped out of the car and pulled my arm. "C'mon, Alicia, let's go."

I yanked away from her. "No. I'm not leaving until I get DJ."

The officer said, "Either you're leaving or you're going with us."

"Are there any laws to protect me? They steal my son and they have all the damn rights."

He took a deep breath like he'd grown impatient with me. "If you want to file a complaint against them, you can, but you have to get off their property."

I ran and sat on the grass. "I'm sitting right here. I'm not going anywhere."

My mother pleaded with me and the officer pulled out his cuffs. I didn't care. I'd go to jail before I'd walk away quietly and that's exactly what I did. My mother followed the police car to the station. I tried to explain the situation to the officers during the ride. They laughed as if I was making this all up.

I had nothing but pictures to prove the truth. They had the birth certificate and some bogus document claiming I gave them full custody. The officers laughed and asked sarcastic questions. I stopped speaking and stared out the window. Dwight and Tracey drove alongside the police car. When I looked at them, they all clicked their tongues at me. Even DJ pointed and laughed. I yelled, "Give me my baby back."

The officers said, "Miss, you can't scream in this car like that."

"But look, they're harassing me now!"

"Who?"

I looked at the same car I was just staring at and strangers were inside paying me no attention. Anxiety began to take over me. I swore they were just there. Why did I feel so helpless?

They concocted this clever plan and I never saw it coming. Suddenly, I began to laugh. How could I be this silly? I laughed harder. I'm much smarter than this. One officer said to the other, "She needs a psych eval."

"I don't. I swear I don't. I know this sounds too crazy to be true, but it is. I swear. My mother can vouch for me."

They ignored me and continued talking as if I wasn't there. "Let's just take her in and let the doctor decide."

Then he turned to me. "Is that your mother following us?" I didn't respond, but he continued, "She's right behind us. Hopefully, the commissioner can see you tonight. And listen to me, if you want to get out of here, don't tell him that story."

I asked, "Does it sound that crazy?"

They laughed and in unison said, "Yes."

I hung my head. Obviously, I sounded like a basket case. I didn't know what to do next. Did I have any rights? All I wanted to do was make this right.

Inside the jail, I prayed. Lord, I swear this is my Scared Straight program. I swear off all men from this point. They are all the same. I became overemotional just thinking about everything.

I sat there waiting to be seen by the commissioner and started thinking about my next move. This was clearly going to be a fight.

I was released on my own recon three hours after I had been booked. My mother was still in the parking lot. She claimed she had been calling Dwight to no avail.

"Ma, this is not going to be easy. They must have been planning this for a long time."

She rested her hand on top of mine. "But you're a fighter. You've always been a fighter. No way in the world you gonna let some country bumpkin ruin your life like this."

"It just feels like someone ripped my heart from my chest."

"Yeah, a little pain ain't never stopped nobody. And it ain't going to stop you. You can't ball up and cry now. We got work to do."

Maybe her desire to fight came from all the years of lying down and letting people walk over her. I was happy she wanted to assist in my battle. I nodded. "You're right. We're not leaving here empty-handed."

We went to court the next day to file for custody. When it came to the address, I wrote the address to the house where we were. I was told that they would send me a court date. I begged the bailiff to help me. It was crucial that I know a date before leaving Jacksonville. My charm got me an expedited court date, one month away. By now, I'd realized that throwing a tantrum didn't help my case, so I accepted the date.

Still, I stayed in Jacksonville for the remainder of that week. After going to their home every day, with no sign of them, I decided it would be best that I go home and return for my court date. It killed me, but I had bills, a child, and a mother to take care of. On the plane ride home, I got these sharp pains in my chest. *Please, Lord, don't let me die without seeing my baby again.*

When we arrived in Maryland, I started to regret my decision to return home. But on the other hand, I was at peace knowing they would never do anything to hurt DJ. Then again, I didn't really know anything about them.

CHAPTER 49

Tracey

I tried to explain to Dwight after I got arrested that this was what I was referring to when I said Alicia'd seek revenge. Considering she was searching for us, we had to hide out and it wasn't right. It was very embarrassing. When I received strange phone calls from neighbors telling me she was posting signs in the neighborhood, I decided to call the cops. I wanted her to feel what I felt.

We went over to Mama Dee's for a barbecue to celebrate our return. When we walked in the door, she snatched DJ from my hands. It was the grandson she'd been waiting for. She didn't say two words to Des and Jordan. Danielle always told me she was partial to boys. That's probably why Danny has such low self-esteem, but I hope she didn't plan on neglecting them. "Mama Dee, do you see the girls?"

She gave them hugs and kisses. Then she popped Dwight upside the head. "Boy, now you know I raised you to make better choices."

He seemed to be real irritated. He'd been slightly

grouchy since we left Maryland. I think he was so frustrated and beating himself up for being so wrong about Alicia. I rubbed his back. "It's okay. Everything is better now. We are going to get through this."

When we moved back into our home, everything was just right. The paint was still fresh. All the pieces fell back into place. Even Dwight came around more and more each day. And our little DJ, he belonged here and not with her.

When we were subpoenaed to court for the custody of Dwight Wilson Jr., I was nervous. I heard that all kinds of crazy stuff happens in court. Danny even said sometimes judges give kids back to drug-addicted and abusive mothers and other times justice prevails. Alicia wasn't all the things that I made her out to be, but clearly she didn't deserve to raise him. And the girls would miss DJ dearly. But I was equipped with all the evidence I'd need to paint the picture I wanted to paint. Ms. Alicia, that's what you get for stealing my husband. I was not having it. *No, ma'am.*

CHAPTER 50

Alicia

The past month was hell. I received one e-mail of substance from Dwight and he sent pictures often with no message included. The icebreaker message told me that he didn't know me. He thought I was a bad mother. He knew I'd used drugs and what he seemed most angry about was that he wasn't the first married man I'd dated. He stated stability and family values as reasons why he and Tracey felt they'd be better parents. I could give a damn. That baby came out of me. He belonged to me. No matter what they thought, I was his mother and it was my job to raise him. Whatever they thought I didn't know was subjective. I'll give him the values I feel he needs.

He suggested in his message that DJ could come visit over the summer, but not until he gets used to the arrangement. What gave him the balls to think this proposal made sense? Each time I thought about that message, I got angry. I got more angry as I packed my suitcase on my way back to Jacksonville. I retained a female attorney in Jacksonville.

Judging from her record and our phone conversations, she knew what she was doing and she saw no reason the judgment couldn't be reversed.

My mother and I arrived the night before the court date. I was so tempted to go to their house and just steal DJ and get back on the plane. Then make them prove that they deserved to have him. My good sense told me that would probably guarantee that I'd never see my son again. I planned to do it and do it right.

My heart pounded when I entered the courtroom. They sat there and neither of them turned around. I sat across the room and envied them. I hated how united they appeared. My knees shook and my palms were sweaty. I could choke Tracey.

My attorney clenched my hand. "Alicia, stay cool. The absolute worst thing you could do is lose your cool."

I nodded and bit my bottom lip. Every muscle in my body was tense. Dwight caught me staring at them. Something in his eyes apologized to me. I mouthed, "Why?"

He hung his head and I just wanted to get him alone. She'd obviously manipulated him. Hell, she manipulated both of us. She fooled the shit out of me. Maybe, instead of hating her, I should give her a standing ovation. Damn if I wanted my son being raised by a master manipulator.

When the judge entered, my lawyer turned to me. "You ready?"

The judge was a relatively young-looking sistah, but she was expressionless. After shuffling around some papers, she put on her glasses and the bailiff stated the case. Wilson vs. Dixon. The court was called to order. The judge said, "Now why are we here, Ms. Dixon?"

I began, "Your Honor, the Wilsons took my son without

permission and they are claiming that I signed over custody and I didn't."

She snickered. "Now, how did they take your son? First of all, how do you know the Wilsons?"

I took a deep breath. "Well, Dwight . . . I mean, Mr. Wilson and I were in a relationship."

"You were in a relationship with this woman's husband?"

"Yes, but at the time they were separated. We had a son."

"This is the child in question, Dwight Jr.?"

"Yes, and when Mrs. Wilson and Mr. Wilson rekindled their relationship, we all participated in raising him."

She huffed. "You skipped a whole lot in there, but go on."

"When they decided to move back here, they packed up and left from right under my nose. I went to work one day and they snuck away. When I tried to report him missing, I found out about me supposedly signing over custody to them."

She turned to them. "Now, let me hear your side of the story."

Tracey spoke, "Your Honor, Ms. Dixon is a longtime drug user and when she drinks and gets high, she says things like she doesn't want to be a mother."

I shouted out, "Oh my God, she is lying."

"Ms. Dixon, please don't blurt out in my court."

I nodded. She looked at Tracey, who was anxious to tell her lies. Tracey smiled innocently at the judge. "I have evidence of her crazy lifestyle." She whipped out letters she claimed were from my lesbian lover and letters from Deshaun. What the hell? It took everything in me not to strangle her. She continued, "I have court records dating back ten years where Ms. Dixon herself claimed to be a chronic drug user."

I looked at my mother and nearly fainted. I always knew it would come back to bite me in the ass. But damn, never like this. I had to say that I was a user because they were trying to put me in jail with Deshaun for possession and intent to distribute. My mother shook her head, and the devil continued, "She is a crazy nymphomaniac, drug addict, and a criminal."

I interrupted, "Oh my God! Are you kidding me?"

The judge raised her hand. "Look, I've asked you once not to speak without permission and I will not ask again. The next time I will dismiss the case."

It was killing me to sit quietly and watch her lie about me. Facing Tracey, the judge asked, "Where did you get this information from?"

"Your Honor, off her computer and out of her bedroom."

My mouth hung open. How could I have gone against all my intuition and fall for this? It was so unbelievable.

"So, did she give you permission to print these letters and search her belongings?"

"No, but she didn't hide it. And her criminal record is public record. She was indicted ten years ago . . ." The judge nodded. "She still corresponds with her coconspirator through letters. She's sent him pictures of the baby and I'm concerned she may be taking him to visit."

I covered my chest. How did she know about my relationship with Deshaun? Why was she making this stuff up? I couldn't dispute anything she said. I just had to suffer through all the lies.

She smiled politely and said, "Yes, more than anything, my husband and I are friends. I moved to Maryland to help him with the baby, because he knew Ms. Dixon was doing a horrible job."

My lawyer said, "Objection, Your Honor?"

"Overruled."

I looked at Tracey and she gave me a conniving grin. "So I agreed to help him and it just so happens, I had to move into the house with him and his mistress."

The judge smiled politely at her. "You are a good woman."

No. She is a bitch in disguise.

Then the judge turned her attention to Dwight. "What do you think about this situation?"

"Well, I would like to have the honor of raising my son. A woman can't teach a man how to be a man. Especially a woman who repeatedly says, 'I wish I could go back to when I was childless.' I don't think Ms. Dixon ever intended to be a mother."

I gasped. He glanced at me and, almost as if he had been hypnotized, he said, "She relinquished custody for a reason."

They were ripping my character to shreds and had the judge eating from their hands. I was a drug-abusing mistress who had a close boyfriend in jail that I communicate with via mail. I used to sell drugs, and I had a crazy lesbian lover. Isn't it crazy how someone can paint such an ugly picture? Before the judge left to deliberate, I knew the verdict. I prayed for a miracle, but what's a prayer without a voice? I was hopeless.

My mother demanded that I hold my head high when I walked into the courtroom, but I felt defeated. Tracey came to court with weapons of mass destruction and all I had was my word, and that didn't amount to shit. The judge looked at me. "Ms. Dixon, it seems that you are very spontaneous. You want this today. You don't want it tomorrow. You want to get high today. You want to be clean tomorrow. Raising a child takes structure and commitment. The problem with society now is that so many people want to turn parenting on and off." She paused and looked at Dwight. "Now, Mr. Wilson and . . . Mrs. Wilson, you spoke about values."

Tracey nodded confidently and I just shook my head. The judge continued, "You want to raise your son. But what kind of morals do you teach him? Do you say it's okay to lie and steal?"

My neck snapped back, as did Tracey's. "From what I can tell, there was a period where you were married to both Ms. Dixon and Ms. Tracey Wilson. Are these records correct?" Tracey shouted, "It was a mistake. He thought we were divorced!"

The judge removed her glasses. "You're a bigamist, Mr. Wilson, and I believe Ms. Dixon. Why would she sign her son over to you after you lied and misled her?" She looked at me. "Did you think he was divorced?"

I nodded. She cleared her throat. "Ms. Dixon, I'm going to return custody to you. Ms. Wilson could have had any jackleg notary verify these custody papers and they will not hold up in my court."

I covered my mouth in excitement and clenched my mother's hand. Tears welled in her eyes. The judge raised her finger, warning us not to get too excited. "But I am going to order you to court-appointed parenting classes. Unfortunately, they will have to be taken in Florida. Will that be a problem?"

"No, Your Honor. Whatever to get my baby back."

Tracey shouted, "He doesn't even know her. I'm the only mother he knows."

"Unfortunately, it doesn't matter. An officer of the court will escort you to the Wilsons' home this evening." She turned to look at them. "You will need to gather his things and have them ready by four o'clock. Judgment in favor of the plaintiff."

Tracey broke down in tears and it appeared that Dwight's eyes watered, too. She cried hard. A part of me knew it hurt her, but the other part said it didn't have to be like this. We could have worked this out. Now, after so much lying and deceit, I wasn't certain that I ever wanted my son to visit them. Dwight stood up and faced me. I stared at him, searching for the man I loved, but he was gone. They headed toward the door. Suddenly, I became overwhelmed with emotion as I watched them walk out of court together. I wished it would have been just as simple as handing him over. Unfortunately, I had to face them again.

My mother and I met the officers outside of the Wilsons' home at four on the dot. I'd bitten my nails down to nubs. I prayed that DJ didn't act a fool when they handed him over. We stood at the bottom of the driveway and the officers knocked on the door. Tracey opened the door; her eyes were puffy and her pale cheeks were red. She held DJ tightly and kissed his face. Dwight rubbed her shoulder as the officer stripped them of DJ. I closed my eyes. DJ squealed like he was in pain and that made me cry. The officer rushed down the driveway to me. I said, "DJ."

He abruptly stopped crying and smiled at me. I grabbed him in my arms and held him tightly, crying and kissing him feverishly. I thanked God for the second chance to prove I appreciated His blessing.

READING GROUP GUIDE

1. Do you think Tracey was too hard on Dwight? Should she have moved to Maryland with him?

2. Do you think Dwight was wrong for moving even when he knew Tracey was adamant?

3. Would you consider Dwight a good man? Why or why not?

4. Did you think Alicia was wrong for pursuing Dwight?

5. Do you agree with Dwight's decision to leave his family to make something work with Alicia? Or was Alicia the easy way out?

6. Do you think Dwight and Alicia's sexual encounter was inevitable? Or is it possible to remain friends under those kinds of circumstances?

7. Would you have been able to share your man with another woman?

8. Do you think Tracey really loved Dwight, or was she in
   love with his money?

9. Did the women have ulterior motives for sharing
   Dwight? If so, what do you think these motives were?

10. How many women do you think could handle an ar-
    rangement like this? And under what circumstances is
    it acceptable?

ABOUT THE AUTHORS

CANDICE DOW is a native of Baltimore, MD, and a graduate of the University of Maryland Eastern Shore and Johns Hopkins University. Before becoming a full-time writer, she worked as a software engineer. She is a member of Alpha Kappa Alpha Sorority, Inc., Rho Xi Omega Chapter in Baltimore, and enjoys mentoring teenage girls. Candice is the author of three novels: *Caught in the Mix*, *Ain't No Sunshine*, and *A Hire Love*. She is currently hard at work on her next novel.

DAAIMAH S. POOLE was born and raised in Philadelphia, PA. She graduated from Temple University with a BA in journalism in 2003. While attending Temple, Daaimah worked almost every job imaginable—receptionist, car salesperson, bill collector, waitress, tutor, and substitute teacher. She would later say she was unintentionally doing character research. Daaimah completed her first novel, *Yo Yo Love*, at the age of nineteen, without owning a computer or knowing how to type. Originally published by Oshun Publishing and later picked up by Kensington Books, *Yo Yo Love* went on to become an *Essence* magazine best-seller. Her subsequent novels, *Got a Man*, *What's Real*, *Ex-Girl to the Next Girl*, *All I Want Is Everything*, and *A Rich Man's Baby* have cemented her reputation as an author on the move. Visit WWW.DSPBOOKS.COM.